SPRING'S CALLING

A SEASONS OF MAGIC URBAN FANTASY NOVEL

SARAH BIGLOW

For Tutu
(1924-2018)
You would have loved to read a book about witches

MARCH 11, 2017

ONE

I fiddled with the squad car radio, finally landing on a late-night radio host preparing to start her show as the clock ticked past 10:30 at night. "Well, my loyal listeners, we are nine days from what some scientists are calling the biggest astrological phenomena in human history. Sure, we've all seen a solar eclipse or a meteor shower but never together in the middle of the freaking day!" a deep alto voice said through the car speakers. "According to most reports, those of us on the East Coast, especially here in the Boston area, will be in the direct path of the eclipse, so get your glasses early and get ready for what everyone is calling a pretty amazing show. The city is reporting that the best place to check this out is down on the Common. So, listeners, let me know will you be there?" she continued.

"It just means that we're going to be doing crowd control," my partner, Jacqueline DeWitt, muttered.

I turned my attention to her. Caramel-skinned with dark hair held in a tight bun at the nape of her neck, Jacquie kept one hand loosely on the steering wheel as she cranked the heater. She only succeeded in filling the car with harsh, cold air. We'd been partnered only a couple months. While I liked her enough, I didn't feel like we were friends.

I wanted to agree with her and bemoan the likely detail, but I already had plans. When I was a little girl, I'd been told about the prophecy that laid out my destiny. I'd have to face off against some great evil when a solar eclipse and a meteor shower fell on the Vernal Equinox. The Equinox was supposed to be a time when the world came back into balance between light and dark magic, neither one stronger than the other. Not like with the Summer or Winter Solstice when power ebbed and flowed toward good or evil. But this year had been different. The cold clung to the world longer than it should have. It was just that much harder to cast a spell. I'd spent the last decade honing my skills in preparation. But all the prep in the world couldn't quell the nugget of fear in my chest.

"You okay?" Jacquie's voice cut through my thoughts, pulling me back to the car and the icy air.

Tiny beads of sweat broke out along the nape of my neck chilling me even more. "Yeah ... just thinking. You're right. Crowd control is going to suck." Even though I liked my partner, I couldn't share my burden with her. The magical community survived because of secrecy.

The conversation was cut short by the dispatch radio sitting in the center console between us. "Units needed at the corner of Kneeland Street and Albany Street."

Jacquie scooped up the radio. "Unit fifty-seven responding, we're two blocks out."

She flipped on the lights and siren and put the car in drive, pulling out into the traffic surrounding the Common. We sped past at least three Dunkin Donuts—rivaled in number only by the Starbucks on nearly every opposite corner—ignored the stoplights and hung a hard left until we reached Kneeland Street, nestled between Chinatown and the theater district. We pulled up to find an ambulance and the coroner's van parked on the street blocking traffic. I spotted the assistant medical examiner, Patricia Karo, bent over an Asian man's body. Climbing from the passenger seat, I pulled my jacket tighter as the frigid air—another sign that the world was out of balance—wound its way through every fiber of my being. A gust of air tugged several strands of auburn hair loose and I brushed them aside.

A pair of uniformed officers cordoned off the area with crime scene tape and shooed a couple of nosy bystanders away so we could get by. Jacquie pulled on latex gloves and went to join Tricia by the body. I kept my distance. Even from where I stood at the periphery of the scene, I could clearly see the man's chest was unnaturally concave, as if something had crushed him from above. A quick glance around the scene didn't present any obvious culprits. Something tickled my magical senses, begging me to pay attention, but I couldn't place it. I turned back to the body lying prone on the sidewalk. I'd never worked a homicide before and my palms grew damp as the weight of the responsibility hit me. I glanced over at Jacquie as she methodically moved around the scene. I could only hope to be as good as her.

For an instant the man was gone, replaced by a woman with a blade protruding from her chest. The scent of fresh strawberries bloomed around me and the white-gold pentacle necklace around my neck thrummed warm beneath my jacket as my magic reacted to the memory. I tamped down on my magic as I blinked away tears. The scene returned to the dead man being poked and prodded by Tricia.

I'd earned my detective's shield two months ago, just shy of my twenty-fifth birthday. I didn't flaunt my skills. I did just enough to prove useful to the brass, to get the right amount of attention so they'd remember me when it came time for promotions. Doing anything more would have been dangerous. The wrong people could have taken notice. Like the Order of Samael or the Authority—the so-called benevolent governing body of the magical community.

My decision to join the force wasn't without ulterior motives. Ten years ago, my mother was murdered. Everyone in the magical community knew it, but she'd simply been buried with little fanfare. Despite obvious signs of foul play, there had been no police report or investigation. The Authority had convinced the outside world that she'd simply died of natural causes. I'd never forgotten the truth though. Ten years was a long time for her killer to walk free. But now the shield on my belt gave me license to hunt them down and make them pay.

But my mother's murderer would have to walk free just a little longer. Another man deserved justice now. I watched Jacquie crouch down and pat down the man's pockets in search of an ID. I stepped away and turned my back to the scene and my uninitiated partner.

Beneath the pentacle I wore a small sandalwood infused charm that helped cleanse my magical palette, allowing me to pick up on any signs of magic in the area. Magic, like anything in the universe, obeyed certain laws. It couldn't be created or destroyed. Just redirected and reshaped. I pressed my fingers to the smooth glass surface and inhaled. With the metaphorical slate wiped clean, I picked up on the cloying scent of rotten garlic and the loamy smell of wet limestone. For a moment, the combination turned my stomach and I fought back my gag reflex. This had been what my senses had been alerting me to. The smells intensified the closer I got to the body and I knew it meant our victim had been killed with magic. A practitioner only gave off one scent, which meant whoever had killed the victim had been working as a team. A person's magical signature was like a fingerprint. But that didn't mean I could pick it out just walking by them on the street. They needed to be actively using their ability or have used it in the last day.

"You want to join the rest of us, rookie?" Jacquie called, holding up the dead man's wallet.

Embarrassment warmed my cheeks and I turned back to the matter at hand. I pulled out a pen and notepad from my back pocket and wrote, "Limestone and garlic. Two killers with magic used in last 24 hours?" After donning latex gloves of my own, Jacquie passed me the man's wallet and I pulled out his ID: Edwin Cho. He lived in Chinatown not far from the scene. Given that it was late evening on the weekend he was likely on his way home. I added his name and address to my notepad.

"Do we have any idea what crushed him?" I asked, addressing Tricia.

She was busy taking pictures of the man's injuries. "Nice to see you, Ezri. That shield looks good on you."

"Thanks." We'd worked together when I was in

uniform and had become friends. Not the stay up late in the night talking about our lives type of friends but friendly enough to have drinks or a quick meal on occasion after a long day.

Both of us caught Jacquie's impatient arched brow and Tricia cleared her throat. "No cause of death yet but I'm guessing it was whatever made these crush injuries. With the right angle and amount of pressure, a grown adult could exert enough force to crush someone's chest like this. I'll know more once we get back to the lab. But this is the second case like this I've seen in the last few days."

"Where was the other victim found?" Jacquie probed.

"I'll send over the files but it was out by the Esplanade. Same crush injuries."

I stowed Mr. Cho's ID back in his wallet and handed it off to one of the uniforms who hung back with an evidence bag at the ready. Limestone clogged up my nose as I got close to Mr. Cho's chest. Not everyone is sensitive to other people's magic and my skills weren't infallible. My twenty-four-hour window for identifying magic had come after years of practice. Based on the strength of the smell, Mr. Cho hadn't been dead very long and his attackers had left the scene recently.

"Do we have a time of death?" I pressed.

Tricia shook her head. "Based on what I've seen

of the body, I'd say only a few hours. Rigor's barely set in. I can give you a more definitive time of death after autopsy."

"It looks like there's some dust or residue on his jacket. Our killer, if they used their hands, might have left some prints."

Tricia snapped a few close-ups of Mr. Cho's clothing. Without warning, a new smell hit me: ashy and sulfurous. I tried to repress my gag reflex again, but I could taste the bitterness on my tongue. As calmly as I could I stood up and started to walk the perimeter. I stopped short a few paces from Mr. Cho's body. A pale woman—her eyes hollow and unseeing and mousy brown hair hanging matted around her face—blocked my path. Despite the lifelessness in her gaze, I knew she saw me, knew *what* I was. The sulfur and ash of her magic bloomed into a fiery corona around her head before she disappeared completely. I blinked a few times until the afterimage faded.

What the hell was she?

"Ezri, you still with us?" Jacquie's voice drew me back to reality for a second time.

Our gazes met—her intense brown to my green— and heat crept up the nape of my neck. I needed to avoid making zoning out a habit. I made a note of the stranger's disappearance before capping my pen. "Yeah, I was just thinking that this is a fairly public area. I mean you've got Tufts Hospital and the orange line just up the way. Someone had to see something but there's hardly anyone out. And there are bound to be security cameras nearby that must have caught what happened."

Jacquie nodded. "I'll put in a request when we get back to the precinct."

Turning back to the body, I asked, "I mean do we know who called this in?"

"I got the call from the paramedics about ten minutes before you two showed up. From what they told me, whoever had called it in didn't stick around," Tricia answered, spreading a black body bag out on the sidewalk.

I hadn't even noticed the ambulance leave the scene, but traffic was now flowing slowly through the makeshift blockade of our car and the coroner's van. With the body now on its way to the morgue and no eye witnesses to speak of, there was little reason to stick around. I peeled off my gloves and made my way back to the car. Jacquie slid in behind the driver seat and looked at me.

"You're going to lead the notification of next of kin."

I swallowed back the lump of nerves rising in my throat. "Are you sure?"

"You've got to start sometime."

I buckled my seatbelt and put Mr. Cho's address into the car's GPS. As we pulled away from the scene, I glanced back at the spot where the woman had vanished. I'd never seen magic like that before. The fact that the scene was steeped in spells set off alarm bells in my head. I wasn't sure what evil I was supposed to be facing—no one had ever filled me in on the specifics—but this couldn't be a coincidence. Mr. Cho's death was linked to what was coming and I needed to figure out how if I had any chance of successfully meeting my destiny.

TWO

We pulled up outside an old brick four-story building in the heart of Chinatown. The few people out on the streets eyed us, giving us a wide berth as we approached the front steps. Faint music—my ears strained to identify it as anything other than Oriental instrumental—filtered out of the partially open doorways of nearby restaurants. Trying to filter the background noise out, I took the front steps three at a time to ring the buzzer for the Chos' unit on the second floor. I wet my lips and went over the speech we'd been trained on at the Academy in my head.

Finally, the intercom crackled and a woman's voice said, "Hello?"

"I'm looking for Mrs. Edwin Cho," I said.

"Yes, I'm Mrs. Cho," the voice replied in accented English.

"Ma'am, I'm with the police. Can you buzz me in?"

Silence answered me. I counted to five before the front door unlocked. I pushed it open and led Jacquie up one flight of stairs and down a short, narrow, wood-paneled hallway. The door to the Chos' unit was already open. A woman with a short, black bob threaded with gray waited for us.

"Mrs. Cho?" I confirmed and she nodded.

"Please, call me Su-Ling."

I held up my badge for her to see. "I'm Detective Trenton. This is my partner, Detective DeWitt. Can we talk inside?"

She stood her ground. "What is this about?"

I sensed Jacquie take a step forward so she was in line with me. I exhaled slowly through my nose and tried to put on a sympathetic smile. "It would be better if we spoke inside."

The older woman studied me for a moment longer until she finally stepped out of the doorway, allowing us entry. I closed the distance and crossed the threshold. The apartment was small—probably only a one bedroom—but cozy. The heating system rattled as old-style radiators hissed to life around the room.

"Please sit." Mrs. Cho gestured to the loveseat pressed up against one of the walls.

I settled on the edge and pulled out my notebook

again. Su-Ling took her time sitting in the armchair across from us.

After one more steadying breath, I said, "Mrs. Cho, I'm so very sorry to have to tell you this, but your husband was found dead a short time ago."

Her hands grasped the armrests until her knuckles turned white. Tears sparkled in her eyes, but she refused to let them fall. "No, you are mistaken."

"I'm afraid not. We found his ID on him."

'Who would want to hurt my husband?"

"We were hoping you might know the answer to that. If you feel you can answer just a few questions for us..." Jacquie interjected.

"I can try." She paused and, after a moment, her bob bounced against her cheeks as she shook her head. "No. No one. Edwin was a good man. Nice man. Everyone liked him."

Clearing my palette again, I inhaled, but all I got was the faint scent of cooking spices and some candles that had been burned on the mantle place not long ago. Nothing that jumped out as even remotely magical. If he wasn't part of the magical community, then why would someone with clear magical abilities target him?

Glancing down at my notepad, I continued. "I'm really sorry to have to ask, but when we found him, he wasn't far from the Tufts stop on the orange line.

Did he work nearby or have a reason to be there this late at night?"

"Edwin was working late. He does sometimes. He called me maybe at six o'clock to say he would be a few hours and not to wait for supper." She dabbed at the corners of her eyes, her composure threatening to slip. "I should have known something was wrong when he did not come home yet."

"If you don't mind me asking, what did your husband do for work?"

"He is a professor. He teaches advanced cardiology at Tufts School of Medicine."

His job didn't seem to give any clue so I tried a different tack. I glanced at Jacquie who was busy taking her own notes on the conversation. "Did Edwin have any hobbies or meet anyone new recently?" Maybe he'd hidden any magical connection from his family.

"No. At least, not that he told me. He was very busy with his students. He didn't have time for anything else."

Not the answer I'd been hoping for. One final question then. "Do you know if Edwin took the same route home every day?" Maybe he'd been more than a target of opportunity.

"I don't know." With that, Mrs. Cho's lower lip quivered and tears slipped down her cheeks, first a few at a time and then so heavily that her cheeks shone in the dim light. "I need to call my daughter. I have to tell her that her father is dead. She's only nineteen. She is away at school."

Jacquie stood up and pulled a business card from her jacket pocket. "I know this is hard, Mrs. Cho, and we are so very sorry for your loss. We'll need you to identify your husband's body when you're ready. I'm going to leave my card if you can think of anything or if you need anything. The address of the morgue is on the back. If you want us to be there, please don't hesitate to call us."

Through her tears, Mrs. Cho took Jacquie's card with shaky fingers and buried her face, weeping softly into her shirtsleeves. Jacquie headed for the door and I moved to follow her. I set my own business card on the table beside Mrs. Cho. My heart broke for this woman. I knew that grief better than many of the officers in the department.

She reached out a damp hand and grabbed my wrist. "Please, just find who did this to my husband."

"I pro—" I bit my tongue. We were trained never to promise something in a case like this. "We will do what we can."

Jacquie and I retreated to the car and I flipped open my notebook, jotting down the limited information we'd gotten from Mrs. Cho before rereading the details I'd gathered from the scene. Why kill a cardiology professor with no magical connections? For a fleeting moment I considered that, while the killers may have been magical, the murder wasn't tied to the impending battle I had to face. But I *knew* deep in my bones that they were connected.

Jacquie's phone buzzed. "Karo came through. She sent over the information on the first victim."

I bent over her phone, skimming the details. Two days ago, Altagracia Mendoza, age 78, was found dead near the Esplanade. Her chest was crushed and no witnesses had been identified.

Scrolling down the report, I said, "Look at this, she was found around the same time of night."

"Same MO but vastly different locations, and at first glance there's nothing that connects our victims. They're different sexes, different ages and races."

I shrugged. "Maybe they knew each other through work or a church group or something." I couldn't help but wonder if magic had been involved in Mrs. Mendoza's death too.

"You did well, Ezri," Jacquie said once we were back on the road heading for the precinct. Our shift was nearly over.

"It was harder than I thought. God, when she broke down crying I just wanted to tell her we'd find the son of a bitch who did this."

"We do our jobs the best we can. Sometimes we win and sometimes the criminals get away with it."

"Don't I know it." I stopped short of sharing anything else.

We pulled to a red light and Jacquie looked at me. "I know you lost your mother when you were a kid and this had to bring up some of those feelings."

I stared open-mouthed at my partner. "How?" As far as I knew, the police had no record of her death.

Jacquie eased off of the brake and kept her gaze on the road. After a tense beat she said, "I did my homework on you, Trenton, when you made detective and I knew I'd be partnered with you."

Something about the answer seemed off. Why inquire about my past? Our gazes met in the rearview mirror and the suspicion building in the back of my mind dissipated under her kind expression. Not everyone in the world has dark motives. "She was murdered and I swore I'd find her killer," I blurted. *Why did I just admit that?*

"I'm sorry. That's a noble promise to make, Ezri, but a dangerous one."

"No one gave her the justice she deserved. That's why I'm doing this job."

"You can't let what happened to you color your judgement. So, if you can't handle this case you need to let me know now and the captain can assign you to a different partner."

"No. I can do this. I'm not going to let my personal issues get in the way of working the case. I know this isn't anything like what happened to my mother."

"Good."

With that one word, the conversation came to an abrupt conclusion. I wanted to know what had prompted her digging into my history, but the dashboard clock read 11:07 p.m. and sleep threatened to cloud my thoughts. We pulled into the back lot of the precinct and Jacquie cut the engine.

"Write up your report, then go home and get some sleep. There's nothing more we can do tonight."

"Yes, ma'am."

By the time I finished my report, the graveyard shift was in full force and Jacquie had left and gone home to her niece and nephew. It was almost midnight and I had no desire to make the drive home at the moment. So, I dragged myself out of the bullpen to the break area and flung myself down on one of the bunks. Sleep wrapped around me like a blanket as soon as my head hit the pillow.

Excitement coursed through me as I headed up the two flights of stairs to our apartment. I could hear footsteps thundering behind me as J.T. and Desmond chased after me. Their voices echoed in the stairwell, but I couldn't make out the words. Whatever they were saying, it didn't matter. We'd spent a good night together, staying up way too late and trying wine coolers Desmond got with his fake ID in secret, but today was my birthday and I was sure my parents were going all out. After all, it wasn't every day your only daughter turned fifteen.

I pulled the keys from my pocket and slid them into the lock. The bolt turned easily and I pushed the door inward. Before I even crossed the threshold, I could smell something wrong. The sweet honey of my mother's magic hung in the air, but there were other scents overlapping it. Too many to pick apart. I wasn't that good.

"Ezri, wait!" J.T. called from down the hall.

I ignored him and went in. The hair on the back of my neck stood at attention as did the hair along my forearms. "Mom? Dad?" I called. No answer.

I crossed the short entryway and past my parents' bedroom and into the living room. All of the air went out of my lungs, robbing me of the ability to scream. My throat burned as my vocal cords tried to make sound anyway. My mother's body lay on the floor, a silver-handled knife wedged between her ribs. A small rivulet of blood trickled from the side of her mouth. Nubs of candles lay around her having long burnt themselves out. The scents of whoever had been in the apartment were overwhelming and, as if they had physical mass, pressed down on me until I landed on my knees on the hardwood.

"Mom," I finally squeaked out, clawing my way across the room to her.

Up close her left hand was coated in blood. She gripped something in her right hand and without thinking I pried it open to find a pentacle necklace. It was the one she'd told me she would give me on my fifteenth birthday, just like her mother had done and so on back through the generations to our ancestors who died during the Witch Trials. I freed the necklace from her stiff fingers and secured it around my neck. Whoever took my mother from me wasn't going to take that legacy from me too.

"Ezri," my mother's voice called.

I looked down to find her staring at me, eyes wide open and glittering with unshed tears. She cupped my cheek with her bloody hand and said, "Sweet girl, they're coming. It's time now. I'm sorry I couldn't protect you forever. Remember her words. And you need to wake up now. Ezri, wake up!"

MARCH 12, 2017

The precinct bunkroom came into view as I sat up in a cold sweat, hair matted to my forehead and dampness soaking my shirt. My hand clutched the pendant as if I were still in the dream. I hadn't taken it off since the day my mother died. I'd had that same dream every year on my birthday since I was sixteen. This was the first time my mother had ever spoken to me. The dream had been so vivid, I could still smell the sweetness of my mother's magic. Why had she spoken to me this time? And how could she have been protecting me if she was dead? I'd never known exactly what had happened that night, but I knew she'd fought her attackers until her very last breath. Her warning stuck out in my mind. "Remember her words." Without even naming names, I knew whose words I needed to remember. Our magical family tree traced all the way back to the Witch Trials. And with that lineage came a destiny for one of our line: *When the world is balanced anew and fire rains down as midday turns to night, the last daughter of Harrow's blood shall rise to stand against the Old Guard's return.*

I was the last living daughter of Theodora Harrow's bloodline. It was up to me to fight off the impending evil force. I now only had eight days until I went toe-to-toe with destiny. The burden of what was coming had weighed on me since I learned that I was the one. Fear had given way to determination. If this is what had to be, then I was damn well going to be ready for the fight.

"You okay?" a bleary-eyed guy in dress blues asked from the doorway.

I hadn't even noticed that I was no longer alone. I blinked beads of sweat from my eyes. "Yeah, fine." I caught sight of the clock hanging above the doorway. I'd been out longer than I'd expected. It was nearly five in the morning. I climbed out of the bunk and returned to my desk where I'd left my notepad. I may not have been on shift anymore but that didn't mean I couldn't do some digging. But first, a shower and breakfast were in order.

I had just made it to my car and cranked the heat —sweat and chilly winter air did not mix—when my phone buzzed with an incoming notification. I immediately regretted checking it. A simple text reading, "Happy Birthday, I miss you, sweetheart," should have cheered me up, but I didn't need the reminder of what I'd lost. It was even worse coming from my father. We hadn't spoken in years. I threw the phone onto the passenger seat and headed out of the parking lot.

On some level, I knew he'd lost the love of his life, but the way he'd acted after her death broke my heart. He'd come home not long after I'd found her and he sent me out again with J.T. and Desmond. When we'd come back hours later, my mother's body was gone. The apartment had been cleaned and there was no sign of foul play. He'd refused to call the police, just saying it had been taken care of. Without a body, it hadn't made sense to have a wake and the funeral was a joke.

I always suspected he'd done it to give me some sort of closure. But I'd never gotten closure. And from that day forward I knew the people I was supposed to trust—the people keeping the magical community together and in order—had betrayed my family. They were supposed to keep us safe from dark practitioners and they just swept a heinous act under the rug, pretending it hadn't happened. I'd walked away from all of them.

So my father's small gesture at connection wasn't the joyous greeting it was meant to be. It only boiled my blood and reminded me that I had a mission still to complete and a promise to my mother to keep.

Muscle memory brought me back home to my

one-bedroom apartment in Brighton. Even on a detective's salary, I couldn't afford to live in the city. But being a little way out was nice. It had the calmness of the suburbs but was still urban enough to keep the need to be close enough to get into the city satisfied.

I climbed into the shower and let the water wash away some of the anger that had bubbled to the surface. I needed to be clear headed so I could show Jacquie and the brass that I was capable of doing the work they believed I could do; the work that magic had helped me do to get me where I was. Using magic had become so commonplace in my life I sometimes forgot that it could have a cost. I never pushed myself far enough to really feel the effects. Or at least I hadn't in a long time. Like any part of the body, frequent use strengthened my magic and my ability to wield it. Long gone were the days of three-day-long migraines and unstoppable nosebleeds from manipulating the power within me. I could alter the speed at which a suspect ran away from me without even breaking a sweat now. Sure, it had raised an eyebrow or two, but other officers had chalked it up to being in peak physical condition. Or at least that's what I told myself.

Another benefit of magic: I didn't even have to bother with a hair dryer anymore. I just heated the water molecules until they evaporated. I pulled my hair back into a low knot at the nape of my neck and pulled on a new blouse and pair of slacks. Clipping my holster and badge to my belt, I poured myself a cup of coffee in a travel mug and headed back out into the early morning air.

The trip to the Esplanade was quick. Most of the city wasn't up yet given that it was Sunday. I pulled up to the corner where Mrs. Mendoza's body had been found and I could see the Hatch Shell in the distance, standing empty and unused at this hour. In a few short days people would gather all over the city, even here, to watch the eclipse and the meteor shower. The biggest lightshow the city would get until the fourth of July fireworks display.

I paced the length of the block where Mrs. Mendoza had been discovered. Like Mr. Cho there hadn't been much blood evidence at the scene. The only sign of something out of place that remained was the last vestiges of the cracked sidewalk where she'd lain, her body crushed like Mr. Cho's. I hadn't stayed around long enough to see if the sidewalk had suffered similar damage at the other scene. I pulled my notepad from my pocket and scribbled a reminder to follow up with Tricia about it later. I spotted a few surveillance cameras overhead set up by the department and made a mental note to check the footage when I got back to the precinct for my next shift.

I moved to stand over the cracked cement and closed my eyes. With slow breaths I let the world fall away from me, one sound at a time. The rush of the very distant traffic vanished first, followed by the other city sounds. The buzzing of street lamps faded out until all that was left were the sounds of my breathing and my heart beating in my ears. I opened my eyes and looked around at the world. I could see the interconnecting yet invisible fabric of magic that blanketed the city. Those threads woven together moved through me, latching on for the briefest of moments to the magic within me before letting go and connecting elsewhere. It was a beautiful sight and I had to believe there were few places in the country where magic was so engrained in a place. Magic may not have been born in Boston but it thrived, even though our kind had been persecuted in this place hundreds of years ago. Humanity had since forgotten about our existence or had turned its ire to other superficial differences. Just another facet of the American Dream.

I studied the ground beneath my feet. I could see that a spell had been used here but it was still too faint to pick out its purpose. I could swear my nose picked up the barest hints of limestone and garlic, but even this connected to magic I couldn't reach back that far in time. It was just a trick of my imagination. Confirmation bias messing with my senses. It had still been worth a shot.

As the world came back into focus and daybreak crested over the nearby buildings, a sense of being watched tickled the nape of my neck. I turned around, right hand hovering over my holster, but there was no one in sight. That, of course, meant little when you could turn yourself invisible with enough force of will. I used a little of my own magic —sweet strawberry tickling my nose—to reach out through the world, probing to see if I could reveal anyone hidden by spells, but nothing jumped out at me.

"Get a hold of yourself," I chided before retreating to my car, pulling an illegal U-turn on the street and heading back toward the heart of the city, a sense of foreboding still prickling my senses.

FOUR

Restlessness overtook me until I sat at my desk forty-five minutes before the start of my shift, reading Tricia's report on Mrs. Mendoza. Her injuries were consistent with being crushed by something heavy and the same strange dust particles had been left on her clothing. To me, that all pointed to the same killer. There was also a note about possible partial fingerprints left at the scene. And like Mr. Cho, whoever had called 9-1-1 hadn't stuck around to be questioned so we had no leads to speak of.

My mood hadn't improved since the morning and the unwanted well wishes from my father. The sense that we were dealing with a serial offender only amped up my annoyance level. I knew there was magic involved. If I could get close enough to whoever was slinging spells, I'd be able to identify them and stop them before they could hurt anyone else. But magic was not an approved departmental method of investigation thanks to having to keep the truth under the radar.

The chair at the desk across from mine squeaked as Jacquie sat down at her computer.

"What are you doing here so early?" I asked, looking up from the report.

She smiled. "I was about to ask you the same thing."

"I just wanted to get a jump on the forensics from the first case, since we won't have Tricia's preliminary report on Mr. Cho until at least tonight."

"Read anything interesting?" She pulled herself around the desk to sit beside me.

"Nothing we didn't already know from our scene. Same injuries, same dust residue and some partial prints. I went down to the scene this morning. There were some nearby cameras. I was just about to call the tech guys and see if they had pulled footage yet."

"Well, don't let me stop you."

I picked up the phone's receiver and punched in the extension, waiting while it rang five then six times. Finally, when my hand was halfway back to the cradle, a nasally male voice answered, "Yeah?"

My hand snapped back, pressing the earpiece to my left ear. "Uh, hi. This is Detective Trenton in

Major Crimes. I was calling to see if you'd pulled footage from the Altagracia Mendoza crime scene."

"Hold on." I could hear his fingers click-clacking over a keyboard on the other end of the call. "Just came in. Haven't had a chance to review it."

"That's fine. Just send it over and I'll take care of it on my end," I said, eager to move the case along. Every minute we didn't have any new information or some new line of evidence to follow the more the bad guys slipped away—and the closer we got to the Equinox with all of this dark magic in play.

"That's not really protocol."

I bit my lip. "How long do you need?"

"Twenty minutes. Maybe a half hour depending on how much of a timeframe the request asked for."

"Great. Just send it over as fast as you can."

I slammed the receiver down harder than I'd intended. Jacquie looked up from her computer screen. "Everything okay over there?'

"Yeah, fine. Just the tech guy being an ass."

"Sounded like he was just doing his job. Can't fault him for that."

"Yeah, I know. I'm just ... frustrated. We've already got two victims and no witnesses. No idea why they were targeted. This surveillance footage could break this case wide open. I just don't want to end up with another body when we could have done something sooner."

"You can't take the whole world onto your shoulders. You have to be patient. This doesn't go like they show in the movies, rookie."

Knowing I needed to calm down, I took a deep breath and exhaled slowly. I let out a tiny bit of will, the fresh scent of my magic washing over me, grounding me. "I took a look through the Mendoza file and I still can't find any obvious connections to Mr. Cho. She was a retired FBI analyst but I think maybe we should go to the university and see if there was a connection there. Maybe she'd worked a case there or something or was a guest speaker."

"I'm going to pull the Mendoza file and make sure we aren't missing anything in the electronic copy," Jacquie answered, as if she hadn't heard me.

Just as she turned away, a new email from Tricia popped into my inbox. I started to call after my partner but she was already out of shouting range, so I settled in to read the report from Mr. Cho's preliminary work-up. As we'd assumed, the same dust particulates had been left on his clothing. I skimmed over the description of what the compression of his rib cage had done to his internal organs and focused on the findings related to the actual compression. She'd found indentations that looked almost like handprints. She'd managed to pull some skin cells on top of the partial prints and they were being run through the local database. That was almost as good as a picture of our killer to work with. I dragged a copy of the report into our system, updating the log, and linked it to Mrs. Mendoza's file. Even the evidence seemed to affirm my belief that these deaths were related, even if the victims themselves didn't appear to be.

I was so focused on the file in front of me that I jumped out of my chair when the phone rang beside me. I took a steadying breath and answered. "Detective Trenton."

"This is Vinnie from the tech department. There's a problem with the footage you requested."

I swallowed the groan in my throat. "What kind of problem?"

"It might be easier if you just came down and I could show you."

"Okay. We'll be there as soon as we can."

Jacquie returned with a slim physical file in both hands but I was already out of my seat, jacket in hand. "We need to head down to the tech guys. There's some sort of problem with the footage."

"Did they say what the problem was?"

"Nope. Just that it would be easier to show us in person."

She grabbed her jacket and car keys and slung the file under her arm. Without a word, we left the precinct and headed for the tech department. Much like how the rest of the department was spread out in different locations, we didn't have a central location for tech support so it was a trek across the city out toward Faneuil Hall and the Old State House. Jacquie pulled into a spot near the front door and we headed inside, another bitter afternoon wind biting at exposed skin. I was still shivering when we got to Vinnie's desk.

He was a beefy guy with a shaved head and gauges in both earlobes. He spun to face us and I could feel his gaze traveling up and down my body. I noticed he didn't give Jacquie the same treatment. I put it down to the more than decade age difference between me and my partner and the fact that I'd turned down the guy for a date. I fixed him with a glare and he backed down.

"What was so important about this video you couldn't tell us over the phone?" Jacquie prompted, taking control of the situation.

Vinnie cleared his throat and double clicked the mouse on his computer a few times. "Here's what we pulled from the surrounding cameras for your victim on the ninth." He hit "play" and a scene unfolded. I watched as people meandered along the street in small groups. I scanned the passersby, trying to seek out our victim.

"That's our victim, right there," Jacquie finally said and pointed to a gray-haired woman.

I tracked her movements like a hawk, waiting for her attackers to surface. She got to the corner where she'd been found and everything went black. Not fuzzy snow on a bad signal, just completely black as if they'd been shut off remotely.

"Wait, what happened? Did someone kill the signal?" Jacquie asked.

"No idea. We've got guys looking at the actual cameras but, so far, they seem like they were operating within normal parameters and we didn't pick up anything messing with the signal remotely. Anyway, the video stays black like this for five minutes and then picks up again." He fast forwarded four minutes and twenty seconds and, sure enough, the video came back up showing Mrs. Mendoza lying on the sidewalk, motionless. I tried to find someone reacting to the dead woman, calling 9-1-1, but no one seemed to notice her.

"What time did the 9-1-1 call come in?" I asked.

Jacquie flipped open the file. "Looks like nine forty-one."

I pointed to the time stamp on the video. "By nine twenty-four she was dead. There are people walking around. And no one called 9-1-1 or even checked to see if an old lady was okay for nearly twenty minutes?"

Jacquie pressed her lips into a thin line and studied the screen. Whoever had killed Mrs. Mendoza had used some serious magic if it not only blinded our technology but people around the scene long enough for the killers to melt into the crowd. I suspected whoever had cast that spell had done so before the killing started. People without magical ability would have just kept walking around them as if they didn't exist. They wouldn't stop to think why they were giving the spot on the sidewalk a wide berth.

"Detectives, I have the footage for your victim from last night ready too," Vinnie said, interrupting my train of thought.

"Play it," I ordered. I had a sinking feeling we were going to find the same black screen when Mr. Cho's death came along, but it was worth confirming.

Vinnie queued up the next video and, sure enough, once we spotted Mr. Cho strolling down the street, the video went black for five minutes and then reappeared. The video showed his dead body lying on the sidewalk and everyone moving around him as though he wasn't even there.

"How can none of them see him there and not do anything?" Jacquie grumbled.

"I don't know," I lied. "But I think it's time to talk to the victims' families and see if there's any connection we're missing because this isn't going to get us anywhere."

Jacquie nodded in agreement.

I turned to Vinnie. "It's going to sound stupid, but can you send me the files anyway?"

He shrugged. "Whatever you want."

"Thanks."

With that, we left Vinnie with his useless video

footage. I wanted to tell Jacquie my suspicions about these deaths and their connection to my impending date with destiny, but bringing non-magical people into the community was frowned upon. Plus, I didn't want my partner thinking I was crazy on my first big case. For now, I'd keep the magic to myself and play along with the rest of the investigation.

FIVE

It was almost five o'clock by the time we got back to the precinct. We hadn't spoken most of the ride. I'd been trying to figure out if there was any way I could use magic to manipulate the video footage and restore what had been blacked out. As Vinnie had said, the cameras had still been recording they just captured nothing. I'd never tried to use my abilities for such a task, but it shouldn't be too difficult. For a fleeting moment, I considered reaching out to the Authority. They'd have someone with this particular skillset. But the moment passed and the anger that had been building for a decade washed over me again. I would not give them the satisfaction of crawling back to them in my hour of need when they weren't there to help a grieving teenage girl in search of answers.

"You've been quiet. Want to fill me in?" Jacquie asked.

"What? Sorry. Just thinking."

"So I gathered. Want to share?"

"No. It's nothing."

She studied me with a quizzical expression, opened her mouth as if to say something but stopped and shook her head. For the second time I contemplated cluing Jacquie in on my magic-based theory of the crime and, again, I kept my mouth shut. The way she looked at me, her eyes narrowed just a little bit and her lips pursed, told me she was aware of my frequent trips into my own head and she didn't like it. I'd been a detective for less than two months and this was my first big case. Sure, we'd all been involved with the marathon bombing but I'd been just a beat cop then. People hadn't expected me to carry the case. Maybe Jacquie had reason to be worried about me.

I followed after her and stopped outside one of the interview rooms. Just beyond the window an elderly man and younger woman sat side by side in silence. Mrs. Mendoza's family. When had the family been called in?

"You got this," Jacquie whispered in my ear.

She backed away and let me enter the room on my own. Despite her encouraging words, I had no doubt she was going to be tracking my every move in the interview.

"Mr. Mendoza, my name is Ezri Trenton. I'm one of the detectives working your wife's case. I'm so very sorry for your loss," I said and sat down across from the pair.

The woman translated what I'd said into rapid Spanish. Mr. Mendoza nodded and said something back that I couldn't follow.

"This is my grandfather, Eduardo. He says thank you for your condolences." The woman paused and, when I didn't say anything else, she added, "And I'm Maribel, his granddaughter."

"Thank you both for coming down today. I know this is a very hard time. But I have some questions that I'd like to ask you if that's okay."

Maribel translated my words in her grandfather's ear and he nodded again. I flipped open Mr. Cho's case file and pulled out a photo of him. "Do you know this man?"

Eduardo pulled the picture close and studied it. I could appreciate he was actually trying to help. I couldn't count the number of times a canvas ended with everyone either outright ignoring me or glancing and shaking their head before moving on.

"No," he said and passed the picture to his granddaughter.

Maribel looked at the photo and pushed it back to me. "He doesn't look familiar to me. Why?"

"Is it possible he knew your grandmother through a church group or book club?"

"I don't think so. Why? Who is he?" Maribel repeated.

"He died last night in a similar way to your grandmother. We're just trying to figure out if there is some connection between them."

The pair of them conversed in rapid-fire Spanish and I waited for them to finish. Finally, Maribel said, "I don't think we know this man. I'm sorry."

Through the glass looking out into the heart of the bullpen I saw Jacquie lead Mrs. Cho and her daughter by. They paused long enough for Maribel and Eduardo to get a look at the older woman but they gave no reaction that they knew her. I didn't register any recognition on Mrs. Cho's face either. This only fueled my belief that these victims were chosen at random.

"I know that your wife was former FBI. Do you know if she had any enemies from her work?"

Maribel translated my question and her grandfather shook his head before answering. She looked at me and said, "She was only an analyst. She didn't go into the field."

"Did she maybe lecture at any of the local universities since she retired?"

"I don't think so."

I jotted down the information—unhelpful as it was—and surveyed the pair across from me. "We're going to need you to put together a list of anyone who may have known your grandmother and any groups she participated in so we can look into them," I said.

"Do we really have to do that?" Maribel asked without filling her grandfather in on my request.

"Right now, we don't have a lot to go on and we need to really look at her life and see what might have motivated the attack."

Eduardo whispered something in Maribel's ear and I thought I caught the word "camera". I braced myself for the question I assumed was coming. "She was found near the Esplanade. Aren't there cameras there?"

"We are working all possible avenues." I reached across the table and placed my hand atop Maribel's. "Please, this would really help us."

She finally translated my request for her grandfather and I watched as he nodded and wiped away some tears from his eyes. Maribel gently patted his forearm and we waited for him to compose himself.

"Yes, we will do this."

"Thank you. And if you think of anything else that might be helpful, anything at all even if it's something small, please call me." I pushed my card across the table to them.

"We will." Maribel pocketed the card, stood up and ushered her grandfather from the room.

The silence of the empty interview room pressed in on me and the hair on the nape of my neck tingled. That same feeling of being watched at the

Esplanade returned, but when I glanced over my shoulder there was no one watching me. Shaking the feeling, I retreated to my desk to find two emails from Vinnie with the requested footage. What I needed to do would have been better at home where I was free of the distractions and prying eyes of the precinct, but I couldn't just go running home to do what needed to be done in the middle of a shift. I'd have to risk it here.

"You got this," I whispered under my breath, opening the file from Mr. Cho's scene.

Much like I'd done at the Esplanade, I let the world fade away from my senses. The hum of voices talking on the phone dimmed. The metallic clack of keyboard keys vanished. Even the smell of day-old breakroom coffee became so diluted I couldn't even tell it was there. All I saw was the video file on my screen. I hit play and watched the video from the beginning. Finally, Mr. Cho appeared and then the screen went black. I rewound and hit pause, debating how to proceed. I touched the screen, focusing on the pixels in just the video, and hit play. The video moved frame by frame in something even slower than slow motion, but the result was unchanged. Just after Mr. Cho came into frame, the video went black. Even playing the botched frames in slow-slow motion did nothing to reveal what should have been recorded there.

"Come on." Letting out a frustrated breath, I

raked my fingers through some loose curls that had fallen out of my messy do. Winding strands of red around my finger, I caught a hint of the magic I'd used to dry it. "Of course!"

I was such an idiot. Why focus on the video itself when I should be focusing on the magic woven into it? The pixels couldn't show me what they'd actually recorded because the magic was still blocking them. If I could undo the spell, I'd be set. "Bet you didn't count on me," I snickered smugly under my breath.

I closed my eyes and reached out, trying to find any evidence that the practitioner's magic was still there. I called up the scents I'd found at the scene into my sense memory, first seeking out the dampness of the limestone. Nothing. Moving on to the garlic, I nearly gagged when my magic brushed up against it. An involuntary sneeze made me jump and nearly broke my concentration. Strawberry blossomed around me and I started to disentangle the other practitioner's grip on the video. Once I got hold of the edge of the magic, I should have been able to just will it out of the video, in a sense healing the video with my own brand of spell. Instead, the putrid scent grew stronger, fighting back as if it were *alive* and still connected to the person who'd cast it.

"Trenton, what are you doing?" Jacquie's voice cut through the battle of wills like a sharp blade.

I blinked the precinct back into focus. The sounds came flooding back and made my ears ache like I'd been standing too close to an amp. I was still sitting at my desk but the video in front of me was a little less black. Whatever I'd been doing was starting to work. Unfortunately, the underlying magic came back full force now that I wasn't actively trying to fight it and it turned completely dark again. I turned to see Jacquie standing over my left shoulder staring at me.

"Sorry, what was the question?"

"I asked what you were doing. You know, rookie, you've been zoning out a lot lately."

"I'm sorry... I guess the case is just getting to me a little."

"I told you if you couldn't handle it, you needed to tell me."

"No, I'm fine, really. It won't happen again."

"Now, what the hell are you doing?"

"Oh, uh, I just thought I might have a way to clear up the footage."

"You've got some magic trick that the tech boys don't?"

If only she knew. A seed of dread took root in my gut and for a moment the possibility that she *did* know nauseated me. I laughed to cover the fear. "Maybe. I need to look into it more." I spun around with my back to the screen. "How did it go with Mrs. Cho?" I suspected I knew the answer already, but I needed the deflection from what I'd been doing.

"She's still pretty shaken, but she'd never seen our other victim before."

"Same with Mrs. Mendoza's husband and grand-daughter. But they're going to put a list together of known associates. Maybe we'll find some link there."

"Maybe."

"Jacquie, what if these killings are just random?"

"What makes you think that?"

"Call it a hunch. I mean, I know we've only just started digging, but if we can't find a link between these two then why would the person who killed them have found it?"

Jacquie leaned with one hip against the corner of my desk. "Maybe we're looking in the wrong place."

I crossed my arms over my chest. "Meaning?"

"Maybe we don't need to go as old school as we've been thinking. We live in the twenty-first century."

"Something tells me Mrs. Mendoza wasn't on Facebook or Instagram," I said.

"You'd be surprised."

I shook my head and turned back around, ready to do some Facebook stalking to see if I could find either of our victims online, when Jacquie rounded the desk and grabbed her jacket off her chair. She gestured for me to follow.

"Where are we going?" I called.

"For a ride. Come on."

I glanced around the bullpen but no one paid us

any attention so I trailed after my partner. I slipped into the passenger seat and waited for her to start the engine, but she sat there, hands resting against the bottom of the steering wheel. After a beat, she looked at me. "Something is going on with you." It was a statement of fact not a question.

"I don't know what you're talking about," I protested.

"There's something other than this case in your head and it's been distracting you all shift."

"I told you last night and I'll say it again, I'm fine. I can handle this case or any case. I know how to separate my personal and professional lives."

"Look, if it has something to do with what you told me about your mother, I want you to know I'm here to listen if you want to talk about it. Maybe getting it off your chest will give you the clarity to focus on this case. Because, I'll be honest with you, right now I'm really not sure you are going to cut it."

Her words were harsh but her eyes showed how concerned she was for me. That look in her eyes reminded me of my mother. Even if she didn't realize it, that look made me feel fourteen years old again. I plastered a confident smile on my face and said, "Thanks, but like I said, I'm good. Now, where are we going?"

"I heard it was your birthday today. Figured I'd treat you to dinner."

I laughed. "You should have led with that."

That hint of concern crept back into the edges of her mouth but she said nothing. She started the engine and pulled out of the parking lot. We ended up eating Chinese out of cartons, sitting on a bench near the Public Garden, overlooking the small lake. It was still too cold to have the swan boats out on the water so they sat docked at the far end. I held my container of Szechwan beef close to my chest for warmth, the spiciness making my nose run. We sat in silence for a long time.

"How are the kids?" I finally broke the tension between us.

"Good. Spending more time with their mom lately."

"That's good." From what little I knew about Jacquie's private life, she'd taken in her niece and nephew while her sister-in-law was in rehab. Jacquie's brother had died in a car accident when the kids were young. She didn't like to talk about her family life at work. Something we had in common.

"Yeah. I think she'll be ready to take them back soon."

"You'll miss them," I said and nudged her shoulder with my free hand.

"Yeah. And what about you?"

I arched a brow. "What about me?"

"Are you seeing your father to celebrate?"

I let out a bitter hiccup of laughter. "He sent me

a text this morning. That's it. Frankly, that's more than I wanted from him anyway."

"He's still your father. He still loves you."

"Maybe, but it doesn't mean I have to let him into my life. I'm doing just fine on my own." I checked the display on my phone. We still had half an hour left on our dinner break. The dream from this morning flitted through my consciousness. Maybe a little visit to family wasn't the worst idea after all. "Do you mind if we make a stop before we head back to the precinct?"

Jacquie closed up her carton. "Where to?"

"To see some family after all."

SIX

I always got the sense that my mother was watching me whenever I visited her grave. Maybe that was just how cemeteries were supposed to be. Jacquie waited for me in the car as I wound my way through bits of scrub grass and weeds to my mother's headstone. It was out of the way near the back of the cemetery and the plot was neatly weeded. A small bouquet of daisies sat propped against one corner. My mother's favorite. My father had clearly been by recently. I stopped in front of the stone and tugged the pendant out from beneath my jacket, the metal warm to the touch thanks to body heat.

"Hey, Mom," I greeted. I didn't expect a response, but a gust of wind picked up in that instant and the honey flavor of my mother's magic bloomed around me. I closed my eyes and soaked in the familiar scent. I could almost feel her wrapping her arms around me as she'd done on many a cold night.

"I'm here, sweetheart." I heard her voice in my head as if she were standing right beside me.

Tears stung my eyes and my vision blurred. I blinked until my lashes couldn't keep the deluge back and tears streaked down my cheeks, running in rivulets over the cleft of my chin and onto my jacket. I had so much I wanted to say to my mother but words failed me. I'd made so many promises yet to be kept. I'd honestly thought by now—after ten years— my mother could be at peace. That I would have closure. But I was no closer to solving the case than I'd been as a distraught fifteen-year-old coming home to find her life in ruins. I dabbed at my cheeks and hitched a breath.

"I don't know where to start. I'm so sorry I haven't found who took you from us yet. I haven't given up, I promise. Things have gotten kind of strange around here. The case I'm working, it's steeped in dark magic. It can't be a coincidence that it's happening now when we are so close to the Equinox, to the prophecy coming true." The pendant pulsed between my fingers. "I can feel the power shifting, Mom. It's fighting hard to find equi-librium. Harder than it has been in years."

"Remember her words." It was like a breath

against the nape of my neck, setting the tiny hairs on edge.

"I couldn't forget Eleanor's warning if I tried."

Most of the branches of our family tree had died out years ago so, when I came along, it seemed pretty damn definitive that I was the one destined to fight the coming evil. As such, the prophecy had been drilled into my head until I could recite it in my sleep. My parents never let me forget the burden I carried having been born a girl. I'd resented it at first, being so young. But it meant more time spent with my mother, learning everything she could teach me about magic. It hadn't been enough. I still remembered finding out what destiny awaited me when I was eight years old.

Winter had settled in, the days growing short and dark. The heat was cranked in our apartment to ward off the cold. I didn't really understand what the change in seasons meant for people like us. Not yet. But I could see as soon as the days changed, my mother's mood soured. She snapped at my father and stormed around the house. They didn't think I saw them fight, but I was keenly aware of the stiff embraces and glares over dinner. I knew what was coming next: divorce. My friend Angie Vazquez's parents had gotten a divorce. She'd said it had started with arguing and one day her dad just didn't come home. So I'd started to prepare myself. I'd even packed a suitcase to be ready for when my parents were no longer under the same roof.

Today had been one of the worst days. They'd shut themselves in their bedroom, but I could still hear their voices rising and falling from behind closed doors. I snuck into the hallway outside their room and listened, ear pressed to the crack between the door and the jam.

"Katie, be reasonable," Dad said.

"She needs to know, Matthew. We have to start now before it's too late," Mom argued.

"She's just a kid. Can't we wait a few years until she's older? Until she can really understand what's happening?"

I could hear floorboards creak. "They say it could happen soon."

"But they don't know for sure. They could be wrong. They have been before."

"My mother told me when I was her age."

"And how'd that work out?"

"I turned out just fine." My mother's voice rose with the last word.

"Because it wasn't about you."

"I didn't know that. Not until Ezri came along."

"How do we even know it's her? She's not the only one left."

"She's the only girl. You know Madeline can't have more children."

The argument had my attention and I didn't

notice the doorknob turn until the door was open and my mother nearly tripped over me. I watched as my parents exchanged furtive glances before my mother bent down to my eye level. "How much of that did you hear?"

I bit my lip, not wanting to admit I'd been snooping. "Am I in trouble?"

Her lips turned up into a smile that didn't reach her eyes. I could see she was trying not to cry. "No. But I think we need to have a talk."

"Are you and Dad going to get a divorce?" It came out before I could stop the words.

"Of course not. Why would you think that?" Dad asked.

"You fight all the time and I know it's about me," I answered, my voice barely above a whisper.

Mom pulled me into her arms and shushed me, her hands patting my back. I let her hold me like that as long as she wanted, even though I still didn't believe my father's words. Finally, Mom stood up and guided me to the living room. Dad trailed behind us, keeping his distance. Mom disappeared back into the bedroom, returning with an old book.

"Ezri, honey, you know how you can do things other people can't?"

"Yes. We have magic."

'That's right. And it has been in our family for a very, very long time." She patted the cover of the book. "This has been in our family for hundreds of years. In it, one of our family members wrote about a very special girl in our family."

I wiped at the tears in my eyes. "Who?"

"It doesn't say her name."

"What does it say?"

She opened the book and flipped through the yellowed pages to the middle of the book and passed it to me. "Here, you can read it for yourself."

I took in the swirls of the penmanship of the author. I turned back to the front page and saw that it was the diary of Theodora Harrow, born 1671. Returning to the page my mother had marked, I read Theodora's words:

Eleanor's parting gift came in the form of events yet to pass. I transcribe them here so that we may never forget her sacrifice or that our blood must live on. When the world is balanced anew and fire rains down as midday turns to night, the last daughter of Harrow's blood shall rise to stand against the Old Guard's return.

I looked up at my mother. "What does it mean?"

Mom pressed her lips into a thin line. Dad remained silent. Finally, she took the book out of my hands and said, "Ezri, you are the last daughter of Harrow's blood. We think that you are meant to do great things and have great power. You can never forget these words."

I blinked back tears, returning to my mother's grave. For the longest time, I'd thought I wouldn't be alone in the battle to come, but as the last decade proved, my assumption had been painfully wrong. I hadn't just lost my mother though. A familiar face I hadn't seen in years flashed before me and I let it pull me back into the past again.

I was thirteen years old and it was a blistering summer day. Desmond and I sat side by side on the porch of the rented house overlooking the Cape. He'd been descended from Eleanor Pruitt, my ancestor's sister, the one who'd made the prophecy that hung around my neck like an albatross. I wiped beads of sweat from my forehead, my hair cropped short. My cousin couldn't have been any more different. Blue eyed and dirty blond, he towered over me, having nearly five years on me in age. I often wondered why he hung out with me at all.

At present, Desmond sipped from a bottle of root beer. He glanced at me and said, "You know, you're lucky."

I let out a laugh. "What for?"

"You have a destiny. You know what's awaiting you."

I couldn't resist an eye roll. "Whatever, Des. I didn't ask for this stupid destiny. Why does it have to be me?"

"Because you were born with the right qualifications."

"You mean boobs?"

He shrugged and tried to hide a smile with his

soda bottle. "All I'm saying is I wish I had what you do. Having magic running in your veins is great, but sometimes I just feel so rudderless. Like what makes me so special that I've been given this power?"

"You can have my destiny. I mean, sure, it's nice to hang out with my mom, but everyone expects me to be this great and amazing person. But I'm just me. I'm just Ezri."

He wrapped an arm around my shoulders, skin sticking to skin in the heat, and leaned in. "I can't take it from you, but I'll be there for you if you need me. I promise."

A sudden chill pulled me out of the memory and back to my mother's graveside. The pendant in my hand still generated significant heat—more than it should have at this point—and I shoved it back beneath my jacket. Another gust of wind blew and I braced against the headstone so it didn't take me with it. My teeth clattered together against the cold and my legs ached from standing still. I shook them out to get the blood flowing again. Fresh tears turned to icy patches on my cheeks as I remembered Desmond's promise. One he'd broken two years later. He'd been part of covering up my mother's murder and I'd lost one of my closest allies.

Footsteps crunched through the stiff grass behind me, sending my hackles up. I clenched my fists and spun on my heel, ready to bring my hands up to defend myself. Tension fled from my muscles as soon as Jacquie came into view. I blew out a breath and tried to shake the sense of anxiety that suddenly settled in my chest, constricting my lungs.

"Sorry to interrupt your visit, but we need to go. We've got another body."

SEVEN

The sun had faded from most of the sky by the time we pulled up at the corner of St. James Street and Berkley Street. It wasn't far from the theater district and one of the numerous law schools that Boston boasted. Like the other two scenes, it was well traveled, even on a weekend. Before I climbed out of the car, I took quick stock of the security cameras that were visible. There weren't nearly as many as at the previous scenes but it was likely that one had captured the killers in action. I fully expected the footage to be corrupted like the others, but that didn't matter. If I could manage to fix one set, I could do all three.

The moment I stepped out of the car, bile burbled into my throat and I ducked back in. Jacquie was already halfway to where Tricia bent over a body. I swallowed and pulled out the sandalwood charm. I inhaled deeply, letting it wash everything else away. I nudged the car door open and took a breath. It wasn't nearly as overpowering and nauseating but I could still smell the dark magic stinking up the scene, even more so than Mr. Cho. We'd just barely missed our killers. Steeling myself, I traipsed from the car to join my partner by the body, pulling on gloves as I went. My chest tightened when I saw the victim—a teenage boy with rust-colored hair. His skin, which had probably been pale in life, was ashen in death.

Tricia looked over at me, dark circles wreathing her eyes. "Meet Preston Elms. Poor thing was only sixteen. Just got his learner's permit."

I crouched beside the medical examiner and took in Preston's body. I could smell the limestone as if he'd been lying in a quarry. The same dust coated his jacket and I could almost see the whorls of a fingerprint in the fabric of his T-shirt. I lifted his right hand—his limb and joints still supple—and found angry red abrasions and what looked like stone chips beneath his fingernails.

"He fought back. It looks like he may have even gotten a piece of his attacker," I pointed out, keeping Preston's hand aloft until Tricia returned with an evidence bag to collect the chips and swab the dead boy's fingers.

Jacquie nudged my knee with the toe of her boot

and I stood up to join her. "We may have access to some surveillance cameras," she said.

"I noticed. But if this is the same killer, and I have to believe it is, they'd have known that. They'd have done whatever the hell they did before to mess with the footage."

"And the killer is escalating. It's barely been twenty-four hours since the last body dropped. There were at least two days between Altagracia and Edwin."

"They're getting impatient," I said. I held my tongue about the fact that the Equinox was rapidly approaching.

"That they are." She turned to Tricia. "Whatever you can get us on forensics as fast as you can would be appreciated."

"Got it," Tricia said with a mock salute that Jacquie didn't catch. I jotted down some additional notes in my notepad like Preston's address—I was not looking forward to another notification—and that I'd sensed the same magic at the scene.

I scanned the people walking by, hoping something would jump out at me. The ones who were stopping by the crime scene expressed only mild interest before being ushered along by uniformed officers. No one obvious stood out as watching and relishing the scene. And it was all well and good that I could pick up on a magical signature, but it meant nothing if I didn't have a person to connect it to. I was about to see if I could latch on to the magic in the area—it was widespread enough that it practically blanketed the length of sidewalk where Preston's body lay—when another fiery figure appeared not twenty paces from me.

Jacquie's back was to her and Tricia was too busy finishing up examining Preston's corpse to notice. As nonchalantly as I could manage, I closed the distance. The woman's eyes were hollow and her hair was coal black. Her clothes looked similar to those worn by the woman I'd seen disappear at the Cho scene.

"Who are you? What are you doing here?" I hissed.

She smiled, withered lips pulling back into a vile grin full of missing and decayed teeth. The same harsh, choking scent of burning flesh and ash clogged up my nostrils and I coughed to try to get much needed air to my lungs. I was close enough to notice the thick rope burns circling her throat. She lifted her right hand, pointing the index finger straight at my chest. Despite not having eyes, I swear she gave me an accusatory glare. The pendant beneath my jacket warmed against my breastbone, as if to protect me from her taunt.

She opened her mouth and a rattling laugh burbled from her chest. No one seemed to take notice of the figure and then, just as before, she vanished. The painful timbre of her laugh still grated on my eardrums and I was certain they were bleeding from the noise. But having gotten this close, I had some idea of who the woman may have been. A faded memory of learning about practitioners strong enough to rise from the grave floated to the surface.

Her smoky signature still clung to my nasal passages and I had to take a second hit of the sandalwood to get myself oriented again. Even with her scent gone, things were a little hazy. The limestone and garlic hung heavy in the air as they had before, but the world felt off kilter.

Streetlights finally came on along the road as the last vestiges of sunlight disappeared. I watched people passing through the small pools of orange light and my brain latched on to a thought from earlier. *There should be enough magic here to let me track the killers.*

Yes, leaving the scene was risky. I'd have to come up with an excuse to tell Jacquie, but it was the only real lead I had. I focused on the limestone and let it gather around me. I had to keep my own powers in check so that they didn't overwhelm what I was trying to find. Finally, a silvery shimmer manifested, one end settling over Preston's torso, the other disappearing off into the city streets. I took off and followed after it.

I ducked under the crime scene tape and settled into a jog, letting the magic lead me north along Berkeley Street. For a moment, it looked as if the killer had tried to duck down a side street half a block away, but the magic veered back the other way, heading straight past the looming sign of a department store and Panera Bread. Before I realized it, I hit Boylston and skidded to a stop.

The main thoroughfare was teeming with pedestrians and several of them stopped to stare at me. In my mad dash more chunks of hair had come loose and I could feel my chest rising and falling more quickly from the exertion. Blocking all of that out, I zeroed in on the killer's signature again, this time hanging a right and making a beeline for the Public Gardens, not far from where Jacquie and I had sat eating dinner a few short hours ago. I kept running until I hit the Common, the shimmer of magic vanishing as quickly as it had manifested to me.

I skidded to a halt not far from the inbound Boylston T station. I could hear the screech of the trains coming into the station from here. Barren trees lined the stretches of the Common to my left. How far back had I actually lost the scent? I spun in a slow circle trying to remember or pick up another trace, but it was gone.

My phone buzzed in my jacket pocket and I yanked it out to see my partner's name flash across the screen with an incoming call. My throat went dry as the line buzzed again, waiting for me to answer. I knew she was going to ask where I'd run off to and I still hadn't come up with an excuse. I couldn't just ignore her call. "Hey, partner," I greeted, hoping my nerves didn't come through.

"Where the hell did you go? One of the uniforms saw you just take off."

Time to bend the truth. "I thought I saw someone loitering nearby, watching the scene. But when I started over they took off and I followed." I was about to add that I'd identified myself as police, but there didn't seem to be the need to build things up that far yet.

"Did you catch them?"

"No." At least that was the whole truth.

"Make sure you note it in your report. Get back to the scene. We need to head back to the precinct."

"Why?"

"Just get back here." The line went dead.

I stowed my phone and retraced my steps. I passed the Gardens and caught a whiff of damp limestone but I knew if I followed up on it now, I'd get more of an earful from Jacquie for disobeying a superior officer. She could escalate it to the captain if she wanted to jam me up. I made a mental note and went another block on Boylston before turning left on Berkeley. I could see the medical examiner's van pulling away from the scene as I arrived. Jacquie was in the driver seat of the car, seatbelt on and ready to leave. Squaring my shoulders, I marched over to the passenger side door and climbed in.

"So why do we have to get back to the precinct?" I asked as Jacquie pulled into the flow of traffic.

"You want to tell me why you went chasing after a suspect without letting me know first?"

I opened my mouth but words failed me. I wanted to say, "Because I was following a magical lead that you wouldn't understand," but knew I couldn't. So I went with, "I didn't want them to get away. We have so little on these cases as it is. I just reacted. I guess I wasn't thinking."

She took her eyes off the road and our gazes met. I shrunk back against the seat under her disappointed demeanor. "That's right, you didn't think. That kind of shit gets you killed in this job. I thought you knew that."

"I do. It won't happen again."

"It better not. And I meant what I said. If you aren't cut out for this, you have to tell me. This case is bigger than we imagined and I can't have you running off putting things in jeopardy. Not with so many people dying."

"I get it. I screwed up and you don't want me messing with making the biggest bust of your career. I'm not some child you have to babysit."

"Then stop acting like it."

I bit down hard on my tongue to keep from snapping back at her. She must have felt the same because the rest of the trip back to the precinct was silent. Tension crawled all over my body. Magic was threatening to ruin this part of my life too.

As I sat down to write my report on Preston's scene, I thought again about whether it would be easier to just bring a non-practitioner into the fold, etiquette and experience be damned. But the way Jacquie avoided eye contact with me batted that idea down. She was mad at me now and telling her the truth would only end poorly.

By the time I finished my report and looked at the clock, my shift was over. Jacquie was nowhere to be seen. I heaved a small sigh of relief as I made my way out to my car and back home.

Despite the clock reading nearly midnight, the moment I crossed the threshold into my apartment, my energy level jumped. I should have been tired, but every nerve in my body was firing at once, telling me that there was work to be done. I had video footage to extract, but there was something else about the murders that bugged me.

The locations had all been very public—too public if you didn't have magic to conceal your crimes. The victims still felt random but maybe the places were the key. I decided handling the video footage was the best option now. If we could put a face to our killers then maybe location didn't matter. Changing into sweatpants and a T-shirt, I climbed onto the couch, laptop propped against my knees. I opened up my work email and found the files from

Vinnie. Dragging a copy of each video onto the desktop, I opened Mr. Cho's video and let the world fall away.

As I'd done at the precinct, I started the video a few seconds before it went black. I pressed my fingers to the screen—thankful for once I didn't have a touch screen—and released a fraction of my magic into the device, letting it seek out the dark spell holding the footage hostage. It took more digging than the last time, but I finally found it.

"Give it up," I grunted through clenched teeth.

The reek of garlic choked me, but I fought back. Unafraid of attracting the wrong attention, I let out a burst of power and soon all I could smell was strawberry. I closed my eyes, imagining the video's pixels were tangible things I could touch. In my mind's eye, I could see them, tethered together and oozing black with the killer's accomplice's spell. I reached out toward the darkness and my hands came away covered in viscous fluid giving off a mix of fresh tar and mulch. Thick vines of dark magic slithered around the hidden images. I felt my fingers curl around the first vine and I pulled as hard as I could. Sharp pinpricks of pain shot through my fingertips and I bit my lower lip to keep from letting the pain get to me. I willed my hands to become hard as stone and impervious to penetration. Slowly, the skin on the palms of my hands and the pads of my fingers turned rough and thick. The vine wiggled beneath my grasp, but it was no longer able to lash out at me. Pulling power from around me, I strengthened my grip and my arm muscles and pulled the vine free, flinging it off into the ether. As soon as it disappeared, the blackness covering the frame vanished, giving me a clear glimpse. But it was out of order and this close up it meant nothing.

I couldn't worry about the order now. There were too many frames to free and even with my magical endurance built up I knew the task ahead of me was going to drain me. After the first vine was freed, the others clung even tighter, giving me no other choice than to fight even harder to get them off.

After what felt like hours, I'd only freed a small fraction of the infected video file. My arms grew heavy with exertion—even fueled by extra magic to keep me going—and my hands ached from all of the pulling. Maybe it was exhaustion setting in, but I never sensed the dark spell caster's presence until thick vines slithered up my body, choking the air from my lungs and compressing my chest.

Another loop circled my throat, violently crushing my windpipe. I could feel my eyes throbbing in their sockets. My brain said to give up and preserve what little air I had left to breathe. It told me that if I didn't struggle, it would be over sooner.

I promptly told my brain to fuck off. I wasn't going to be killed by a computer virus turned sentient. As best I could, I took in one big breath and held it. Black spots popped in my vision, but I ignored them. Instead, I turned my thoughts to changing the way my body was constructed. All magic is the manipulation of molecules and the vines would have a much harder time keeping hold of me if I wasn't solid. One moment I was a flesh and blood human being, the next I was simply light, filling the space in my mind's eye with brightness.

The vines withered on contact and, even though I didn't have a corporeal form in that instant, I smiled. The presence of my adversary sharpened into the shadow of a person. I couldn't make out a face—they weren't that stupid—but it was a generally male shaped figure. Just as I'd suspected.

"You want to go, asshole? Let's go!" My voice bounced from every angle in the space.

I directed the parts of me that used to be hands toward the figure's shadowy face, fingers materializing enough to claw out his eyes. He vanished before I could reach him.

"You are more formidable than we thought," a voice sneered. It could have been anyone or a group of someones speaking in unison.

"Your first mistake was assuming you knew me," I replied.

"We will see. But even your blood can't save you in the end," the voice spat.

The figure disappeared completely and the voice

faded. I stayed as particles of light for a while longer, but nothing else came to attack me.

The world around me slipped out of view and, before I knew it, I was back in my apartment, the laptop dangling precariously from my lap. I set it down and surveyed the space around me. I swallowed and cringed, my muscles sore as if someone really had been squeezing the life out of me. I examined my chest and felt what could be welts ringing my torso. My fingers ached and I spotted smears of blood on the screen of my computer and my index fingers on both hands were stained crimson.

Great.

I took a few minutes to let my body adjust to being back in the real world and in one piece before I went to wipe the blood from the computer. I had used my abilities plenty of times to stop bad guys in the last five years, but I'd never flat out fought someone with power. That had never been what my parents had taught me. Maybe if the Authority hadn't given me the middle finger all those years ago I would have learned what it felt like to fight someone else who was evenly matched in magical ability.

Time to see whether I'd actually made any real progress. The video file was still mostly black, but there were slivers of video where none had been before. I stared, expecting them to vanish now that I wasn't magically in contact with the file, but they remained. I'd managed to actually make some progress. Too bad it had kicked my ass.

I staggered to the bathroom and checked myself out in the mirror. There was a small bruise wreathing my throat and deep purple bruises were already forming around my ribs. I could cover my throat with concealer and I'd just have to be careful moving around. I popped a few aspirin for the pain. Some people could do amazing things with healing magic, but I wasn't one of them.

Minor, mundane cuts I could handle. Wounds caused by magic were a different story. J.T. had been able to heal—or at least he was on his way to learning his birthright—but that was a long time ago. I'd done enough dredging up of the past for one day. Gingerly, I retreated to bed. I prayed tonight I could just fall into a dreamless void and sleep. At least tomorrow was my day off.

EIGHT

I almost got my wish. My head hit the pillow just after five in the morning and if I dreamed, I didn't recall them. But I started awake as my phone skittered along the table beside my bed at half past eight. It was a precinct number and my heart leapt into my throat, throbbing painfully as I scrambled to answer.

"Detective Trenton," I answered, my words still sluggish with sleep and my throat still aching from the fight only a few short hours ago.

"Sorry to call on your day off, Detective," the dispatcher said. "But Captain Beech insisted you and Detective DeWitt report to the precinct this morning at nine thirty."

I swallowed—it was less painful than when I went to bed—and blinked a few times, trying to shake the tiredness from my body. "Did she say what it's about?"

"I'm afraid not, ma'am. That's all I was told."

"Thanks." I ended the call and stared up at the ceiling, immobile. I really needed sleep and time to heal, but the captain would only have called us in if it was case related. So I crawled out of bed and took a lukewarm shower, wincing only a few times when the water pressure was too much for my battered body.

It was almost nine o'clock by the time I ended up in Monday morning traffic on Commonwealth Avenue. Working the second shift had its advantages. Generally avoiding rush hour was one of them. I kept an eye on the clock the entire trip. By the time I walked into the precinct my phone's screen told me it was 9:27. Jacquie was sitting at her desk, staring intently at her computer screen. I was halfway to my desk when she swiveled to face me, her caramel-colored eyes looking nearly as sleep-deprived as mine.

"You look like shit, partner," she said. Apparently, her anger had dissipated with a few hours of sleep. That or my bruises gave her some sense of sympathy.

A small weight lifted from my chest. "Thanks. Do you have any idea what's going on?"

"Not sure. But we've got company in the conference room." She hooked a thumb over her shoulder.

The door was ajar and I could see people in blue jackets crowded around one end of the table. "She called in the Feds," I whispered just as Captain Beech stepped from her office, waving us inside.

"We'll find out," Jacquie answered.

Every time I found myself in the captain's office, I felt like was being called to the principal's office—even if it was for something good. So, like always, my gut tightened ever so slightly and my neck muscles tensed. Despite the fact that there were two chairs waiting for us, both Jacquie and I remained standing at attention as Captain Beech rounded the desk.

"I apologize for calling you both in on your day off, but this case has gotten bigger than we expected. So far we've been lucky that most news outlets haven't reported on the murders or connected them."

"We're working as hard as we can, ma'am," I said.

She held up a hand. "I know you are, Detective. But we've had three dead bodies in nearly as many days and no indication that our killer is close to being done with whatever their agenda is. We need some fresh eyes on this. That's why I've called in the FBI."

The door opened behind us and, instinctively, I turned toward the sound. A tall man with enough pomade in his hair to rival a Ken doll strode in. He wore an expertly fitted black suit with a white dress shirt and skinny black tie. He could have walked off the set of a *Men in Black* movie and I wouldn't have been surprised. Despite too much product in his hair, he had a sort of elegance in the way he moved and I caught myself admiring the gentle slope of his nose and chin.

"Detectives Trenton and DeWitt, this is Supervisory Special Agent James Taggart. He's going to be assisting us with the investigation."

Jacquie shook his hand first. I followed suit and the moment our fingers touched, electricity jolted up my arm. His grip was firm and my already aching fingers throbbed under the pressure. He caught and held my gaze for far longer than necessary.

"Pleasure to meet you both," he finally said. Something about his voice sounded familiar and my brain struggled to place it. The clipped cadence bore a hint of the voice I'd encountered disentangling the magic from the video footage, but that was ridiculous. The killer wouldn't imitate an FBI agent. What would a Fed get by killing random innocent people? There was something else familiar about Taggart, like I'd seen him before, but my brain was overloaded trying to solve too many problems to add the mystery to the list right now.

"Let's get started," Captain Beech said.

Taggart released his grip on my hand and I tried to cover the pain as my fingers throbbed. I shoved it in my pocket and focused a little energy into the skin, urging the pain to slip away. I was halfway to the conference room when I felt a hand on my shoulder.

Jacquie came up beside me and said, "Don't let

them psych you out. This is still our case. They're here because one of the victims was one of their own. But the captain's right. We don't have any leads and we need the extra eyes. Maybe we've missed something."

"Yeah, maybe," I muttered.

We joined Agent Taggart and his team in the conference room. Both of the whiteboards in the room were in use. One was covered with a brief breakdown of each victim—photo, location and date of death—while the other held a map of the city with little colored flags denoting the locations. There was a rough circle drawn around the three points and a small black "x" drawn in the center of the three points.

One of the blue-jacketed agents—a woman who looked to be in her 30s with jet black hair trimmed to just below her chin and watery blue eyes—stood beside the map. "We think we've triangulated the killer's comfort zone," she announced.

I studied the map and wasn't impressed. It was too simple. Sure, geographic profiling was a useful skill and had helped to catch killers plenty of times, but this felt *unfinished*. They still had almost a week before the Equinox and, if it were me, I wouldn't have stopped at just three. I did have to give them some credit for emphasizing the geography since I'd come to the conclusion that location was the key to these killers.

"How do we know that's it?" I asked.

The agent looked at me, her mouth slightly agape. "Excuse me?"

"How do we know we won't have any more victims? The killer is getting more brazen. The time between bodies is shortening. Whatever is driving these acts is ramping up, not slowing down. I just think it's too early to think we can narrow it down."

"Well that's your opinion, Detective." The way she said the last word made my skin crawl, as if the title I'd earned was somehow useless.

"Let's hear the detective out," Taggart interrupted.

"And what about the video surveillance? Has your team managed to make any headway with that?" I pressed.

"Well, we've got our best analysts on it."

"So, you've got no more than we do. How about the first victim, Altagracia Mendoza? She worked for your agency. Have you any leads there you want to share?"

She opened her mouth to snap back at me, but Agent Taggart stepped up and placed a hand on his subordinate's arm. "Agent Mendoza's work is classified. But we have our people looking into any potential leads there and we will of course share anything we find with you. For now, why don't we focus on the 'why' of these three victims? Perhaps if we can determine their connection, we can stop the killer from claiming another life."

"This is where we could really use some help. So far, the families of the first two victims haven't been able to provide any helpful connections," Jacquie interjected.

"What about the third victim?" Taggart kept his attention on me.

"We have the boy's parents coming in this morning for an interview," Captain Beech said, much to my surprise.

"Let us know when they arrive. We'll speak with them."

Captain Beech nodded and ushered Jacquie and me out of the room. "You two should stay for the interview. This is still our case."

"Understood," Jacquie said.

As soon as the captain was out of earshot I turned to my partner, a cold drizzle of sweat snaking down my neck. "We never notified the family."

"Third shift handled it. But don't worry, I made sure they gave both of our cards. I've also let Marcy in reception know to page us when the family arrives."

"You want to get into the interview room before the Feds," I said with a smirk.

Jacquie winked. "I have to admit, I wasn't expecting you to pick a fight with a Fed two minutes after being introduced, but I'm with you, there's no way in hell we are getting sidelined from our own investigation."

I watched as the woman I'd snapped at earlier came striding out of the conference room, hands shoved in her pockets. Taggart remained in the room, bent over some files on the conference room table. The tip of his tie brushed the bottom of the paper and for a moment he looked up and our gazes met again. He gave me a brief smile before turning his attention back. I felt heat creep up the tips of my ears. I was clearly imagining things.

"Do you want to take the lead on the family interview before the Feds kick us out?" Jacquie asked.

I shook my head. "No, you go ahead. I actually realized I have to check on something."

"Check on what?"

"Something for the case. I'll let you know if anything comes of it. Let me know if you get anything from Preston's parents."

I didn't wait for her to respond. I weaved between the morning shift coming in with their coffee mugs. The fact that I'd barely slept caught up with me and I couldn't stifle a yawn. I wasn't going to let Taggart and his team steal this case out from under me. Sleep could wait until the killers were caught.

NINE

Battling rush hour traffic out of the city wasn't nearly as harrowing as my trip in, but it still took me nearly a half hour to get back to my apartment. Mercifully, you couldn't go more than a couple blocks without hitting a Dunkin' Donuts so I'd grabbed a bagel and a large coffee before heading inside.

Some part of me knew it was all in my head but that first sip of coffee set my synapses blazing, jolting me awake more than I'd felt in days. It wouldn't last long. I intended to take advantage of it. My laptop sat askew on the living room table where I'd left it in the wee hours this morning. My throat and ribs ached, as if to signal a revolt if I tried to attack more of the video footage. Knowing I wasn't in a place to handle more abuse—at least not without a lot of extra protection before I started—I traipsed into the bedroom and pushed aside the lower row of work pants and jackets in my closet, rummaging until I found the two printer paper boxes hiding in the back. Dragging them out sent a cloud of dust into the air.

"Note to self, clean the closet once in a while," I said, coughing, before getting a grip and hoisting the boxes into my arms.

I dumped the boxes on the edge of the couch, dusting off my blouse and pants before opening the top box. When my mother died and I took my magical education upon myself, I'd gathered all of the family journals, secreting them away from my father and the Authority. At least I assumed they didn't know I had them, otherwise they'd have come knocking down my door to get them back.

An unexpected wave of sadness washed over me as I studied the carefully preserved leather-bound diaries of the witches who'd come before me and for a split second I was that eight-year-old holding Theodora Harrow's words in my hands for the first time. Four hundred years of lives and spells condensed to one 11 ½" by 18" box.

Setting the lid aside, I moved on to the second box. My mother had kept a lot of books and other bits of local history from the time of the Witch Trials for the Authority. Lucky for me, she'd kept them at home and I'd gotten my hands on them before the Authority came looking. I wasn't entirely sure what I was looking for, but the locations of our murders now were somehow significant back when Theodora and Eleanor were alive. It was the only lead that made any sort of sense.

Gently, I pulled out the thick tomes on magical lore from around the world. Our brand of magic came along with us to the Colonies, but that didn't mean it was the only kind out there. Setting it on the floor beneath the table, I moved on to the next layer of materials—hand drawn maps of Massachusetts circa 1690. The height of the persecution of my kind. I spread the first map out on the table, careful not to pull it for fear it would tear. Whoever had done the cartography had been spot on and it amazed me how I could still pick out the edge of the Charles River running through what would become downtown Boston. Even some of the named cities and towns were still in their current locations. Over the landscape, I spotted tiny red circles. I lifted the map up to the light and saw that there were minute burn marks through each of the spots.

"That's weird," I muttered.

There was no other sign of burning or damage to the map. I brushed the tip of my thumb over one of the dots and for a moment it burned, giving off the same choking ash and sulfur smell of the women at the crime scenes. The burning subsided after maybe thirty seconds, but the deepness of the red on the map remained. In fact, red scorch marks brightened all over the map. Smoke to my right caught my attention and I turned in time to see the journal on the top of the pile in the first box starting to smolder. I pulled it free and blew on it, hoping whatever magic I'd just invoked didn't set everything else ablaze. The pages began flipping open of their own accord to reveal what I assumed was a ledger of sorts. Text—in the same flowing script as Theodora Harrow's—burned bright against the page. As I ran my finger across the words, they dimmed enough for me to read:

Agatha Warren – hung by the neck until dead for poisoning children. Date of Death: 2 July 1690.

I studied the entry again. There was no suspicion on Agatha's part. Someone—another witch or a fearful local—had decided she was guilty and punished her accordingly. Out of curiosity, I turned back to the map and traced my finger across another of the red scorch marks. In my lap, the ledger grew warm again and another entry, this one dated from March of 1689, ignited. This woman, Margaret Keene, had also been hung, this time for cursing the town clerics.

Setting the map back on the table for the time being, I turned my attention to the other entries in the ledger. By and large all of them recorded hanging deaths of women who had used magic for dark purposes. *Is there one somewhere marking the losses on our side too?* I knew that Eleanor Pruitt's name would be on that list. She'd been born a Harrow just like Theodora so, for hundreds of years, the two branches of the family tree never knew which would bear the prophesied Savior. Not until I came along.

My eyes blurred from lack of sleep and too much concentration. The coffee was definitely wearing off. I blinked the map back into focus. Maybe it was my mind playing tricks on me, but the lines crossing the map denoting longitude and latitude sharpened into focus. Everything else seemed to fade to the background.

"Of course!" I snatched up my laptop, hastily pulling up the department database. My fingers flew over the keys, pulling up the GPS coordinates of the crime scenes. I plotted them in Google Maps and made the digital map as big as possible. Balancing the computer on my lap, I scooped up the old map and studied it. I followed the curve of the river to where the Esplanade would be today. Sure enough, an angry red scorch mark sat at the intersection of the same coordinates as Mrs. Mendoza's scene.

Excitement coursed through me, the nape of my neck and upper lip growing damp with sweat. I bit my lower lip to keep myself under control. One shared point could be a coincidence. I scrolled to Mr. Cho's crime scene and checked the coordinates. My heart beat double time against my ribs as I traced my index finger on the map, finding another angry circle in the same location. With my pulse now thrumming in my temple, I checked Preston's GPS location and found a third mark.

An involuntary whoop erupted from my mouth. Our killers were taking lives on spots where dark practitioners had been hung. It all made sense now. The two women I'd seen vanishing in brimstone had to be the souls of the women who'd been killed. Evil or not, my heart broke just a little for their deaths. Magic was not inherently good or evil so everyone had the same potential to use it. They could have just as easily been kindred souls to my family. Now I just had to figure out where the next attack was going to occur and what they were planning.

A broad grin broke out over my lips. Let the FBI chase their tails trying to link the victims. I had the real ammunition in my hands for solving the case. The pinpoints of the physical map glowed bright again. There had to be a few dozen spots spread out across its surface. Now that I knew what I was working with, maybe I could get ahead of the killers and stop them before they struck again.

TEN

Time passed but I was hardly aware of it. I was studiously going over the ledger in Theodora's book, matching the scenes of execution to points on the map and keeping detailed notes. The video files of the crime scenes taunted me from the taskbar on my computer. I knew I should try to make progress, but diving into the past and into what my ancestors faced seemed a more enjoyable use of my attention and energy, not to mention it carried less chance of physical harm.

As the sunlight shifted through the pair of windows in my living room, casting light along the way on the sun's descent into evening, my stomach rumbled and I forced myself to take a break and warmed half of a leftover panini in the toaster oven. Munching it one-handed I turned on my phone expecting to see missed calls from Jacquie or maybe even Tricia with new information on the physical evidence. I had a missed call and a voicemail from Jacquie from an hour ago. Pressing the phone to my ear I listened.

"Trenton, it's your partner. I don't know where you've run off to, but people are going to start taking notice soon. Call me back."

I hit her number on speed dial and waited. It rang four times before flipping to voicemail. "You've reached Jacqueline DeWitt. Leave a message and I'll get back to you when I can."

I waited for the beep and said, "Hey, Jacquie, it's me. Sorry I missed your call. I'm following up on a lead that's taking longer than I expected. I'll be back as soon as I can."

Hanging up, I tried Tricia's work number. We usually worked the same shift and it might be too early for her to be back at the lab but I could hope. The line rang for a sixth time and then, "Medical examiner's office, Tricia Karo speaking."

"Tricia, it's Ezri."

"Oh, hey. I see they've got you working overtime on this too."

"Seems like it. The captain's called in the FBI for an assist on our cases."

"I'm not surprised. My boss has had calls from the federal crime lab asking questions too."

My throat went dry. "They aren't asking you to turn over evidence, are they?"

Tricia laughed. "Not yet. And even if they did, you know I keep backups of all the reports."

"Speaking of, have there been any new results back? DNA or fingerprints from the victims' clothing?"

"We ran the prints but so far nothing. The DNA is going to take a few more days."

"Damn. What about that dust? Any luck identifying it?"

"Yes, but don't get too excited. It's granite and it's pretty common in a lot of the statues in the city. It could have come from someone cleaning or doing repair work on a statue or other granite structure."

Adele's "Hello"—the tone I'd programmed for higher ups in the department—interrupted our conversation. "Tricia, thanks for the update. I appreciate it. I've got another call I need to take."

"Sure thing. Chat later."

I ended our call and accepted the incoming call. "This is Detective Trenton."

"Detective, it's Captain Beech. Where are you right now?"

I started to tell her that it was my day off and I was at home, but I stopped short. This case was all hands on deck no matter whose day off it was. So I gave her a version of the truth that was in line with what I'd just told Jacquie. "I'm following up on a possible lead about the geographic profile, ma'am."

"I need you back at the precinct as soon as possible."

"Is everything all right, Captain?"

"Come right to my office when you get here."

Heat snaked up my neck and settled in the tips of my ears. Once again, I had the distinct feeling I was being called in to be reprimanded. She said nothing else to me and I ended the call. Despite my brain telling my body I needed to move, it took me two tries to get my feet to cooperate and for me to get to my car.

Numbness seeped into every pore on the drive back into the city. The sun had dipped below most of the buildings in downtown by the time I found a parking spot at the precinct. I wiped sweat from my palms and tried to shake the nerves building with every step as I entered the building. The bull pen was eerily empty. Had everyone gone on a coordinated dinner break just to freak me out? Even the Feds had disappeared from the conference room. Acid sloshed in my belly as I walked past my desk and knocked on the doorframe to Captain Beech's office.

"Come in and close the door."

I pulled the door shut behind me as I stepped over the threshold and paused, unsure whether to stand or sit. This time she gestured for me to take a seat and I perched on the edge of the seat nearest the door. Easier to make a quick exit if necessary. The captain closed a folder on her desk and looked me in the eye. "How are you doing, Ezri?"

I blinked, confusion buzzing in my brain. "Fine."

"I have some concerns with how you've handled yourself so far with this investigation."

"Did Jacquie say something about me leaving the scene yesterday? I already apologized to her and I assured her it wouldn't happen again, ma'am."

The captain held up a hand for silence. "It doesn't matter who raised the concerns. But they are legitimate. You've displayed some erratic behavior recently that needs to be addressed and I can't allow it to continue unchecked."

I averted my gaze as she continued. "Leaving your partner without notification. The way you treated our federal partners. At best, it's just unprofessional. At worst, insubordination."

My muscles turned to water as I sat there. I'd been following leads and defending my case. The rational part of my brain said that the captain was right. Seen by an outside observer, I had been acting a little off lately.

"What happens now?" The defensiveness left my voice.

"You're to report to the department's psychologist for evaluation tomorrow morning at eight o'clock. Upon a satisfactory report, you'll be permitted back to work. Until then, you'll be on leave with pay."

Arguing would only prove her point more and so

I clamped my mouth shut and tried my best to stand without my legs giving out beneath me. Captain Beech stood and moved to open the door for me.

"It goes without saying that you can't be involved with the case until you're reinstated."

"Y-yes, ma'am. I understand."

Angry tears pricked the backs of my eyes but I wouldn't let them fall. Not here, not ever. I was stronger than that. I squared my shoulders and held my head high as I marched through the bull pen. It was sparsely populated now, but no one gave me a second thought. Like everything else I'd endured in the last ten years, I would get through this hiccup in my career too. I wanted to be mad at Jacquie but she'd been doing her job and looking out for me.

Needing a distraction when I got home, I turned off my computer and set aside the map and ledger in one of the boxes. Instead, I dug into the first box, finding a manila folder that looked out of place among the rest of the antiques. The folder contained a couple sheets of lined paper with my handwritten notes about my mother's death scrawled on them. At the very bottom of the box, a bulky plastic bag containing the knife I'd found in my mother's chest sat untouched. I hadn't been aware enough not to touch the handle, but I could easily exclude my own fingerprints from any other sets that might be there. I could see myself pulling the blade free, casting it aside in my horror and grief. When I'd realized no one was coming to take the evidence and get justice for my mother, I'd bagged it up and secreted it away until I could find someone to test it. I hadn't built enough rapport with the forensics people until recently.

"Tricia," I breathed and scooped up the folder and the bag and stuffed them in a shoulder bag. I texted Tricia to meet me for dinner on her break. If I got lucky, she'd agree to run the blood and finger-print analysis for me off the books. At the very least, seeing her would keep my mind off my impending shrink visit in the morning. I had no love for the profession, especially when my father had tried to get me to seek therapy in the wake of my mother's death. I'd been so angry at the world back then I hadn't given it a real chance. Eventually, my father gave in and I'd stopped going.

"THANKS FOR MEETING ME," I said and slid into a booth across from Tricia a short time later.

"Well, it's not drinks but it will have to do," Tricia set her menu aside. She slid out of the booth and pulled me into a fierce hug. "Happy Birthday a day late." Her sharp brown eyes traveled from my face down and back up again.

We sat. I toyed with the corner of the laminated

menu, summoning the courage to ask what I'd come for. "So, uh, I kind of have a favor to ask."

"Is it illegal?" She laughed.

"Yes."

She stared at me for a minute and then said, "Shit, you're serious."

"I wish I wasn't." As discreetly as I could I took out the knife and slid it across the table to her. "I need you to test this for fingerprints and DNA.'

"First, where did you get that?" She kept her hands away from the plastic.

"My mother's chest ten years ago."

"Fuck, Ezri, I ... I'm sorry."

I averted my gaze. How I wished people would stop telling me how sorry they were and actually *do* something about it. "Please, can you test this off the books?"

"You know I'm not supposed to run tests unless it's associated with a case."

I rubbed at the crease between my eyebrows, frustration building. "And my mother's death was never logged as a homicide. I could file a report now; that way you'd have a case number to link it to."

"Wouldn't that be suspicious?'

"It's all I've got," I answered.

She took the bag and slid it down on the booth seat beside her. "Look, I can't make any promises, but I'll see what I can do."

I smiled at her, tension melting from my body. "You have no idea how much that means to me."

Tricia smiled but it barely showed. I'd pushed her and it might not pay off. Panic started to worm its way into my thoughts, sending shocks of tingling nerves down my arms. One touch of the sandalwood charm and a little dab of magic and the tension receded. For now.

"So, are you still seeing that doctor? What's his name, Marcus?" I asked, suspecting we both wouldn't mind a change of topic.

Her head whipped up and this time the smile was genuine. A faint blush colored her cheeks. "Off and on. Currently on. It's hard with both of our schedules, but when we're together we definitely enjoy ourselves."

"I'm happy for you."

"How about you? Still rocking the single life or has someone caught your eye?"

It was my turn to smile. "Definitely still single and not in the market to change that any time soon. The new gig has a lot more responsibility and I just don't feel like I'm in a place to meet anyone."

"Cops date all the time. You'll find the right person."

J.T.'s face flashed before me, stirring up long-buried feelings. "Maybe." I paused. "Let's order. I know you're on the clock still and really busy. I don't want to keep you too long."

"Don't worry about it. I can use the break. But I get the feeling you don't want to talk about work."

"I swear sometimes you're a mind reader. Things at work aren't great right now." I waited to see if Tricia prompted me for more. She didn't. Instead, she flagged down our server and we placed our orders.

"Did you at least take a minute yesterday to celebrate the fact that you've been alive for a quarter of a century?"

"Not really. I went and visited my mother's grave. Since she died birthdays haven't really been my thing."

"I get it. What about your dad?"

I bristled. "What about him?"

"I guess I just figured you'd see him."

"We haven't spoken in years. I'd rather not talk to him or about him if that's okay."

"Okay. I hear you. I'm just saying if it were me, with all that time gone by, maybe I'd try to reach out. You're both adults now and maybe you can find some common ground."

I nearly choked on the straw in my mouth. "That's a fantasy, Tricia. That man and I have nothing in common and never will. Please just drop it."

"You're right, it's your relationship. I shouldn't tell you how it works or what you should do with it."

In an instant, my shoulders grew heavy with the guilt of lashing out at my friend. She'd been trying to be empathetic. She didn't deserve the brunt of my anger and inner drama. "I'm sorry. I'm just cranky with everything going on. Sometimes I let things build up until they just bubble over and I take it out on people who don't deserve it. It's just, with the anniversary of my mother's death and the shrink visit, I'm going a bit crazy."

"Shrink visit?"

I'd let too much slip. No taking it back now. "I'm on leave until I'm cleared by the department's shrink. My partner accused me of erratic behavior and so the captain thinks I'm not fit for duty."

Tricia propped her hands under her chin. "Don't hate me for saying this, but maybe it will be good to talk to someone. You clearly have a lot of stuff on your mind right now. Maybe having a neutral person to unload on will do you some good."

I wanted to tell her she was wrong, that therapy wasn't the answer for me, but maybe all of these people telling me it was good for me was a sign. I'd never been the best at asking for help, not since my mother's death. "I don't hate you. And I should go in with an open mind. I mean I'm off the case until I'm cleared so I need to make a good impression."

"I've heard he's cute," she said and winked.

"I'm in enough trouble with the department as it

is. I can't add inappropriate relationship with another employee to the list."

"Just keep an open mind," she repeated with a snicker.

The conversation turned to less dramatic fare as our food arrived and we tucked in. Just as the sky outside took on a purple-blue hue, Tricia's phone rang. She scooped it up, opening her wallet in the same gesture and tossed a couple of bills on the table. More than enough to cover both of our meals plus tip.

"You don't have to do that," I protested.

"Consider it a birthday gift. I have to run. They need me back at the lab."

I slipped on my jacket and said, "Thanks for this. I'll walk you out."

We parted ways outside the restaurant, Tricia going to the parking garage around the corner and me wandering up toward Boylston Street. Arlington church wasn't far off, sitting opposite the Public Garden. The sight of it triggered a sense memory of the damp limestone signature coming from the Garden and I weaved through pedestrian traffic to stand at the entrance to the park. *Is our killer using the park as cover to fade into the crowd? Is he one of the many homeless who call the area a temporary shelter, even on the bitterly cold nights? And who is his partner?* These thoughts jumbled in my head as I walked. A gust of cold night air ripped through my jacket and I pulled the fabric tighter. It did little to ward off the chill as I entered the park and strode past the lake with its dormant Swan boats. The paths were devoid of foot traffic. Most people preferred the wider space of the Common one block over.

I found a measure of peace here. As if to give Mother Nature the middle finger, some of the trees had budding leaves on some of their topmost branches, saying, "Spring is coming whether you like it or not." Magic, like nature, could be resilient, always fighting to exert control. It's why our powers were so tied to the seasons. The potential for magic flows through everything. Every leaf, every rain storm and gust of air.

I reached out to the air around me, sending the molecules vibrating faster to create a pocket of warmth. Maybe it was all in my head, but I swear as soon as the hint of my own magic hit my nostrils, the damp smell of limestone surfaced. I tried to follow it past a row of lifelike statues but they all had the vague scent, as if they were drying out from a quick evening rain.

"Get a grip, Ezri," I chided myself. I was so desperate for answers that I was making things up just to play the hero.

I don't need to play at being a hero. I'm supposed to actually *be* one. I'd never been clear on who exactly I'd be facing down, but these deaths raising up the spirits of dark practitioners had to be part of it. And I was all that stood between their plan and keeping humanity safe.

No pressure.

MARCH 14, 2017

I slept in fits and starts. My brain wouldn't shut off, fretting about the case and when the killers would strike next. And what had pulled Tricia from our dinner? Was there already a fourth victim I knew nothing about? One and two o'clock in the morning came and went. By the time my alarm went off at six thirty, I'd managed maybe three hours' sleep. I did my best to cover the fading bruise on my throat and made myself presentable, ready to honestly give the session with the shrink a shot. Out of routine, I clipped my badge to my belt.

I kept my head down as I walked into the precinct, ignoring my colleagues as I marched up to the second floor and down to the very back of the building. The sign on the door read, "Dr. Fellowes." My heart skipped a beat.

There are plenty of people in the city with that last name.

I knocked once before the door swung inward and a familiar face greeted me. Surprise more than anything kept my feet rooted to the floor. Otherwise, I'd have been halfway out of the building before he even opened his mouth.

It had been ten years, but Desmond looked the same as he did when I was a teenager except with a few added laugh lines around the corners of his eyes. How had I not known he'd ended up here serving the same department as me?

"It's been a long time, Ez. Please, come in," he said, not letting me ruminate on how I'd been blind to his presence for all these years.

I wanted to tell him to fuck off with his familial demeanor. We were distant cousins after all, even if our families had been close. I wanted to turn and run, but I was still frozen in place.

"It's you." The words sounded miles away to my ears.

"Come in and we can talk."

I inhaled and slowly blew the breath out, silently begging my leg muscles to respond to my brain's command to move. Sure, there was a 50/50 chance I'd go back downstairs, but it would be better than standing there on the threshold dumbstruck. Finally, my feet moved and I followed my cousin into the office.

It had a surprising warmth to it. The furniture was understated and the artwork on the walls was definitely Desmond. He'd always loved abstract art. He sat behind his desk, inquisitive blue eyes tracking my every move. I eased the door most of the way closed but remained standing.

"I'm not going to bite, I promise. You can sit down." He gestured to the leather sofa opposite the desk.

"This is a conflict of interest. You aren't qualified to assess my fitness for duty."

"I know it's been a while since we've seen each other, but I can assure you I'm licensed." The smirk on his face only made me want to punch him.

"You're family. You aren't objective."

"We're distant relatives. To most people it wouldn't even count. Please, sit down. I want to help you."

I flipped him off for good measure but settled on the side of the sofa farthest from him. He watched me and I met his gaze with a glare. He didn't flinch. So we sat there staring each other down until he blinked.

"Why are you here?" I finally asked.

"Shouldn't I be asking you that question?"

"I mean why are you here in the police department?"

"Contrary to popular belief, you don't own the

department, Ezri. You don't get to stick your name on it and claim it as your own."

I closed my eyes and took a deep breath, trying to quell the anger in my chest, burning to be released. "Fine. But shouldn't someone else be doing this?"

"I can have one of my colleagues take things over but, given the timing of things, I think you'd rather have someone in the know on this side of the desk."

I clenched my hands into fists in an effort to disperse some of my nervous energy. "Can we just get this over with so I can get back to work?"

Desmond leaned back, elbows propped on the edge of the desk, one hand rubbing his chin. "I'm not going to just rubber stamp you back to work."

I was on my feet before I realized my brain had given the command. "I don't need this shit right now. Not from you."

"For God's sake, Ezri, sit down." His facial features remained neutral, despite the harsh tone of the words.

"How can I trust you after everything you did?"

I expected him to deny what he'd done, but he said nothing. His face fell, though, and I could see unshed tears in his eyes. He almost looked as if I'd slapped him across the face.

"Ezri, please sit down. I think we are long overdue a chat. Forget I work for the department for a minute. Can we just be family?"

His puppy dog eyes were working their way into

my heart, urging me to give in. But the wounded girl that had shaped me was revolting in my head. I stood immobile for a while longer, letting head and heart fight it out. Eventually, my heart gained the upper hand and I sat back down. "Okay. Fine. Let's talk."

I wanted Desmond to stay behind his desk to ensure there was a barrier between us. I wasn't ready for him to be in my personal space just yet, but he didn't seem to care. He moved to sit beside me on the sofa, hands cupping his knees.

"Why don't you tell me what happened? All I've got is that you exhibited erratic behavior at a crime scene."

My shoulder muscles tensed. "I was following the killer's magical trail. But I couldn't tell anyone because normal people can't know that magic still exists. The Authority's rules, remember?"

"It must be difficult trying to do your job and not being able to tell the people around you the truth."

I couldn't resist an eye roll. "Yeah, it is. I know that these cases are wrapped up in some pretty heinous dark magic, but I can't tell that to anyone, so the rest of the department and Feds are left spinning in circles trying to find connections between people where none exist."

"What do you mean by that?"

"We haven't found any obvious connections between the victims yet, but maybe it's not about the people. I think it's tied to the locations, but I haven't figured out what their end game is yet." I didn't want to talk about it anymore. I wanted to be anywhere but with him.

"Other than the case, how've you been?" he asked, giving me mental whiplash with the sudden change in the conversation.

I shrugged one shoulder. "Fine."

"Come on, we used to talk a lot. Hell, there were times I wished I could have shut you up."

"I'm not a kid anymore, Desmond. You were my idol, but not anymore."

"I'm sorry you feel that way. But I genuinely am interested in what you've been doing."

"You mean they haven't been keeping tabs on me?"

"If they have been, they didn't tell me."

Somehow, I doubted that. "There's nothing really to tell. I went to college, got my degree and joined the force. End of story."

He snorted. "You were always smart, Ez, but not even you could have made detective this fast without help."

My gaze narrowed. "What are you accusing me of exactly?"

"As I said, you're smart. If I had to guess, I'd say you used your particular talents to get ahead."

"It's not against the rules. And I was helping people."

"I'm not saying you did anything bad. It's quite

resourceful of you, actually. But there's so much more you could be doing. If you just—"

"No."

"Let me finish."

"Forget it. I'm not going back there. Not after what they did. After what they cost me."

Desmond rubbed the bridge of his nose. "You were so young then. There's so much you didn't understand. So much you still don't get. If you just let them explain, if you let them help you, it would be so much easier. I think we both know a fight is coming."

"Nothing would make me ask them for help. And I've been doing just fine on my own for years."

He gestured to my throat. "I'd say someone beat you pretty good there. We could show you how to defend yourself."

I swallowed, the muscles still sore. "It's not that bad."

"Do you know who hurt you?"

"Nope. But I'll be ready next time. And I'm doing things you couldn't dream of. So tell the Authority to keep their noses out of my business."

He let out a prolonged sigh. "I can't do that. You may not trust them, but you need them. And, more importantly, they need you. The prophecy is going to come to pass soon."

In six days.

"They aren't the ones with a destiny."

"But the outcome of whatever battle you fight affects them. Why pass up their help if it gives you an edge?"

"I just can't. I've managed on my own for the last ten years."

"Come with me to the Authority. Just talk to them. Do that for me and I'll sign off on your reinstatement paperwork."

My blood ran cold and again I was on my feet. I let some of my will bleed into the world and Desmond went flying over the back of the sofa, slamming with a concussive 'whump' into the far wall. "You're going to blackmail me?" My voice reverberated off the walls.

Desmond didn't answer right away. He gingerly pulled himself to his feet, favoring the side that had collided with the wall. Spearmint permeated the room as he approached me. I'd almost forgotten the scent of his magic. There'd been a time as a child when I'd loved that smell.

"No, of course not. I'm offering a win-win situation. We get our Savior back and you get back to fighting for your victims."

"You're unbelievable."

"Whether you want to acknowledge it or not, these are desperate times, Ezri."

"Believe me, I know that. We've got three innocent people dead and I'm pretty sure whoever is behind it is raising the spirits of dark practitioners. I need to be back at work. I need to stop whatever this spell is they're building."

"Then come back. All I am trying to do is help you. Come back into the fold and you might learn that what you think is the truth about what happened with your mother is just your perception."

"I know what happened." I could feel my defenses coming back up. The intent to strike out again rippled over my skin like waves, ready to crash. I tried to calm myself. Lashing out again wasn't going to do me any favors, not when he literally controlled when and if I got my job back.

"Still, we have resources you don't. Resources you can't possibly expect to get here where no one really understands what's happening. The video footage alone is baffling the department's techs."

"How do you know about that?" A little of the fire died down in my chest.

"I've read up on the case. Like you said, this is deeply rooted in magic. In our history and the history of this city."

"Then let me get back to work and save this city from more heartbreak."

"I told you my terms. I'll give you some time to think about it. But don't wait too long. We are on a bit of a clock."

I bit back the angry retorts that were fighting to come out. They wouldn't help the situation. He'd made it perfectly clear where he stood. I needed to be on the case, but how could I go back to the people who'd let such a horrible thing happen to my family and not seek justice for it? How could I believe anything they had to say?

They'd say anything to win me back, even if it was full of lies. Desmond had seen something in these people that made him stick around, but he didn't seem intent on sharing. Not here. Besides, he'd never been the one to bear the burden of being the Savior. He'd never really known what it was like to know that someday everything would come down to you being able to fight back.

He moved in, arms open as if to give me a hug, and I brushed past him. I wasn't ready to be embraced by him. I yanked the door open and stepped into the hallway. I half expected him to come after me, but no footsteps sounded on the hardwood behind me. I chanced a look back over my shoulder and he'd returned to his desk. Our gazes met one last time.

"I'll think about it." It came out barely above a whisper.

TWELVE

The moment I was out of Desmond's office, I took off at a sprint down to the first floor and back out into the open air. I didn't acknowledge any of my co-workers or the jacketed federal agents milling around the front of the building. I hadn't even stopped to see if there was anything new with the case. Not that I was allowed to know, but that didn't stop my curiosity from taking the reins sometimes. How had the interview gone with Preston's family? Had the lists produced by Mrs. Cho and Mr. Mendoza yielded anything helpful?

I paced back and forth in front of the entrance letting the cool air calm my anger, hands shoved in my jacket pockets, until a uniformed officer I didn't recognize approached me.

"Can I help you?" she asked. Her tone carried an edge of suspicion.

I moved the hem of my jacket enough to flash her my badge. "I'm good. Thanks."

"Sorry, Detective. I didn't realize," she said, her tone immediately melting in an apologetic lilt.

"It's okay, Officer. I should probably get going anyway."

Not excited by the prospect of sitting at home on my hands, I took the long way back to my apartment. I wound through the back streets of Brookline and Allston until I pulled into my parking space, having killed an extra half hour. It had given me time to calm down a little. The mere thought of Desmond no longer sent hot lances of rage rippling through my gut. Frustration still lurked at the back of my thoughts, though, settling into a pulsing headache at the base of my skull. I detested not being involved in the case. But they didn't know I had the video files. If I could actually recover some of the footage maybe Desmond's evaluation wouldn't matter. They'd need me back.

I bounded up to my front door with renewed purpose, ready to take on the killer's slimy magic. As I turned the key in the lock, the tiny hairs on the back of my neck flared. Leaving the key in the lock, I spun to face an empty hallway. I caught a whiff of lavender and charged toward the source. I swiped my right hand in front of me and came up against something like a barrier. Someone was hiding behind an invisibility spell. I curled my fingers as if to pull off a blanket, exerting just enough of my own power to counter the spell.

A girl with a dark purple pixie cut hovered six inches off the ground, her body translucent. Her outfit screamed Goth in its over-the-top use of black. Double cartilage piercings adorned each ear.

"Who are you?" I felt a barrier of my own encase me.

The girl set her feet on the ground becoming mostly solid. She held her hands up defensively. "Whoah, don't take my head off."

My hand inched toward my hip, ready to un-holster my weapon when I realized I hadn't brought it with me. "I'll ask you one more time, who are you?"

"Honestly, not the question I was expecting. But my name is Kayla."

"Who sent you?"

"Desmond."

"Fuck him," I growled, my ire reignited. "I don't need a damn babysitter."

"Look, I'm just a messenger, okay? All he said was to just make sure you stay out of trouble and, when you're ready, I'm supposed to let him know to come get you."

"And how would he know how to find me?" I snapped.

She rolled her eyes. "Your personnel file, duh."

Her explanation was logical enough, but I still didn't like Desmond sending someone to follow me. "Well, you can tell him I'm not going anywhere with him." I waved one hand dismissively in her direction. "Go on, go float on back to him and tell him that."

"You know, for the Chosen One, you're kind of a douche."

"Thanks." I turned on my heel and marched back to my door. I only dropped the protective barrier once I was inside and the door was locked.

Sure, it was only a minor impediment for a Whisperer like Kayla, but it still gave me a modicum of security. I'd only met one or two Whisperers in the time I was being trained by the Authority, but they'd given off a devil may care vibe. Living practitioners who'd had their magic go wrong, they'd been something of a Boogie man and cautionary tale for children in the community. Don't overuse your magic or you'll end up invisible to everyone you love.

The perversion of their own magic did come with the ability to pass through any solid surface virtually unseen, especially to modern technology. When I'd joined the force, I'd come to suspect many turned to crime given how easy it would be to get in and out without being seen. It helped, too, that they could make themselves completely invisible to people without any magical talents.

I stood by the doorway and waited until the floral

scent of Kayla's magic dissipated. I couldn't be entirely sure she was gone, but I was going to have to chance it. I had more important things to do than worry about some errand girl. The living room was in the same disarray as I'd left it and I shoved the boxes and map aside, settling my laptop on my knees like I'd done before. Time to unmask these killers.

The vertebrae and cartilage in my neck snapped as I loosened the muscles. I wasn't going to be caught off guard again by the son of a bitch on the other end of this spell. I opened the video file and built up the magic around me, folding it in layers over my body like armor. In my mind's eye, I dove through the pixels and back into the virtual existence of the video file.

The stink of the tar grew more intense the closer I got, as if whoever was fueling the spell had purposely increased its potency since our last encounter. I clawed at the vines, freeing them with brute strength. As they slithered away and vanished, the muck beneath began to thin, revealing the hidden frames below.

I was making good progress when something sharp and heavy slammed into my back, knocking the air from my lungs. I stumbled face-first into the tar, coughing as it poured down my throat, choking me.

I spit but nothing came up. I took shallow, weak breaths, doing my best to take in oxygen through my nose. Whatever had knocked me down came swinging again and this time I managed to roll out of the arc of the blow. A mace fashioned from the vines collided with the space I'd just occupied, ripping through the fabric of the magical reality.

Still choking, I did my best to conjure something —anything—to defend myself. I pulled from the world around me, fashioning it into the one weapon I knew how to use: a gun. It felt solid in my hands, reassuring. I waited for my attacker to swing again, aimed the muzzle and fired. The vines exploded into shards of green, disappearing as if they'd never existed.

My assailant howled in anger. Or was it pain? Had I struck him, too, with my bullet? I took aim again at the sound of his voice and fired off another shot. This time it was definitely a cry of pain. With my attacker distracted, the tar thinned enough in my throat to spit out and I could breathe again.

"Come on you bastard!" The words tore from my throat, leaving it aching and raw.

The wails of pain subsided and, no matter what I tried, he stayed out of view, shrouded in shadow. This world was mostly of his making after all. I turned in a slow circle, waiting for the next attack to come. On my second rotation, something came speeding out of the dark, landing a shot to my jaw. My head snapped back and stars burst in my vision. The pain didn't hit me yet, thanks to the barrier of my own magic around me. I should have thought to cast the spell over my entire body.

Stupid.

My opponent took advantage of the weakness and slammed another fist-like manifestation into my face. Blood dribbled down my chin from a split lip. I stood perfectly still, waiting for them to make a move. When the fist came flying into view, I used my own force to grab it inches from my face and slammed it into the ground. Whoever was behind it wasn't physically attached to the magic and the fist melted into liquid, slipping through my fingers as easily as water.

The shadows quivered at the edge of my vision, turning into a behemoth, trundling toward me at full speed. Moments before the thing would have turned me into a pancake, I dematerialized into rays of light like I'd done last time. The creature passed through me—not a feeling I ever wanted to experience again—and vanished.

I turned to the vine-covered video frames to find the work I'd done was holding, but the rest of the tar and vines had thickened and hardened. I heaved for breath as the thought dawned on me. This had all been a distraction to keep me from accomplishing my intended goal. I summoned what strength I had left that wasn't devoted to keeping my armor up to claw at the tar. My hands came away covered in muck and blood. The pain receptors in my hands were numbed by my own magic. I was sure I'd feel the agony later, but I needed to try to finish what I'd started.

I changed tactics. Instead of brute forcing my way through the protection spell on the video, I tried altering it at a molecular level like in the real world. I plucked a few molecules of tar from the rest and imposed my own will upon them, turning them to tiny granules of sand before hardening to glass and shattering.

"I've got you now."

The length of tar in front of me quivered, glistening as it changed form. So close now. Just a little further.

Pain erupted in my left leg and I listed to one side as it gave out and refused to bear my weight. I looked down to find blood oozing down my calf. What looked like a piece of stone protruded from the wound. Something had pierced my armor. Limping, I turned to face my attacker, but the void of the magical construct greeted me. I wiggled the chunk of stone free, wincing as the blood flowed more freely and dizziness threatened to topple me. I diverted some of my magic to keeping the wound at bay.

"You aren't going to stop me. I'll just keep coming back and fighting!" My voice was swallowed by the silence around me.

Then something whistled through the air at top speed. My magic was beginning to fail me and I wasn't fast enough to avoid the second projectile before it found its mark between my shoulder blades. Pain radiated from the point of impact and my body gave in. I fell—new pain in my elbow joined the rest of the agony—and the world disappeared, sending me into a freefall back to reality until consciousness eluded me.

THIRTEEN

I wasn't sure what roused me at first until I moved my left leg and pain seared through my nerve endings. A guttural groan burbled in my throat.

"You're awake," a semi-familiar voice said.

I cracked one lid to see a hazy figure with purple hair leaning over me. My vision cleared to reveal my apartment in disarray and instinct kicked in. I tried to move to defend myself from the intruder—my head was fuzzy but I was pretty certain I hadn't invited Desmond's little spy in—but everything went slanted and I collapsed back on the couch.

"Whoa, calm down, Savior lady. You're hurt pretty bad."

I swallowed the cotton feeling from my mouth. "K-Kayla."

"Well, at least whoever used your face as a punching bag didn't mess with your memory. Didn't make your personality any better, but some things I guess are just immutable."

"Why ... why are you in my apartment?" The world started to right itself and I sat up. The pain in my calf blazed anew and I bent double to fight the nausea.

"I came back hoping you'd have changed your mind about Desmond's offer and when you didn't answer..."

"You broke into my home."

"Is it really breaking in if I just passed through the door like it didn't exist?"

"You could have called for an ambulance."

"Don't tell me you really wanted some normal paramedic treating magic-based injuries."

"How did you know?"

She handed me a towel and I pressed it to my leg. While I waited for her to answer I took stock of my other injuries. My jaw was tender from the blow I'd sustained, but nothing felt broken. I'd have one hell of a bruise later and I could taste blood in my mouth from the split lip. My fingers weren't nearly as shredded as I'd expected. The protection spell I'd put together had done its job. My neck and back, on the other hand, ached with every breath I took.

"The place reeks of your magic. And since you were alone, I doubt you were beating yourself up," Kayla finally answered.

"Look, thanks for the assist"—I pressed the towel

tighter around my leg wound—"but I've got it from here."

Kayla rolled her eyes. "You don't have to do everything alone, you know. Heroes know when to ask for help."

I wanted to tell her off, but the injuries would be easier to assess and bandage with more than two hands. "I don't suppose you know any healing magic?"

She smirked. "I know a thing or two."

I rolled up my pant leg—the dry-cleaning bill was going to be a bitch—and surveyed the wound. The puncture was maybe half an inch in diameter. I couldn't tell just how deep it went. I tried flexing the muscle and blood trickled out. Unceremoniously, Kayla grabbed my injured leg by the ankle and yanked it straight so my foot was propped against the edge of the table. Lavender tickled my nose as she pressed her hands to the wound. It stung as the skin started to knit back together.

"That should heal up in a few days." She surveyed the rest of me. "Not sure there's much I can do for your face. Maybe urge the bruising and swelling on a little faster. But you really should see an actual Healer if you want to be in fighting shape any time soon."

"Whatever you can do," I said. Magic could solve a great many things but even it had its limits.

I half expected her to smack me when administering her healing touch, but her fingers were light against my skin. The pain dulled to a manageable level. Maybe it was a side effect, but the pain in my neck and back eased a little too.

"I know it's none of my business and you're probably going to tell me to fuck off, but what were you doing that got your ass kicked?" she asked.

I had every confidence that Kayla had orders to report back to Desmond whatever I told her, and he would no doubt chide me for still working the case even though I was under orders not to. But in that moment, as the pain and her magic ebbed and flowed through my body, I found my tongue loosened.

"We've got some magically altered video footage I'm trying to restore." I reached for my laptop and my elbow twinged. A red welt marred the skin, I probably hit it on something when I passed out. Kayla pushed the computer within my grasp and I pulled up the file I'd been working on. "See, the file is corrupted, but I've been able to slowly peel away the magic."

"I know some guys who could handle that for you in a day."

"I can do it on my own."

"Not from where I'm sitting." She tugged at a loose thread on her vest. "But, right, you're all anti-Authority. Can't possibly have them help with a magical problem. It's not like the whole world is on the brink of hell breaking loose or anything except, you know, if you believe the prophecy that some evil is rising and if you don't stop it we're all screwed."

"You've done your duty. You can go now," I snapped.

She opened her mouth to protest but was cut off thanks to my computer's inbox beeping loudly with incoming messages. I pulled the machine toward me to find new video footage for a location marked as the Orpheum Theater. Heat flushed through me as I realized what this meant: we had a fourth body.

I scrambled for the map and book ledger, ignoring Kayla as my brain spiraled into overdrive. I nearly dropped the computer twice as I tried to pull up a new browser tab to find the GPS coordinates of the theater. I caught Kayla hovering out of the corner of my eye, but she stayed silent as I worked. Three typos later, I had the GPS coordinates on my screen. Pulse throbbing painfully in my neck, I scooped up the map and checked for the latitude and longitude markers, finally finding them. As expected—and feared—they intersected at an angry red mark. I didn't bother to read the entry detailing what evil woman had lost her life in this place. I knew all I needed. More video footage would be on the way and the case was hitting dead ends everywhere they looked. I hated to admit it, but Desmond was right. I needed help.

There had to be a pattern emerging. Ignoring Kayla for a little longer, I fiddled with the GPS coordinates on Google Maps, inputting the three other scenes. I connected them and cold sweat prickled on the nape of my neck. It almost looked like an inverted pentagram. A shiver ran down my spine. It shouldn't be a surprise that they would corrupt a symbol of good magic for their own purposes.

Finally, I set the map aside and fixed my attention back on the Whisperer levitating half a foot from the ground. "Okay."

She blinked, as if I'd startled her from a trance. "Okay what?"

"Okay, tell Desmond I'll go to the Authority. But I can't promise anything beyond that."

Kayla grinned from ear to ear. "Baby steps, Savior girl. Baby steps. Be back in a flash."

Kayla needed to update her definition of "a flash". The purple-haired pest didn't rematerialize until almost nine o'clock. At least it had given me time to eat a proper meal. That alone helped my body fight through the aches and pains. Like the last time—I'm assuming seeing as I wasn't exactly conscious—she just waltzed through my locked front door as if she owned the place, earbud dangling from one ear, the cord snaking down into the pocket of her jeans.

"You really need to learn the concept of knocking before you just enter someone's house, especially one with a gun and a license to shoot you."

"And here I thought we had a connection." She let out a girlish chuckle.

"When does Desmond want to meet?"

"He's downstairs in the car. He muttered something about not wanting you to turn him into a human pin ball for entering your space or whatever."

"At least he respects some boundaries," I grumbled before donning a jacket and tossing my laptop in a messenger bag and heading downstairs. I glanced behind me as the elevator doors began to shut and found Kayla standing there, immobile. "Are you coming?" I prompted.

"Oh, no. This is a you and Des thing."

The pet name struck me as odd. He'd never let anyone but me call him that when we were younger ... except his *girlfriend*. "Fine, whatever. But you aren't waiting in my apartment. Go do whatever it is you normally do on a Tuesday night."

"Got it, boss." She vanished with only a hint of lavender left in the air.

I shook my head and shouldered the front door open. I didn't have to guess which car belonged to Desmond. In all the time I'd known him, he'd only driven one car—a Mini Cooper, complete with stripe down the middle. I never understood why he loved the thing so much. I found it cramped as hell, even as a young teenager. I paused a moment to collect myself, not entirely ready to be trapped in a car for at least twenty minutes with him with no way out. He flashed the headlights at me and I forced my feet to move. My leg spasmed with every step, but I grit my teeth and kept going. I even managed to get into the passenger seat somewhat gracefully.

"I'm glad you reconsidered." Desmond put the car into drive and pulled out onto the road, heading out of the city.

"You didn't give me much choice."

Awkward silence filled the car between us until finally he asked, "Do you want to tell me what changed your mind?"

"Another victim was just found."

"God, I'm so sorry."

"For once, it's not your fault."

He shook his head, strands of blond hair brushing the tops of his eyebrows. "Even if you aren't having issues with work, I wish you'd realize that there are issues about your past you haven't dealt with. Holding on to them isn't healthy and it could hurt you if you aren't careful."

"If they can help with solving the case, fine. But I'm not getting into the rest of it with you or them."

Desmond said nothing and turned his attention back to the road. As we drove, the pain from the wound in my leg intensified. Damn, I should have at least grabbed some aspirin before leaving my apartment. As we moved on to the Mass Pike out toward Newton, my stomach started to twist in nervous knots. I hadn't been back to the Authority's base of operations in a decade. Had it changed much since my last visit or was it stuck perpetually in the early 1900s with its wall sconces and ornate woodwork?

"So, should I assume the bruises are case-related?" His voice cut through my thoughts.

My jaw ached in response to his question and I couldn't resist brushing my fingertips against the sore spot. "Yeah. But I'm fine."

I caught the side-eye he was giving me. "You were favoring your left leg on your way to the car too. We can have a Healer take a look at it."

"Thanks."

"So, you want to tell me what tried to kick your ass?"

The stubborn part of me didn't want to share the details. For one thing, I'd assumed my disclosure to Kayla had made its way to Desmond's eager ears. And I still didn't trust his interest in me. But the way he glanced at me, concern making his eyes crinkle at the corners, reminded me of the cousin I'd grown up with. The one who'd once told me he envied my burden as the Savior. I'd spent so long distancing myself from everyone in my past that the possibility that I didn't actually have to do this alone put the tiniest chink in the wall I'd built around my heart.

"I told you about the video files that were magically corrupted, right?"

"Yeah."

"I went back in to try to fix more of the files, but whoever cast the spell was waiting for me. I think I winged him though. So at least I got a few licks in this time. But if I'm honest, whoever he is, he's stronger than anything I've dealt with before. I'm hoping it's just the waning effects from the Solstice and things will even out in a few days with the Equinox." Otherwise, I wasn't sure I would be ready to fulfill my destiny.

"Have you actually made any progress?" He was digging now, trying to keep me talking and distracted.

"Some but ... maybe I should focus on finding the killer's next target. There will be plenty of time to decrypt the evidence after the fact."

"Well, we've got people who can help with that so you don't have to wait forever to get the information. I'm assuming you've been trying to decrypt it to get a look at the killer."

"Killers plural. There've been two magical signatures at every scene I've been to."

I expected him to comment or at the very least dig for more information about the killers. He said nothing and when I turned my attention to where we were, I found myself staring up at the mansion that housed the Authority. The exterior had definitely not changed. All brownstone with cream window accents. The towering wrought-iron gate flanked by rows of hedges at the base of the circular drive remained as well. I'd always wondered what the neighbors thought of the revolving door of guests arriving at all hours of the day and night.

Desmond rolled down his window and

punched in the six-digit passcode. The gates swung inward on silent hinges and we pulled up to the top of the circular drive. My hand trembled as I undid the seatbelt and climbed into the cool evening air. Being back in the grounds sent another shiver down my spine. A lump caught in my throat and my legs turned stiff and rooted to the spot. I was vaguely aware of Desmond coming to stand beside me. The presence of his hand on my wrist, squeezing tight, freed me from my brain's self-imposed immobility.

"There's nothing to be afraid of. I promise." His last words cut deeper than I'm sure he meant them to.

"Jury's still out on whether your word's any good," I muttered but allowed him to guide me through the front doors.

I stopped short in the front hall. My brain was trying to impose the memory of what this place had been in my youth over the updated, sleek design. Gone were the dimly lit sconces and tiny alcoves leading to the library to the left and the kitchen and dining room to the right. Now, recessed LED lighting lit the space, washing everything with a rosy glow. The spiral staircase to the right leading up to the main hall had been stripped of the gaudy carpeting and was now polished hardwood, stained an inviting cherry wood color.

"You've missed a lot since you've been gone,"

Desmond whispered in my ear and nudged me toward the stairs.

I shifted my bag to the other shoulder and took the stairs slow and steady, letting the sound of each footfall ground me. I was back here. It wasn't a dream or my mind playing tricks. Reaching the top of the stairs, I paused to take in the upper floor. Unlike the first floor, it hadn't changed nearly as much. The floor was still carpeted in thick beige shag rugs. I looked around, expecting more people to be mingling, but it was eerily quiet and empty.

"We can use the meeting hall." Desmond's voice echoed in the space.

Taking a steadying breath, I marched forward and gave the double doors a solid shove inward. They opened to reveal the same setup as the last time I'd been there: thirteen chairs in a semi-circle with a single chair facing them. I crossed the threshold and nostalgia bowled me over, dragging me back into the past.

Heavy snowdrifts piled high outside the first-floor windows below us. J.T. and I were supposed to be studying down in the library, but we'd snuck up to the meeting hall unnoticed. Sunlight reflected off the untouched mounds outside, catching in the blond of his hair. We sat side by side in the two chairs in the center of the semi-circle, hands clasped together. He leaned in, his sea-glass-green eyes half open, and kissed me. Excitement spread from my chest down into my belly. It wasn't that we hadn't kissed before. But this space was almost sacred. That added element of illicitness made me giddy and I pulled away giggling.

"You okay?" His hand tightened around mine.

I looked around. "We shouldn't be doing this in here. They'd freak out if they found us."

He smirked. "Where's your sense of adventure, Ez? We'll be running things one day and we can do whatever we want. Make our own rules."

"Yeah. First rule, don't make people feel like they've got to join up."

"What do you mean?"

I pulled my hands free of his and pulled my knees up to my chest, chin resting atop them. "Think about it. We don't have a choice in whether the Authority tells us what to do and how to use our magic. Don't you want that freedom?"

"I guess I never thought about it that way. I just figured this is kind of our birthright to be here."

"That's the problem. Not everyone knows where their magic comes from. We should be free to use it however we want."

"That's dangerous, Ezri. Look at the Order. We don't want them running around unchecked."

"I'm not saying we shouldn't punish the people who use it for evil, but if people aren't hurting themselves or anyone else, why should they have to even tell the Authority that they exist? You can't honestly *tell me you like having them breathing down your neck, watching everything you do. Every spell you learn."*

He mirrored my position and, after a long pause, said, "Of course I'd like more freedom, but could you imagine going through all of this without their help? Facing what you're facing. Why would you ever want to be in the magical world without them having your back?"

"Ezri, did you hear me?"

The memory of J.T. faded and I was back in the room with Desmond by my side. I pinched the bridge of my nose and turned to him. "Sorry, what?"

He let out a sigh of annoyance and motioned to a young woman with a blonde bob and hipster glasses who I guessed was a few years older than me. "This is Avery, one of our best tech people."

The other woman crossed the distance and extended her hand to me. "Avery Stohl. I can't believe I'm meeting you. Me, meeting the Savior."

I gripped her extended hand—covered in a thin sheen of sweat—and arched a brow at her excitement to meet me and the fact that she knew who I was. "Uh, yeah. Sorry, how do you know about that?"

She waved her free hand. "Everybody knows who you are around here. I mean I couldn't pick you out on the street, but everyone knows you."

Great, my reputation precedes me. I freed my

hand from Avery's grasp. "So, you're good with technology?"

Avery laughed. "She's funny. I routinely kick technology in the ass. Des didn't mention what you needed help with though."

How many girlfriends does he have?

Desmond gave a conspicuous fake cough and took a few steps back. "I'll leave you two to it then."

I rounded on him. "And where are you going?"

"I have a letter of reinstatement to send off."

My irritation that he was once more abandoning me ebbed a little at the mention of my reinstatement.

"You're really going to tell the captain to let me back in?"

"I said I'd help you out if you came. You did, so I am."

"You still think I have issues."

"Oh, I know you have issues, Ezri. But until you're willing to hash them out, I don't think there's much else I can do."

I blew out a breath. "I'll work on it."

"Good. I'll be here when you're ready," he said and left the room.

Avery motioned for me to follow her out of the meeting hall and down a corridor I didn't remember. She said nothing as she led me through the passageway into an open space filled with desktops, laptops and an array of tablets.

"Jeez, did you rob an electronics store?"

Avery grinned. "Nah. The Authority is moving into the twenty-first century. You'd be amazed what people are trying to do with magic these days. Magical hacking is totally a thing. Not that I condone it or anything."

I set my bag down and pulled out my own laptop, adding it to the jumble of electronics on the nearest table. "If I'm honest, it doesn't really surprise me. People always find new ways to hurt each other."

Avery nodded. "Right, Des mentioned you're a cop."

"You two sound awfully friendly. From what I remember he only let his girlfriend call him that."

Color flooded Avery's cheeks, burning bright red against her otherwise pale skin. "It's still new, but we've known each other for years."

"I don't remember you."

"You never hung with the nerds so we wouldn't have crossed paths. And Des and I really started getting close after..."

"After I left."

She nodded, tugged at the ends of her bob and didn't look at me. "Right. Of course. So, uh, what's the problem exactly?"

Flipping my computer open, I pulled the files up and hit play on the one I'd been working with. "We've got surveillance footage of several murders; except, well, we don't. They've used magic to corrupt the files. I've been able to fix bits and pieces, but whatever spell they used, it's like a living thing. Or maybe it's still connected to the caster. I don't entirely know."

Avery quirked a brow at me. "You've been doing this on your own?"

"It's not like I can ask the techs in the department for help. They don't know magic exists."

"Right, but you don't ever go into tech alone when magic's involved."

Her judgmental tone sent my hackles rising. "Maybe *you* don't."

"Tell me what happened when you went in."

I massaged the wound in my leg and my fingers came away rust colored. "Like I said, it was as if the spell was alive and it could sense when I was trying to undo it. No sooner had I started picking apart the magic than something was trying to kill me."

Avery nodded as if she'd heard all of this before. "And that's why you don't ever go in alone. We don't know why exactly, but when technology and magic mix, you always need two people at least. One to combat whatever the damage is and one to watch their back and take on whatever defenses might have been left behind."

"You may want a whole team when you go in there." I held up my bloodstained fingers.

"Noted. Is it just the one file?"

"No. It's four."

Avery's eyes widened behind her glasses. "Four people are dead and magic's involved?"

"Looks like it."

"Why haven't we heard about this?"

"Because solving murders isn't the Authority's job?"

"I mean we like the general public."

"Not my department."

The techie went silent and I could see the wheels turning in her head, trying to decide whether to ask more questions or just accept what I'd given her and move on. Finally, she cleared her throat and said, "Right. Of course. We'll get right on it. Do you need the computer back?"

"Yeah. Just copy the files."

Avery flitted around the room, grabbing cables and connectors I'd never seen before. She grabbed my laptop with one hand—my heart may have stopped beating entirely as she balanced it in her palm—before setting it down. She strung cords from one machine to another and I stood in silence, watching as she made sense of whatever was going on. She only looked up when the door behind us opened and a balding man in his late 30s waltzed in.

He gave me a silent nod and settled in behind one of the computer setups. "What have they got us doing now?" His tenor voice came out in a whine, which seemed in direct contrast to his beefy frame.

"Morgan, behave. We're helping a police investigation," Avery said with a not-so-discreet nod in my direction.

"Since when do we help cops?'

"Since the Savior's asking," she snapped.

Morgan stared at me, mouth agape. "S-sorry. I didn't realize. Whatever you need, any time," he stammered. He practically launched himself out of the chair.

"I swear to God, if you bow I'm going to arrest you for being a douchebag," I warned when his knees were only a few inches from the floor.

In an awkward duck walk he backed up and narrowly avoided landing on the floor. He opened his mouth to speak again and stopped. Instead, he situated himself back in the chair, spun so he wasn't looking at me anymore and put on a set of earphones.

"Let me know when you finish. And thanks for doing this," I said to Avery and shouldered my bag with the map and diaries in it.

Avery blinked, as if woken from a daze, and scrambled to unhook my computer and relinquish it back into my custody. I slid it into the bag as well and showed myself out. Finding my way back to the meeting hall proved easier than I'd thought. I found Desmond standing by one of the windows looking out at the grounds.

"Have you been waiting here the whole time?" I asked, stepping up beside him.

"No. You should be getting a call from your

captain shortly telling you to report back to duty tomorrow."

"Thanks."

"Come on, we should get you checked out by a Healer."

My stomach gurgled unceremoniously as we headed for the double doors. "Dinner wouldn't be a bad thing either."

"I think we can manage that."

A short while later, we found ourselves sitting side by side in the kitchen, platters of sandwiches in front of us. I tried not to eat like a beggar getting a meal for the first time in days, but I'm pretty sure I failed. I was halfway through my third sandwich when a dark-skinned teenage boy wandered in followed by a woman who I immediately identified as his mother. They shared the same inquisitive brown eyes and high cheekbones.

"Ezri, this is Belladonna and her son Adrian. They're going to take a look at you."

My shoulders drooped at Desmond's words. It was silly, but in some small way I'd been hoping for J.T. to walk through those doors. It would have been poetic to get all my reconnections to the past done in one day.

Adrian sidled up to me and bent down so his nose was uncomfortably close to my face. "Someone punched you pretty hard."

"I hadn't noticed. And aren't you a little young to be giving me a medical opinion?"

"I'm in training." He looked over to his mother and she smiled a big, toothy grin.

She rounded the table, pushing the tray of food out of reach, and nudged her son out of the way. Gently, she pressed the tips of her fingers against the bruise on my jaw. I tried not to wince. "He wasn't wrong," she finally said. "I can reduce the swelling a little, but ice is probably best. And some ibuprofen for the pain. Where else are you hurt?"

My ribs ached more than they had in days. I reached for the hem of my shirt but stopped mid-motion. Breaths came in shallow rasps as I stared at her. Adrian continued to leer at me and heat crept up the nape of my neck. Belladonna glanced at her son and swatted him away. She gestured to him and Desmond saying, "Right, the two of you, out now."

Desmond stood without comment, but Adrian opened his mouth to protest. His mother gave him a swat on the arm and he backpedaled, following Desmond out of the room. I let out a long breath and pulled up my shirt to reveal the welts on my side.

"Girl, you really took a beating, didn't you?"

"Hazards of the job," I said. This time I couldn't cover the pain as she poked and prodded at my side.

"You didn't get this chasing bad men down alleyways. These were caused by magic. Dark, powerful and potent by the looks of it."

"You aren't wrong."

"Anything else I should know about?" she asked.

Bending over, I hiked my pant leg up to reveal the bloody bandage covering the wound in my calf muscle. She peeled away the wrapping and let out a hiss. "And you're still walking around with all of these injuries?"

"I'm tougher than I look."

"Right, let's get to work."

She flitted around the kitchen, grabbing an icepack from an industrial freezer and producing some ibuprofen from her pocket. Sitting back down beside me, she pressed her hand to my cheek and the tantalizing scent of cinnamon filled the air. Out of habit, I let a little of my own power slip out, a defense mechanism I wasn't entirely conscious of. Bella murmured something under her breath I didn't understand and my magic receded, letting her work. The ache in my jaw dissipated. The icepack and meds weren't a bad thing either.

I expected her to move down my body, but she propped my leg in her lap and probed the skin around the wound. The haze of her magic made it hurt less, but little lances of pain made their way through my nervous system and to my brain.

"What did this?" she asked.

"It felt like a piece of stone."

"There's someone else's magic at work here. Fair warning, this is going to hurt. A lot."

I opened my mouth to tell her I'd be fine when she clamped both hands over my leg and fire erupted everywhere her skin touched mine. A guttural scream ripped from my throat, bile churned and those three sandwiches threatened to make a repeat appearance. My left hand sought purchase on the table and my fingers dug into the faux wooden edge, the skin of my entire hand blanching until it resembled a corpse.

Sweat broke out on my brow and trickled down my face, dripping off my nose and landing in big splotches on my blouse. I could feel wet patches blooming under my arms, too, and I could hardly catch my breath. Something foul filled the air, only to be beaten back moments later by the sharp taste of cinnamon.

"That should heal by morning now." Belladonna's voice was miles away.

The world blinked in and out of focus, small, black dots popping everywhere I looked. Something cool materialized against my forehead and I sunk into whoever was behind me propping me up.

Slowly, the world righted itself. The burning died away and my stomach settled. I twisted around to find Desmond sitting behind me, worry lines tugging at his lips.

"Thanks," I rasped.

He said nothing but held me tighter. Belladonna

pressed a glass of water into my hands and I drank quickly. With my body no longer revolting against me, I took stock. My ribs didn't hurt and my leg, while tender to the touch, was no longer bleeding. The bandage was less elaborate, which had to be a good thing.

"Your phone's been ringing incessantly for the last twenty minutes," Desmond said.

I dug it out of my bag to see several missed calls and a voicemail from the precinct. No doubt the captain reinstating me as Desmond had promised.

Belladonna set a bottle of pills on the table beside me. "Take two before you go to sleep. It will help you heal."

I pocketed the medication and said, "Thanks again."

"Try to stay out of trouble."

I laughed. "Not likely, but I'll do my best."

Adrian appeared briefly to stuff sandwiches in a bag and ferret them away somewhere. He fixed me with a curious stare before vanishing again, leaving Desmond and me alone once again.

"So, your girlfriend's interesting," I said, finishing the glass of water and pushing myself up so I could straddle the bench facing him.

Color spread over the bridge of his nose and he smirked. "I like to think so. If you stick around, I think you two would get along."

"I like her more already than your little spy."

He laughed. "Kayla is an acquired taste."

"You've got that right." I spun the empty glass in my hands. "So, you're happy?"

"I am. Though I'd be happier with you back in my life."

"I'll work on that too," I said and I meant it. He could have held out and kept me off the case for as long as he wanted. But he was being nice to me. He was more like the Desmond I remembered than I wanted to admit.

"Come on, I'll drive you home," Desmond said, offering his hand to help me up.

I hoisted myself up on my own, testing my leg. It seemed to hold my weight well enough. A few hours' sleep and Bella's magic coursing through me should heal the rest of it. He led the way back out in the night air. His was the only car left in the circular drive.

"It's changed more than I expected," I admitted once we were back on the road.

"They aren't the villains you make them out to be, Ezri. These are good people who are trying to help their community where they can."

"They're still being told what to do, how they can practice their craft."

"The Council thinks it's safer that way."

"They haven't changed, have they? Still the same people."

"For the most part, though I've taken over my mom's seat and ... yours is still waiting for you."

"Then I can't be a part of it. You aren't going to change my mind. Thank you for the help with the case, but that's all I'm getting from them. I don't trust them."

"Whether you trust them or not, they need you. Like it or not, their future rides on your shoulders."

"But it's my destiny, not theirs."

"You may have turned your back on them, but they haven't forgotten you. Avery was right, everyone here knows who you are. They can help you. I can't believe you're meant to do this all on your own. I think we both know that the Order is behind whatever is coming."

The Order of Samael—the Authority's bitter enemy and primary cause of the Salem Witch Trials. We'd been taught that the Order had used the trials as an excuse to thin the ranks of good practitioners. But the mass hysteria had ended up taking plenty of their people too. They were also fond of branding their members: a triple spiral to represent life and a scythe for their supposed power over death.

"Then they should have thought about that before they let my mother get killed and covered it up," I muttered.

I turned my attention to the passing traffic outside and the thick, cloud-filled navy sky above. Rain was imminent. Being back in the boundaries of the Authority's domain had set my nerves on edge more than I'd expected. But it also hadn't been quite as horrible as I'd anticipated either. For his part, Desmond didn't pester me the rest of the ride. He pulled up outside my apartment building and put the car in park.

"If you need anything else, case-related or not, just let me know."

"Yeah. I will. And, Desmond, thanks for clearing things with my captain."

"You said you will try talking out your issues. Please, don't let things fester any longer," he answered.

I opened the car door but didn't get out. I craned my neck to try to catch a glimpse of a certain purple-haired punk girl. Nothing immediately drew my attention and I couldn't sense her magic nearby.

"Kayla's gone," Desmond said, as if reading my mind.

We sat awkwardly for another few minutes before he reached over and pulled me into a hug. I didn't fight him. Maybe he was right. Maybe I did need this connection in my life. He finally let go and his eyes shone with unshed tears.

I gave him a weak smile. "See you around." I eased the passenger side door closed and headed inside. Once I was safely back in my apartment I played the waiting message on my voicemail.

Captain Beech was letting me back to work for my next shift. Relief flooded through me; endorphins and residual traces of Belladonna's magic coursed through my body, relaxing me far more than I had been in days.

MARCH 15, 2017

Belladonna's pills worked like a charm—and I wasn't entirely sure they weren't fueled by magic because I got ten solid, dreamless hours of sleep, rolling over and peering gummy-eyed at the clock just before nine o'clock the next morning. Lying beneath the blankets, I took stock of the injuries that had plagued me for the last few days. My throat and ribs felt better and at first blush the swelling on my jaw had gone down significantly. I twisted into a position where I could reach my leg and prodded the bandage with the tip of my finger. The muscle ached but no more than just a pulled muscle. As I climbed from the bed, a thought began to nag me.

I'd been so focused on trying to uncover the killers' identities through the video footage that I'd ignored the uniqueness of the primary killer's magical signature. Everyone I'd ever met had the scent of something naturally occurring in the world. Limestone—while naturally occurring—didn't always smell damp. I caught my reflection in the mirror and studied myself as I tried to put the missing piece into place. There had to be something about this killer to explain the strangeness of his magic.

"Come on … what is it?"

I didn't get a chance to let my brain work through the problem before my phone blared with an incoming call. I snatched it from the bedside table and paused when I saw Jacquie's cell phone number on the display. The hit to my pride surfaced, but I forced it down and answered, "Hello."

"I just got a call from the medical examiner. She finally got the results back on those fingerprints and skin cells from the victims."

"And who did they belong to?"

"She wouldn't say over the phone. She wants us to go over so she can tell us in person."

"Like … now?"

"She hinted that sooner was better than later and to come without the FBI escort if possible."

That didn't sound like Tricia. Sure, she didn't like people honing in on her playground, but to completely ice out the Feds seemed dangerous from a career standpoint. Pushing my doubts to the side, I said, "I'll meet you there. Just give me a half hour."

"See you there, partner."

The casual way she ended the call, as if nothing had happened, seemed odd. But if I was back in her good graces, then I'd take it. As I dressed and clipped my badge and service weapon to my hip, excitement rose in my chest. We actually had a tangible lead after nearly a week of dead bodies and nothing concrete to go on.

Traffic seemed to bend to my buoyant mood because I made it to the morgue in record time, leaning against the hood of my car when Jacquie pulled in.

"Care to fill me in on what I missed?" I asked. I had to pretend I didn't know about the latest victim.

"We had another body drop yesterday. And I hate to say it, but even with the FBI's help, we're still no closer to finding a link between our victims. Not that lack of evidence is stopping Agent Taggart."

"What's that supposed to mean?" I pressed as we went inside, flashing our badges at the front desk.

"I heard rumblings he was planning a press conference for this morning. I've got no idea what he's going to tell the public. So far, we've been lucky to avoid the murders ending up in the news cycle. I worry it's just going to cause panic. Right now, it's contained."

I agreed with her sentiment that it seemed foolish to hold a conference now when we really had nothing of substance to share with the public. The fact that people were dying was enough to set people on edge and take matters into their own hands. Fear ignited people's prejudices and prejudice only led to rash decisions and horrible consequences. "What does the captain say about all of this?"

"I think she's as frustrated as the rest of us. She knows we're doing what we can with the little information we've got. We've had uniforms out canvassing all of the scenes, but no one is coming forward as a witness."

"What if it's not about the people but the place itself?" I could nudge them in the right direction without coming out and saying magic was involved or, in fact, was the root motive for the killings.

We stopped at the door separating the autopsy suite from the in-house lab and I studied my partner's face. The normally smooth contours around her lips and eyes were wrinkled as if she'd been deep in thought. "I'm not sure what you mean. They're all public places, but nothing about them seems connected."

Not in the present anyway. "It was just a thought," I said, trying to play my suspicions off, pushing the swinging door inward.

Tricia jumped to her feet as soon as we walked in. Machines around the room blinked and beeped as they processed samples and did whatever else they were programmed for. I never was the best with science. I noted the dark circles under my friend's eyes and the frantic energy with which she flitted around the lab.

"We're here. What's so important you couldn't tell us over the phone?" Jacquie asked.

"You don't have the Feds with you, right?" Anxiety modulated her voice up a few steps, making it high and breathy.

"No. Just like you asked," I said.

"Good. Because what I've got is going to sound crazy.' Tricia picked up a tablet and flicked her fingertip across the screen. "Just so you know, I ran the samples three times to be sure."

"Just show us what you found," Jacquie insisted.

Tricia turned the tablet to show us a missing person's photo from nearly five years ago. The notation at the top of the photo indicated the case remained unsolved. Then-twenty-four-year-old Kevin Ellery had gone missing in November, never to be seen again. "What does a missing person have to do with our case?"

"His fingerprints and DNA were on all four bodies. It took me a while because the fingerprint scan was missing from the electronic file so I had to go digging through cold case storage for the physical file."

"What's the crazy part that you didn't want to bring to the FBI?" I glanced up from the photo.

"The skin cells I managed to pull the DNA match from *were* the stone dust. I can't explain it. It's like this guy was turned to stone and he left residue behind."

I didn't blame her for not wanting to bring this to the FBI. To a normal person it would sound insane. But it sparked something in the back of my memory. Something I'd once read about how magic can affect some people. Abuse it too much and it could literally change you at a molecular level. Like Whisperers but worse.

What did you do, Kevin?

"Even with the ... weirdness, you're certain this evidence is conclusive?" Jacquie interjected.

"Yes. Whether it holds up in court is another story. Any halfway decent defense attorney will rip apart the DNA evidence and claim it was corrupted somehow in the lab. If I didn't know my lab was pristine, I'd be inclined to agree with them."

I stepped away from the pair of them and studied Kevin's electronic casefile. He'd been reported missing around Thanksgiving by his mother. There'd been very few leads to go on. A girlfriend who hadn't seen him in weeks and a job that assumed he'd abandoned employment because he hadn't shown up in days. Because he wasn't a "newsworthy" victim—read not under eighteen and female—the police assigned to the case appeared to have given up pretty quickly. I scrolled through to find his mother's address.

Hoping she hadn't moved from Jamaica Plain in

five years, I copied the address into my phone. "Thanks for this, Tricia." To Jacquie I said, "Let's take a ride and pay Mrs. Ellery a visit."

Jacquie started for the door. I was about to fall in step when Tricia called, "Ezri, one second."

I gestured for my partner to go on ahead and stayed put until it was just Tricia and me in the room. "What's up?"

"That ... thing you asked me to do. I got results."

My heart hammered against my ribs and excitement began to build. "And?"

"There were two sets of fingerprints. One was yours."

"Shit, I should have warned you about that."

"Considering you asked me to run it, I assumed I could exclude you."

"The other set?"

"I don't have a match in the system, but they matched the blood on the blade."

"Wait ... what are you saying?"

"The only other person to touch the knife was your mother. I'm sorry, I'm sure this wasn't what you were hoping for."

"Thanks for trying anyway." I left the lab in a daze, trying to process the new information. Had whoever killed my mother made her do it herself? Had they worn gloves?

I found Jacquie waiting outside by my car. She

gestured to the driver seat and started for the passenger side.

"It seems you've got a feeling about this," she said as we buckled in.

I pushed the new questions about my mother's death to the back burner and climbed in. "What would make a missing person resurface in the same city he was last seen in five years later and start killing random strangers?" I questioned.

"Maybe if we can figure out why he went missing in the first place, we'll get some answers about now."

I hoped she was right. If we found Kevin, I was certain he'd lead us to his accomplice. And maybe then I'd be able to stop the evil from rising in only five days' time.

SIXTEEN

My mind raced the entire drive through the city. What had Kevin done that would turn his DNA to stone? How long had he been using his magic? Was he on the Authority's radar or had he been aligned with the Order? Where had he been the last five years? My brain kept jumping back to the question of motive. What would lead a seemingly normal guy to kill four people in the middle of a crowded city street?

A headache thrummed behind my eyes by the time I pulled into the driveway of the two-story row house. The wooden wraparound porch was in dire need of a new paint job and I noted a few missing shingles from the roof. I took the rickety steps two at a time and rang the buzzer by the door, waiting for a response.

One minute. No answer.

I tried again, this time adding a knock to the beige-coated door.

Movement from the bay window to the right caught my attention. The flutter of a curtain falling back into place and a face disappearing from view. I pulled my ID from my pocket, ready to present to whoever came to the door. Finally, the hinges squeaked. The door swung inward just enough for that same face—a haggard looking woman—to be visible.

"Whatever you're selling, I'm not interested."

"Are you Mrs. Ellery?" I asked.

"Who are you?" Her eyes narrowed with suspicion.

"I'm Detective Trenton." I showed her my badge. "This is my partner, Detective DeWitt. We'd like to talk to you about your son, Kevin."

"He's been gone five years and no one gave a damn about him. Why do you care now?"

Jacquie cleared her throat and moved so that she placed herself closer to Mrs. Ellery. "We have reason to believe your son may have been seen in the city recently. It would really help us if we could speak with you."

Mrs. Ellery studied us in silence. The corners of her mouth worked as if she wanted to accept Jacquie's statement and the sliver of hope it promised.

"Mrs. Ellery, we know the investigation into

Kevin's disappearance went cold. But we have a chance to find him. Please, help us," I pleaded.

She blinked, her eyes welling with tears. She pulled the door open wide enough for us to pass through, leading us into the living room to the right. The interior of the house was in similar disrepair as the outside. The wallpaper in the short foyer was faded and dated. The furniture in the living room could have come straight out of a second-hand store. To my surprise, the mantle held photos of Kevin—based on the photo from his missing person file—and only him. No smiling portraits or candid family shots. Mrs. Ellery gestured toward the worn loveseat tucked beneath the bay window. Jacquie and I sat side by side and I pulled out my notebook.

"What can you tell us about the last time you saw your son?" I began.

She fidgeted with her hands, twisting her fingers together so tight I was surprised the joints didn't snap and pop from the exertion. "That was five years ago and I told the police everything back then."

"Well, we'd like to hear it from you now," I pressed.

"It was a few days before Thanksgiving. Kevin had been talking for weeks about coming to spend the holiday with us. He'd been spending it with his girlfriend and her family the last few years ... since he graduated college. But then he called and said it would just be him. They'd had some sort of fight. But then Thanksgiving came and he didn't show up. I called the police the next day because I knew something was wrong."

"Did you reach out to his girlfriend at all?"

She shook her head. "I suppose the police did, but I got the impression they'd broken up. If I'm honest, I never really cared for her so I wasn't too upset that they'd ended things."

"Could he have gone to be with other family? His father perhaps?" Jacquie interjected.

I tried to hide my confusion at my partner's question. I made a show of jotting down notes to check the original case file and follow up on the girlfriend.

"We were still together then. We don't have any other relatives in the area. So, no, he wouldn't have gone anywhere else for the holiday. You said Kevin's been seen? Where? When?"

Time to tell her the truth. "Actually, Mrs. Ellery, Kevin's been linked to some current crimes we're investigating. Have you had any contact with your son recently?"

She blinked in silence, her mouth agape. "No."

"No hang-up phone calls or emails from addresses you don't recognize? No sign that he might be reaching out to you?"

"No, nothing like that."

"What about his ex-girlfriend? Has she been in touch?"

"No one's been in touch with me. And why would my son be involved in crimes?"

"That's what we're trying to figure out. We know he's in the city now. Was there anywhere he liked to go to maybe clear his head?"

"He liked the water. He'd go for walks a lot by the river. I don't know exactly where."

"Near the Esplanade?" Jacquie probed.

"Maybe."

"Did he ever spend any time downtown near Chinatown? Did he maybe have friends there?" Jacquie was on the edge of the loveseat, pen poised over her notepad.

"He could have. He didn't really tell me where people lived."

"What about the Public Gardens?"

"He liked the Swan boats. When he was younger, he always told me that he thought they were romantic." Tears trickled down her cheeks, but she made no attempt to wipe them away. "What are you going to do if you find Kevin?"

"If he's involved in the crimes we're investigating, we're going to have to bring him in," Jacquie said. She produced a business card and set it on the end table to her left. "If you can think of anything else, please call. We'll be in touch if we need anything else or have more questions."

That was my cue to stand up and pocket my notepad. I had one other question I needed to ask but it wasn't for mixed company. I turned to Mrs. Ellery and asked, "Do you mind if I use your bathroom?"

"Sure. I'll show you."

Jacquie arched a brow at me as if to say, "What are you up to?" I discreetly held up one hand to wave her off and followed Mrs. Ellery out of the living room and upstairs to the second floor. We stopped outside a door and she crossed her arms over her chest.

"You're more than just a police officer, aren't you?" Her tone carried a hint of accusation.

Feigning ignorance, I said, "I don't know what you mean."

She jutted her chin in the direction of my necklaces. "I know magical items when I see them."

Now that she'd admitted to knowing about its existence, I launched in. "I know Kevin has magic. We didn't just find his DNA at our crime scenes. His magical signature was present too. If you have any idea what happened to your son, if it's magic-related, you need to tell me."

"I suspected he was practicing ... testing out his gifts. I gave up using my magic a long time ago, when I got married and Kevin was born. Back then, my family was enough to satisfy me and I just wanted to fit in. It had been so long since I'd even thought about my abilities, I didn't even consider Kevin had inherited them."

Two thoughts occurred to me simultaneously:

magic passed down maternal lines so she had to know he'd get magic and how in the hell had she gotten off the Authority's radar for twenty something years?

Mrs. Ellery took a breath, her arms relaxed to her sides and she met my gaze head on. "There's something you should see."

Her hand trembled as she reached for the closed door beside us. After a moment to steady her nerves, she pushed it inward, revealing a neatly kept bedroom done up in green hues. The bed was partially unmade and, without asking, I understood. A part of her wanted to keep it exactly as her son had left it with the hope that one day he'd return.

"I can go in myself," I said in a hushed tone.

She nodded and pointed to the desk nestled beneath a window. "The photo in the silver frame."

I crossed the threshold and picked up the photo of Kevin and a girl I assumed was his ex-girlfriend. At first blush, it was an ordinary photograph of a happy couple. But I didn't need Mrs. Ellery to point out what was so telling. The girl wore a sleeveless dress and tattooed prominently on her left shoulder was a triple spiral with a scythe.

I turned to face Mrs. Ellery, photograph in hand. "She was a member of the Order?"

"I can't be sure. I mean sometimes kids when they're young see something they like, not knowing what it means, but if she was a willing participant... Oh God, could they have hurt my son?"

I set the picture down and left the room, pulling the door shut behind me. "I promise, I'm going to do what I can to find your son."

"Please don't hurt him. He was a good boy."

"I can't make that promise. I'm sorry. He's mixed up in some pretty serious crimes that he's going to have to answer for."

I started back down the stairs to rejoin Jacquie in the car and stopped midway down. "Was Kevin ever involved with the Authority?"

"I don't think so. I'm not sure he even knew what he was doing with his magic. Like I said, I gave that up when he came along and I never talked about it with him. And they left me alone."

"Thank you. I'll be in touch." I made a mental note to check in with Desmond to see if the Authority had any record of Kevin.

"What was that about?" Jacquie asked before I closed the driver-side door.

"I had to go to the bathroom," I lied. The engine roared to life and I pulled out of the driveway and into the street. "Do we have a last known on the ex-girlfriend?"

Before she could answer, both of our phones beeped. Jacquie swiped her screen and looked over at me. "The ex-girlfriend is going to have to wait."

"Why?" I didn't bother to check my phone.

"We just got an alert. Taggart is going live on NBC right now with a press conference."

I pulled a U-turn in the street and headed back the way we'd come until I found an empty parking spot and pulled in. Jacquie pulled the live stream up on her phone and we sat watching. Even on the small screen I could see the cameras flashing as reporters hung on every word. Taggart walked out to stand at a podium perched on the front steps of the State House, the gold dome glistening and reflecting the noon-day light overhead. He looked smug as he stood there, surveying his audience. Maybe it was just the look he always had, but it still made my fist itch to plant one right on his beak-like nose.

"Thank you all for coming. Together with the Boston Police Department's Major Crimes Division, the FBI has been investigating a series of homicides throughout the greater Boston area. Due to our combined efforts, at this time, we have identified a suspect, twenty-nine-year-old Kevin Ellery." The photo from Kevin's missing person's file flashed on the screen. "Anyone with information on Mr. Ellery's whereabouts is asked to contact the police tip line on the number below. We are urging the public to exercise extreme caution at this time. If you observe the suspect, contact police immediately. Do not approach him. He is considered armed and extremely dangerous. Thank you." The flurry of follow-up questions turned into white noise as

Taggart turned from the podium. As his hands lifted from the edges of the podium his jacket sleeve rode up and I caught something smudged and dark on the soft flesh of his left wrist.

"Do you see that?" I asked. I immediately snatched the phone and tried to zoom in, only to remember it was a live feed.

"See what? A half-assed press briefing that is only going to send the public into a panic and inundate us with false leads for days?" Jacquie quipped.

I gave a noncommittal sound as I tried to commit what little I'd seen on his arm to memory. I'd only caught the faintest edge, but it looked like the whorl on the bottom of the Order's brand. So far he hadn't given me any reason not to trust him, but if he was with the Order, there was no telling what he'd do to throw us off the real scent of our killers.

SEVENTEEN

With a few swipes, we had Kevin's ex-girlfriend's address and were on the road, heading back toward my own stomping ground. If the information we had was accurate, she was in a fourth-floor walk-up out near Boston College. We pulled into a free spot and, armed with Kevin's file, we rang the buzzer. No one came on over the intercom system, but we got lucky and an older gentleman came out of the building a few minutes later. He gave us a courteous nod and held the door open for us.

Déjà vu hit me as we walked upstairs. It wasn't the same as notifying Mrs. Cho of finding her husband's body but the trek up to question a potential witness filled me with the same nervous energy. I reached the apartment door first and banged hard twice. I heard footsteps from within and took a step back, reaching for my badge, when the door swung open with enough force to send it slamming into the opposite wall.

"What do you want?" a guy in his thirties with a scraggly beard and buzzcut demanded.

"We're with the police," I answered and held up my badge.

His eyes went wide and he coughed. "The pot's legal. I swear."

"We're looking for Gabrielle," I said, ignoring his marijuana-fueled confession.

"She's at work."

"And where would that be?" Jacquie interjected.

"A little hole-in-the-wall Italian place in the North End."

I tried not to roll my eyes. "You realize that describes almost every restaurant in the area. We're going to need a name."

Buzzcut disappeared into the apartment and appeared with a business card for a restaurant I hadn't heard of. "Great. Thanks."

"So, we're cool about the pot, right?"

I smiled. "Have a good day."

We were halfway down the stairwell when Jacquie asked, "How do you feel about an early lunch?"

Just before 11:30 we sat in the back booth of a cramped restaurant with sticky laminated tables. I wasn't expecting greatness from the cuisine, but we'd specifically requested to sit in Gabrielle's section so our trip was at least headed in the right direction. A busser brought by glasses of room temperature water before Gabrielle stopped by. Time had deepened the scowl lines around her mouth and her hair was shorter and done in a pixie cut, which mildly resembled Kayla's, but it was definitely the girl from the photo. Despite the chilly weather outside, she wore a shirt that showed off her shoulder and the faded tattoo. The sight of the mark in person sparked panic, tightening my chest so it hurt to breathe. Almost on autopilot a burst of strawberry-scented magic erupted around me. The waitress's nose flared and she took an almost imperceptible step away from me.

"Are you Gabrielle?" I asked before the girl could speak.

"Yeah. What can I get you?" The flatness of her tone gave away how bored she was standing there having to wait on us.

"A few minutes of your time to answer some questions," I said, flashing my badge.

Her back went ramrod straight and her eyes darted side to side, as if to check if anyone had noticed. "I can't really talk now. My boss can't know you're here."

"We're just patrons asking about the lunch specials," Jacquie said in a soothing voice.

Gabrielle's shoulders relaxed a fraction of an

inch and she dug the tip of her pen into her pad so forcefully that I could see it pierce several sheets of paper. "Talk fast then."

"We know you and Kevin Ellery were together a few years ago when he went missing. You were his girlfriend."

"Ex. We broke up."

I leaned forward a little. "Why?"

"He was getting too possessive. I told this to the police before like a long time ago. Why are you bringing it up now?"

"Have you seen the news this morning?" I prompted.

She shook her head. "Did something happen? Did they find Kevin?"

"Not yet. But he's a person of interest in some pretty serious crimes. When's the last time you talked to him?"

"Like five years ago when we broke up. If he's mixed up in crimes, that's on him. I don't have anything to do with him anymore." She craned her neck in the direction of the kitchen and then looked back at us. "Can you please just order something?"

I flipped through the menu and ordered the meat lasagna. Jacquie went with the chicken parmesan and I silently prayed we didn't end up with food poisoning. As it turned out, despite the subpar décor, the food was pretty decent. As we ate, I glanced across the table at my partner, working up the courage to speak.

"We're good, right?" Jacquie asked first.

The forkful of lasagna fell back to the plate as I stared at her. How had she known I'd been psyching myself up to ask the same thing? "I think so. I mean I assume you were the reason I had to pay a visit to the department shrink, but I get it. I was acting a little crazy. And I am working through some shit about my past. It's a work in progress but I'm trying." It wasn't the whole truth, but I'd made the promise to Desmond that I'd try.

Jacquie set her knife and fork down. "I was just trying to look out for you. I get that it's been hard. You're young and you've made it this far by doing some good police work, but a promotion like this is a big chance. I just don't want to see you throw that away by being overzealous. I've seen up and comers climb too high and fall and I almost got taken down in the aftermath. I just needed to know I had a partner whose judgment I could count on."

"I'm sorry. I ... I didn't know that."

"No reason you should," she answered and turned back to her food.

"I'm sorry about whatever happened."

She gave me a thin-lipped smile. "It was a long time ago. Not long after I made detective myself."

That confession only made things worse. I hated lying to Jacquie about the existence of magic. About this case, everything. Her fears about me losing my shit had been rooted in her own experiences, which only solidified that I couldn't tell her now. She needed to believe I was okay. Maybe once this case was done, I'd tell her everything, magical secrecy be damned. Maybe then the guilt on my conscience would lessen.

I shot a look over to where Gabrielle stood, texting on her phone. "Do you believe her that she hasn't seen Kevin in five years? And now she's over there furiously texting somebody."

Jacquie nodded. "She's hiding something, that's for sure."

"How much you want to bet the person on the other end of that text thread is Kevin?"

"No way to know from here." Her mouth hung open like she wanted to say something else, but she stayed silent and turned back to her meal.

She may not have had a way to tell what was happening with Gabrielle, but I did. Glancing over my shoulder, I spotted Gabrielle heading through the row of booths toward the front of the restaurant. Inhaling, I focused on her, sharpening my hearing and manipulating the soundwaves around me just enough to catch that she was going for a break. I watched as she stepped through the front door, took a few strides from the building and lit up a cigarette. I slid from the booth and started to follow.

"Where are you going?" Jacquie asked, catching my left wrist in her outstretched hand.

Thinking fast, I spotted a dessert display case near the front of the store and said, "Checking out dessert."

I weaved through the other servers and settled in front of the display. It was as good as I was likely to get cover wise and its proximity to Gabrielle meant I could expend less energy trying to spy on her. She paced outside, phone pressed to her ear, taking drags from the cigarette. The pendant around my neck warmed as I extended my range of hearing through the glass panel of the door and windows, pulling in the sound of her voice.

"Cops showed up at work asking about Kevin. What the hell is going on?"

Static and crackling white noise answered her, setting my temples throbbing. I massaged the spot right above my left eyebrow and waited for it to pass.

Finally, Gabrielle spoke again. "One of them's got magic. I could feel it. Why are they looking for Kevin? What aren't you telling me?"

More static and my vision started to blur. But by Gabrielle's response I knew that she wasn't working with Kevin. There was no reason she'd fake that kind of confusion on a phone call she didn't know was being eavesdropped on. My heart sank a little at that realization. Here I thought we were getting closer to answers and we were just hitting more dead ends.

Gabrielle ended her phone call and the buzzing in my brain dulled. She stamped out her cigarette and I darted back to the table, sliding on the fake vinyl seat just as the door closed behind her.

"See anything good?" Jacquie asked.

"No, not really." Before I could say more, my phone buzzed in my pocket with an incoming text message.

Sliding the phone from my pocket, I took a cursory glance at the screen. A message from Desmond asking me to stop by the Authority headquarters as soon as possible. That couldn't be good.

"Hey, I hate to do this, but I need to follow up on something."

"Great, let's go."

"I need to do this alone. It's an informant who gets jumpy if I show up with anyone else. And I don't know if he's even reliable. I don't want to drag you all over the city if it isn't going to pan out." God, I hated how easily the lies came to me.

Jacquie stared at me for a minute and I waited for her to call me on my bullshit. "Okay. You'll need to drop me at the morgue so I can get my car and then I'll head back to the precinct and see if anything of note has come off the tip line. But you let me know the second you've got actionable information."

"I swear, you'll be the first person I call."

EIGHTEEN

A million different scenarios ran through my brain on the trip back out to Newton. Had they finished unscrambling the video files already or had they run into some unforeseen problem? Was Desmond going to try to recruit me back into the fold again? The uncertainty of what lay beyond the exterior of headquarters sent anxious jolts of energy through my body, making my skin prickle with electricity. I zapped myself twice on the door handle before I was even in the foyer.

Desmond waited for me in the hallway, a solemn look on his face. That wasn't good. The last time I'd seen that expression was at my mother's sham of a funeral when I learned no one was going to give her justice. I stopped a few feet from him, arms at my sides even though my instinct told me a fight was coming and I needed to protect myself.

"What's going on? Your text was pretty vague," I said, trying to keep my tone neutral.

"The Council wanted to talk to you."

"Not a chance in hell." I did an about face and was two paces from the door when I felt an invisible hand grab me around both wrists and yank me backwards, spinning so I was facing Desmond again.

"You aren't running away from this, Ezri. You may not like them and that's fine. But things are happening regarding the Prophecy and they need to know what you know."

I pushed a little of my own will into the mix, breaking his hold on me and sending him staggering back a couple paces. "You mean you haven't told them everything I shared with you? I assumed you were their spy in the department."

Anger flashed across his face. A rare expression that darkened his normally handsome features. "Grow the fuck up, Ezri. We all have to do things and deal with people we'd rather not. And you might be surprised. They have some suggestions that might help your case."

"Just so you know, my partner was already suspicious of me running off. I had to lie to her to get here. If they jeopardize my relationship with her, I'm going to be pissed," I snapped. Even more pissed. I had taken one step toward the spiral staircase when he caught my left arm and guided me toward the library. My brow furrowed at the change of venue.

"They aren't meeting upstairs?"

"For this, they felt the library would be better suited."

Great, a lecture.

I managed not to roll my eyes as Desmond led me into the room with its two walls of floor-to-ceiling bookshelves. Photographs of past generations were peppered among the shelves, propped up by the spines of pristinely kept tomes. The faces were just a blur as I took in the floor-to-ceiling tinted windows.

The last time I'd been in this space, the handful of tables had been placed evenly in the center of the room with their little green-shaded lamps situated dead center of each table. Today, the lamps sat unlit and the tables were pushed together to make one long rectangle. Thirteen chairs wreathed the table.

I counted only eleven people sitting in the room. They were all faces I recognized from my youth. Raymond Wallace—a slender man with a full salt and pepper beard and sharp brown eyes—had been the one to come to our apartment when my mother died. He'd shown little sympathy for our loss. It took all the willpower I possessed not to send him flying through the windows behind him and out into the street. J.T.'s mother, Bethany Somers, sat in one of the seats. She wouldn't meet my gaze.

Desmond sat down in one of the remaining chairs and it became clear that the last one, at the head of the table, was for me. The moment I sat in that seat, the Council would be complete again. They all stared at me expectantly, as if the prodigal daughter had finally returned home, ready to forget the sins of the past. Well, I wasn't ready to bury any hatchets or share conciliatory hugs with anyone.

"Ms. Trenton, thank you for coming on such short notice," Wallace said in his scratchy tenor voice.

"It's Detective," I said through clenched teeth. I refused to sit.

"Of course. My apologies. It's just we don't use such formal titles here. As you may recall."

"If it's all the same to you, I'd prefer you stick to the formal title."

He nodded and looked around the table. "We've been keeping an eye on the deaths in the city of late. And after the press conference by the FBI we felt we needed to speak with you directly."

"I'm listening."

"Please sit down." Belladonna's calming voice drew my attention. I hadn't noticed her sitting in one of the chairs.

I tasted cinnamon on my tongue and grit my teeth, trying to fight her magical nudge. Knowing that arguing would only prolong things, I sat on the very edge of the chair, ready to make a speedy exit if necessary. Wallace retrieved a thick volume from somewhere out of view—a side table or bag I couldn't see—and slid it across the table to me. I caught it and noted the page about one third of the way through the tome, marked with a red sticky tab. All eyes followed me as I turned to the marked page on Gargoyles. A quick skim of the entry confirmed what I'd at least suspected about Kevin. Gargoyles were usually the result of overuse of magic but could also be the result of a dark practitioner's curse. Super strong, they typically moved freely under the light of a full moon. If the curse was placed on them by another, they could be controlled by that spell caster. The sketch beside the entry depicted a man frozen in stone but with exquisite detail of the clothing and facial features.

"Kevin Ellery is a Gargoyle," I said to no one in particular. It explained almost everything about him. Why he'd gone missing five years ago. Someone had either cursed him or he'd done something so bad to land himself encased in stone and it also explained why he was resurfacing now. If he'd been cursed, someone could be reanimating him outside of the full moon to do their bidding. He may be an unwitting participant in all of this.

"We suspect he may be involved with the Order," Wallace said.

"He's definitely got a history of magic. And his ex-girlfriend was a member." There was something else that my brain was trying to connect to this new piece of the puzzle.

The Public Gardens!

"Where do Gargoyles usually end up in the city?" I asked, turning my attention away from Wallace and on to Belladonna.

"Public spaces mostly. It's easier to fit in with other statues. I've seen a few near the Copley branch of the Public Library."

"This is actually helpful. I think I have an idea of where he might be."

"Perhaps you should focus on where he will strike next," Wallace said.

"If I can find him before he attacks, then it doesn't matter," I said.

"Except you know he's working with someone else. You said there were two magical signatures at the scenes," Desmond interjected.

"Find the fifth location and stop them there. Maybe I can catch both of them before they can finish whatever it is they're planning," I said, following what I guessed was my cousin's logic.

Wallace cleared his throat. "We were hoping you had some idea of what that might be."

"I can't see the future. All I know is they're killing people and, from what I've seen at two of the scenes, they're resurrecting the spirits of dark practitioners killed during the Trials."

Wallace stroked his beard in thought, never taking his eyes off me. I took several calming breaths before saying, "Look, I think it's time you shared what you know about this prophecy I'm supposed to fulfill. I get that's it's coming and the time will be here in a few days when the meteor shower and the solar eclipse happen. But you've got to know something about what the evil is I'm supposed to put down."

"All we know is the Order has long desired to bring their forces back into the world."

I couldn't resist an eye roll as Wallace prattled on. "Could you be more specific?"

"Both sides of this war were born out of the same group of Druids back in Ireland. We suspect whatever ritual they're planning will try to invoke that ancient magic at the very least," a gray-haired woman with wire-framed glasses answered before Wallace got the chance. If memory served, she was Marjorie Hampton, one of the researchers from my parents' day.

"That could explain why they're raising dark practitioners," Belladonna murmured just loud enough for me to hear.

"Can we get back to how you'll find this fifth location? And how do you even know these other deaths occurred on hanging sites of dark practitioners?" a dark-skinned man with a mop of thick, black curls interrupted.

I shrugged. "I may have a map and ledger of where every dark practitioner was hung. They fit the locations of the crime scenes down to the longitude and latitude. I think it's forming an inverted pentagram so finding the last point shouldn't be difficult."

Wallace glowered at me. "Very well. We would like you to report back once you've apprehended Mr. Ellery and his accomplice."

"I don't work for you. Besides, once they're in custody, it's out of my hands." Deciding this was enough of being a team player, I stood up and left the room.

I paused in the foyer, expecting to hear footsteps thundering after me. Silence was my only companion. I still stayed put for a few minutes longer and sensed the presence behind me before I saw who it was. Bethany stood there, looking at her hands.

"I just wanted to tell you how sorry I am for everything you've been through," she said in a hushed tone. She'd never been one to speak louder than a whisper. Back before everything had gone to hell, she'd been like a second mother to me. Snippets of memories of movie nights at the Somers' house flashed through my mind.

I tugged at my jacket sleeve as a distraction. "Thanks. I should really go. I need to follow up on a couple leads and I told my partner I'd let her know if I found anything of importance."

"Right. Look, Ezri, I know things between you and J.T. ended badly, but I wanted you to know that, no matter what, I'm here if you need anything. I understand you are hesitant to trust us again, but we really do want the same thing."

"And what is that exactly?"

"To stop the Order from executing whatever their plan is, no matter what it takes."

Including my life.

"I'll keep that in mind. But I really should go."

She took a step toward me and lifted her arms as if she wanted to hug me, but I shied away from the gesture. She stepped back into the library awkwardly. Desmond passed her as she disappeared from view.

"Walk you to your car?" The anger had left his voice.

I nodded and we walked out to the circular drive together. We paused at the driver side door. He studied me with those piercing blue eyes. "Want to tell me how you have a map of all those locations?"

"It was with my family's journals."

"It's supposed to be in the library archives.'

I shrugged. "I didn't take it. Look, if it means so much to them, I'll return it when this case is solved. Right now, it's my only real lead to finding the fifth scene."

"Please be careful. I don't want to lose you after just getting you back, little cousin."

"Thanks for the concern, but I'll be fine."

He frowned and gestured to my leg and ribs. "You aren't indestructible, oh Chosen One."

"I'm healing. It's barely even noticeable anymore. Desmond, relax. I'm tougher than I look."

He didn't seem convinced, but he smiled at me. "I sound like a broken record, but I'm glad you're back."

"Don't get used to it."

I climbed into the car and shoved the key into the ignition. As the engine purred to life, so did my phone with an incoming text from Jacquie. "Tip line is off the hook. Get anything yet?"

'Checking one last thing and I'll get back to you.'

I left headquarters behind and in the rearview mirror I caught Desmond holding his phone up to his ear.

NINETEEN

Afternoon was rapidly turning to early evening —the kill window—by the time I got back to my apartment. The time between kills had been steadily decreasing and even with the entire public looking for Kevin, I doubted he would be deterred. And if he was still working with his partner, people could be standing right next to him and not even notice.

There were a handful of spots on the map that looked like they could be in the vicinity of the fifth point on the pentagram, but I needed to view them in comparison to the spots we already had. I tried pressing the map to the Google map on my laptop, but the backlight of the screen made it impossible to see and my eyes crossed from the effort.

Some frustration and fighting with the install disc for a never-used printer later, I had a Google

Map printout and far more success. Tracing the dots of the other four crime scenes, all but one of the remaining potential sites was ruled out, leaving one that sat squarely at the intersection of Charles Street and Tremont Street in Downtown.

Excitement coursed through me at the realization that I was one step away from catching our killers and thwarting the Order with a few days to spare. The energy flooded every nerve in my body and synapse in my brain, urging me onward. Halfway back to my car I called Jacquie.

"I have a lead on a potential attack site," I said, the words tumbling out of my mouth as I climbed back in the car.

"Where?"

"Charles and Tremont."

"How'd you figure this out?"

"Does it matter? If I'm right, we can catch them."

"I'll meet you there."

"Where's our friendly FBI shadow?"

"Taggart hasn't been around for a few hours."

His absence sent up red flags in my brain. If he was, in fact, working for the Order, then he could try to head us off.

"Okay, just meet me there," I said and ended the call.

Whatever good traffic karma I'd been having all week deserted me on my trip into the city. The sun was well below the buildings around me as I fought through the pedestrians milling around the theater district off Tremont Street.

"Come on, move," I groaned as the light finally turned green.

My car tires screeched as I took the turn onto Stuart Street harder than I probably should have. Only two more streets and I'd reach my destination. I prayed I wasn't too late.

One block up, I abandoned my hope of getting to the site by car. I pulled into an available spot and took off on foot, weaving through people heading to and from nearby restaurants. I stopped with Charles Street in sight. I took a moment to clear myself of all the residue of Belladonna's and Desmond's magic from my senses and body, ready to follow anything that leapt out at me. With hurried steps, I traversed Charles back up toward Tremont, scanning every face for recognition.

One minute everything was empty, devoid of magic. Then, as if I'd run headlong into a brick wall, my senses were overwhelmed with the familiar scents of our killers. Dizziness gripped my body and I swayed on the spot, fruitlessly grasping for something to steady myself. I felt the spell caster's intent wash over me, trying to direct me away from whatever horrors were going on within its boundaries, but I pushed through, exerting enough of my own power to break through the barrier. I felt it harden around me and shatter like glass. Whether it was permanently gone I couldn't tell. My attention was focused on the dead body lying prone on the sidewalk. A middle-aged woman with jet-black hair and way too much make-up lay there, chest concave and blood trickling from her mouth. I was too late.

Training kicked in and I un-holstered my gun, holding it low to my side. I scanned the surrounding area, but no one was in view. Whoever was powering the misdirection spell had to be close by, but there was no visible sign of them. And for all I knew, the spell was protecting Kevin's appearance from view too. I knelt by the body and pressed two fingers to the woman's throat. No pulse but the body was warm. Her death had just happened. The air was thick with Kevin's magic and another familiar scent.

Brimstone and burning flesh.

Another sightless spirit stood just out of reach. Her dark lips curled into a sinister smirk and she actually waved at me. Trying to see through the decomposition, I thought she could have been young, maybe even a teenager, when she'd been hung for her crimes. With more flourish than her predecessors, the girl waved both arms and flames whooshed up around her like a cloak, obscuring her face before she vanished.

"Damn it."

I dug my phone out of my pocket with one hand, the other still gripping my service weapon. Without looking, I hit the second speed dial on my contact list —the precinct—and waited while it rang.

"Dispatch," a vaguely familiar male voice answered.

"This is Detective Ezri Trenton, Major Crimes. I need to call in a homicide at the intersection—"

Pain radiated down my spine and stars flashed before my eyes. Dark spots popped and everything went weak. Intellectually I knew I'd fallen face first into a dead body, but my nerves had stopped sending signals to my brain. Sluggishly I tried to turn over to confront my assailant, but everything was too fuzzy and I could only make out a vague shape. My nose was still working and the wretched scent of garlic smothered me. My attempts to lift my gun failed and then a new origin of pain overtook the throb at the base of my skull. Something like ripping cloth hit my ears and then something red poured down the front of my shirt. If my brain hadn't been so rattled, I would have seen the punch coming in time to block it. As it was, my head thudded against the concrete and everything went dark.

I OPENED *my eyes to blinding brightness. The shock to my retinas overwhelmed me and I shut them again as fast as possible. I counted to ten in my head and cracked one lid a second time. Introducing the*

light slowly seemed safer. The light dimmed but never fully faded. Where was I?

"Hello?" I called out through parched lips and a raw throat.

"Sweet girl, I'm here," my mother's voice said from right beside me. My head whipped around and there she was, kneeling at my side looking exactly as she had the last time I'd seen her alive.

"Mom." Tears poured down my cheeks, dripping in fat drops off the tip of my nose. I reached for her and she wrapped me in a tight embrace. "I miss you so much."

"I miss you more." She wiped away the tear tracks with her palms as she'd done when I was a child.

It didn't matter where we were because I had my mother back. She was okay. As her hands broke contact with my cheeks I became aware of another presence. Something was wrong with my senses because I couldn't pinpoint the direction of their approach. My shoulder muscles tightened in response to whoever was coming, but my mother's hand pressed down hard on my arm, reminding me that I wasn't alone. I could face whatever came next.

A woman appeared before us and she looked familiar. Her slate-grey eyes reminded me of Desmond's, but her russet-colored, shoulder-length hair was all our side of the family. It was held back at the nape of her neck and she wore a simple dress. She couldn't have been more than a couple of years older than me. I tried to place her, but my thoughts were still sluggish.

"I know you," I murmured, still trying to get my voice to work right.

A sad smile ghosted over her lips as she moved to sit cross-legged on my other side. "We have not met face-to-face, but I've known you were coming for a very long time."

"Theodora?"

She shook her head and a cloud of sadness drifted over her face. "No. I am afraid not."

There was only one other option. "Eleanor. You made the prophecy about me."

Tears sparkled in her eyes, but she didn't let them fall. "I knew I would never live to see Theodora's heir fulfill her destiny."

Her words took a moment to process through my sluggish brain. "But it talked about a Harrow daughter. You were both Harrows before you married. I've seen the family trees. Theodora didn't marry until after your death."

She patted my left hand gently with both of hers. "I never told my sister, I did not have heart enough to tell her that it was her line that would battle the darkness and not mine. I could not burden her with that knowledge."

I looked to my mother. "Did you know?"

It was her turn to shake her head. "No. None of us could have known that."

"I wasn't fast enough to stop them," I said, the realization like bitter acid on my tongue.

"What are you talking about? You have plenty of time. Still four days before the Equinox," Mom said.

"Whatever ritual they're planning, they've got the bodies they need. I wasn't quick enough to stop them. Even though I knew who the killer was and I figured out where he'd be, I failed." There was something else I should have been angry with myself about but it was a huge blank.

Eleanor's touch tightened on my hand. "Your mother is correct, my dear. You have time yet to stop them from finishing their purpose."

"I don't know what they're planning to do with the spirits they've summoned. I mean they seemed almost corporeal near the end. I've heard that you can make a trade with a life for a life, but that still doesn't explain what they want to do now."

Mom smoothed strands of hair from my face. "That doesn't matter. All that does is that you can stop them. You know where they'll be at the height of the Equinox. You will stop them, Ezri. I have faith in you. I always have. From the moment my heart told me that you were our Savior, I knew you wouldn't fail. You have our blood running through your veins. You are meant for this."

"We are always with you. You just need remember that and you will never be alone in this battle to come. You must remember that," Eleanor murmured.

"I will."

Shadows danced just beyond the edges of the brightness surrounding us and for the first time since I'd opened my eyes sounds filtered through, hitting my eardrums with a delayed reaction. Steady, rhythmic beeping and the murmur of low voices. I strained to hear what they were saying, fought to identify the speakers, but everything was out of focus. Everything but the two women at my side. Eleanor let go of my hand, but I still felt the power of her touch warm me. The heady smell of burning rosemary filled my nostrils and every part of me warmed with the magic she'd wrapped around me. My mother leaned over and kissed my forehead, leaving her mark too.

"We'll see you soon, dear girl. But right now, you need to wake up!"

MARCH 16, 2017

TWENTY

It took what must have been only minutes but felt like years to obey my mother's command. I focused on the steady beeping to pull me from the brightness and back into the real world. I kept my eyes closed for a long time, trying to take everything in with my other senses. My head was elevated but in a comfortable position. My fingers brushed against something soft and as I inched my hands closer to my core I determined someone had put a blanket over me. The overwhelming odor of honey clung to my skin, my hair and everything around me. It was as if someone had dunked me headfirst into a honeycomb. That scent brought back memories and I opened my eyes. The room came into focus and I found myself in a small bedroom with wood paneled walls and nondescript beige curtains that were drawn tight against the outside.

"Where ..." My throat was still sore. It hadn't just been a figment of my imagination.

The door leading out of the room was ajar and footsteps thudded on wood flooring. The door swung inward to reveal two people I didn't expect to ever see in the same place: my ex-boyfriend and my partner. J.T.—looking just as handsome as he had as a teenager—moved to check my vitals while Jacquie took up residence in a chair at my bedside.

"Glad to have you back with us, partner," Jacquie said.

The scent of the honey had given me a clue as to my caretaker, but what was my partner doing here? Wherever here was. Had he done anything to make Jacquie suspect that magic was real? I tried to sit up, but pain seared through my core and J.T. put a firm hand on my shoulder, forcing me back to a flat position.

"You need to keep still or you're going to pull stitches." Our eyes met and the hurt and anger I expected from our breakup was nowhere to be found. Only a touch of sadness amidst a lot of concern. Then again, just because my feelings had festered for a decade didn't mean he'd even thought about me in years, despite his mother trying to reassure me earlier.

"Where am I?" I tried again.

"Headquarters," he answered. He held up a hand to shut me up before I could say anything else.

"Don't argue with me. We're lucky we got you here in time."

I nodded mutely and looked to Jacquie. "This is ... um..."

"I know who J.T. is," Jacquie interrupted. "And you're going to have a lot of questions and we'll answer all of them, but right now you need to rest. You lost a lot of blood and things are moving faster now. With all five spirits resurrected, it's only a matter of time before the Order enacts their plan."

Her words made sense to me on a basic comprehension level but coming out of my partner's mouth baffled the fuck out of me. I suppose there was the possibility J.T. and Jacquie had crossed paths on the job, given that he was presently wearing an EMT uniform. But how had she learned about the Order and their plans? Who'd told her about the spirits I'd seen being resurrected at the crime scenes? I rubbed at my forehead, which only made the rest of my head throb in agony.

"Someone needs to tell me what the hell is going on. And maybe some heavy-duty Advil. Not necessarily in that order," I grunted through the ache in my skull.

J.T. produced a couple of white capsules and some water and I downed them. I didn't expect them to take immediate effect, but, then again, he could have augmented them with a little touch of something extra. The throb began to dissipate almost instantly.

"How long was I out?" It had been early evening last I recalled.

"A while. It's about six in the morning," J.T. answered.

Nearly twelve hours. The pounding in my head intensified for a moment before receding again.

"What do you remember?" Jacquie asked, ever the detective.

"I think I deserve some answers first," I replied. "How do you two know each other?" I gestured at Jacquie. "And how do *you* know about the Order?"

J.T. cleared his throat and made a move toward the doorway. "I'll let you two hash this out. There's a call button on the side of the bed if you need anything, Ez. I'll be back to check on you in a bit."

My heart sank as he disappeared from view. I'd been so mad at him when, really, we'd both been so young and I had pushed him away in my grief. Seeing him now all grown up tugged at feelings I'd thought had died with my mother. I beat back the rush of schoolgirl questions dancing around my thoughts and turned back to Jacquie.

"Spill it. What do you know?"

Jacquie cleared her throat but wouldn't meet my gaze. That only made me nervous. Finally, she looked up and said, "I knew who you were before we were partnered together. About the magic and the fact that you were supposed to be this Savior. The Authority pulled a few strings to make sure we were partnered together."

"Why? What do you have to do with the Authority?"

"It turns out my sister-in-law has magic. So the kids might develop it one day. Your friend Desmond came to me a while ago and brought me into the fold."

"He's not a friend. He's my cousin. Well, distant cousin," I corrected on impulse.

"Right, sorry. It's hard to keep it straight. It seemed pretty impossible when I first found out, but even for those of us without powers, it's pretty damn impressive."

"Why didn't you say anything before?"

"The Authority swore me to secrecy. There were so many times I wanted to tell you. But they'd warned me you had trust issues when it came to magic and they needed you to trust me."

I let out a hiccup of hysterical laughter. "There were so many times I wanted to tell you about magic too. It would have made everything so much easier. I guess the Authority had more influence over both of us than we realized."

She nodded in silence. "And I'm sorry I had to tell the captain about you acting erratically. But the Authority made it clear they needed you back into the fold before the Equinox."

"Well, maybe you weren't wrong about that part. I've got shit I need to work out. And maybe talking to Desmond won't be the worst thing."

"I do hope you get the answers you're looking for about your mother."

There was something else I needed to tell my partner, but the alluring scent of J.T.'s magic tugged at my consciousness, urging me to return to the depths of my dreams where the pain and heartache of reality were just a distant memory. Jacquie finally stood up and moved to the doorway and stepped over the threshold, leaving me with just a silhouette of her body. The edges started to go fuzzy and I gave in to the pull of the drugs. Right now, I could only hope sleep would take me back to my mother's arms.

When I woke the next time, the sky outside of my only window was still bright, if a bit dimmed. Damn, I wished I had a clock to keep track of how much time I was losing from sleeping. I didn't remember any dreams this time, but I did feel a little better. No one came to check on me right away and I enjoyed the solitude, taking the time to assess my body. I reached up with one hand and gingerly pressed the back of my head. The memory of getting clocked came back to me, along with the smell of recently dead human remains and the gag-inducing smell of my attacker's magic: garlic. It had been Kevin's accomplice. There was a small comfort in that. Given what we'd seen of the other bodies, I probably wouldn't have been alive if Kevin had taken a swing at the back of my head. But why hadn't he stuck around to make sure he'd finished the deed?

Next, I pushed the blankets down to thick sweatpants covering my lower limbs. I pulled the fabric of my shirt up to my breasts, exposing a wide swathe of medical tape and bandages. The ghost of the attack flashed before me, the feeling of the blade slicing through skin and muscle again and again and I couldn't hold back the bile. Someone had thought to leave a bucket at the bedside and I managed not to make a mess. My whole body shook from the effort and something oozed toward my leg. I groped for the call button and slammed it with my fist.

"How are you feeling?" J.T. asked as he walked in, stowing his phone in his back pocket.

"Ugh," I moaned.

He took the bucket from my sweat-slick hands and settled me back down against the pillows. His fingers probed at my stomach and he peeled the dressing away to reveal a horizontal line of dark stitches, one of which had torn and was now leaking blood.

He worked without speaking. Donning latex gloves, he pressed a cool cloth to my forehead and snipped the offending suture out, replacing it in a matter of seconds. Even he couldn't work miracles with magic, not with something so destructive. He eased the tape off the rest of my stomach and reapplied a new dressing before pulling the blankets back up over my torso. He started to leave again when I reached out to him, unintentionally snaring him in a loop of magic. His right hand jerked back in my direction and he looked back.

"Stay with me?" My voice was coarse.

He dragged the chair over to the other side of the bed and sat down with the back of it facing me. Some habits apparently never died. We stayed like that, contemplating one another for a while in silence. It wasn't awkward like it had been before Jacquie's departure.

"I'm so glad Jacquie was there to get to you when she did."

"She was there?"

"Yes, she was."

I vaguely recalled calling her about the location. "Oh, right. She told me she got pulled into the Authority because of her sister-in-law and her niece and nephew."

"I'm not sure exactly what happened but, yeah, she's been working with us for a while now. It's good to have normal people on the payroll who are in the know. It means you don't have to try to explain away things that don't quite make sense without magic as the go-to answer."

"I wanted to tell her the truth so many times. I just wish she could have told me too."

He shrugged. "The Council told her to keep her mouth shut."

Heat touched the tips of my ears. Once again, the Authority was trying to tell me what to do. "They didn't have that right."

"I don't blame you for being pissed at them, but you're going to have to put a pin in it for now, okay? We need you focused on stopping the Order. We've got less than four days before the Equinox and no one knows for sure what the eclipse and the meteor shower are going to do to the changeover in the balance of power."

"That's what they're counting on," I muttered.

"Which, again, is why we need you ready to fight. You won't be completely healed, but you'll be damn close."

I reached out and grasped the fingers on his right hand. "Thank you for saving me."

He smiled and for a moment he was that fifteen-year-old boy I'd fallen for all those years ago. "It's my job, Ez. Besides, you may have forgotten about me, but I never stopped thinking about you."

"I didn't forget you."

"It sure felt like it. I get that you were grieving, but you pushed all of us away. We wanted to be there for you. I wanted to be there."

"I was so angry about losing my mother and the fact they covered it up, I guess I lashed out at everyone around me."

His lips parted as if he was going to speak, but no

words came out. After a shaky breath, he said, "I can't imagine losing someone that close to you."

"I had a dream about her, you know. Lots of dreams really ... reliving the day I found her, but this one was different. She came to me and told me I wasn't alone."

"You aren't alone. You never have been."

"Eleanor Pruitt was there too. She said she always knew it would be my line that would bring about the prophecy."

"No pressure," he said with a smirk.

I returned the expression. "How much longer do I need to stay here?"

"I know we're working against the clock, but you still need time to rest and heal."

"The longer I lie here the closer the Order gets to finishing their grand plan. And I still have an open serial homicide investigation to solve. I think I know where to find Kevin, I just need to get there."

"Just stay a few more hours, okay?"

"Yeah, okay." I hated having to surrender to his medical judgement. But, if I was being honest with myself, I didn't think I could really get around on my own right now.

I pressed my free hand against my stomach muscles, cushioned by the dressing and blankets, and my stomach gurgled. I gave J.T. a plaintive look. "Can I at least get something to eat? I'm starving."

The lasagna and our run-in with Gabrielle seemed ages ago.

"Sure. I'll have something brought up."

He pulled his hand away from mine and stood, leaving the chair sitting there with the back still facing me. With one final smile, he left me alone. Except I wasn't alone. I hadn't noticed it before—maybe I'd been too hopped up on drugs and magic to feel it—but there was a presence in the room. It tickled the tiny hairs on the backs of my arms, but it lacked any malintent. Whoever or whatever this entity was, it wasn't going to hurt me.

"Kayla?" I whispered. I didn't want to see that little purple-haired punk, but she was the only person I knew who could turn invisible on a whim.

No answer. She wasn't one to hide on me. My brain tried to formulate other options, but magic other than J.T.'s washed over me like warm water, cleansing me without having to make the effort myself. I could swear the lingering scents of Eleanor's and my mother's magic were among the flavors working their way into my skin. I touched the exposed flesh of my forearms and electricity jumped from the hairs to the pad of my finger. I expected to jump at the jolt, but something deep within me had kept that response from making the journey from my brain to the nerves in my extremities.

"Ezri, are you all right?" Desmond's voice pulled me from the moment. I hadn't heard him come in.

"I think there's someone else here," I said in a hushed tone.

He set a tray of soup down on a dresser and looked around. "Where?"

"Everywhere. I can feel them."

"I don't sense anyone else here. Are you absolutely sure?"

As soon as the words left his mouth, the warmth dissipated. My muscles still felt taut with the electrical current, but the smells had died. "Maybe my head is still messed up from the attack," I said.

"Whatever it was, did it feel evil?" He moved the tray to my lap and turned the chair around, settling in at my side.

"No. Whatever it was, it didn't want to hurt me. It felt almost familiar."

"Well, this place is rife with magical echoes of those who came before us. I wouldn't be surprised if we had a few ghosts lurking around."

"Yeah, maybe." I spooned soup to my lips and swallowed greedily. Never before had chicken soup tasted so divine. "Is Jacquie still here?"

"I'm not sure."

I downed a few more mouthfuls before asking, "Did you know she knew everything?"

"I knew they had someone else in the department who was helping to guide you back in our direction, but I didn't know for sure who it was."

The skeptical part of me wanted to distrust him,

but with everything facing us, the time for dishonesty had passed. He'd done his part because the Authority had told him to, just like Jacquie. As, I'm assuming, had J.T.

"When I was unconscious, I had a dream. Or maybe it wasn't a dream. Whatever it was, my mother was there and so was Eleanor. She told me something that you should know."

Desmond's eyes lit up at the mention of his ancestor. "I'm listening."

"She knew something about the prophecy that she never told anyone. It was always going to be Theodora's lineage, not hers, that fulfilled the prophecy."

"Why would she put her own lineage in danger?"

"I don't know. As a distraction maybe? If the bad guys were going after both of their descendants there was a chance Theodora's heirs would still survive."

"That's insane. She was going to her death the night she made the prophecy. So, in a way, she was getting out of it. She didn't have to see her family die," he said, a hint of bitterness in his tone.

"Sacrifice doesn't make sense sometimes. I remember when I was younger, you told me how you wished it had been you. Now we know it never could have been. Lucky me."

He didn't say anything and I concentrated on finishing the soup. It wasn't a huge energy boost, but it was enough to keep me going a little while longer. And there was something I needed to do before time slipped away too fast. "Desmond, I need you to do something for me. Two things really."

"Okay."

"I need you to find Kayla. Show her Kevin Ellery's photo and tell her to see if she can find him. Start in the Public Gardens. He's a gargoyle so she needs to check all the statues."

"Done. What else."

"I need you to find Jacquie and get her back here. I was at the last scene when I was attacked. We need to figure out who it was and arrest their ass."

"I'll see what I can do. Do you need anything else?" He gestured at the tray.

"No. Thanks for sticking with me ... and I'm sorry I've been such a bitch to you for so long."

"It's what family does, even if you're stubborn as hell sometimes. And thanks for not dying on us. It would suck to be down a Savior when we need her the most."

I laughed and my muscles tightened against the stitches. I winced and tried to relax. "Don't make me laugh."

"Now I know you're going to be fine."

He leaned over and gave me a gentle, one-armed hug before spiriting the tray away. Left alone again, my thoughts turned back to the case. I still had a problem to solve and I wasn't going to let being nearly sliced and diced stand in the way. Kevin and the Order may have made all of their innocent sacrifices, but they were still waiting for the Equinox. There was still time to win this fight. The first priority was finding Kevin and my would-be killer. Then we'd find where the Order was planning to conduct their creepy resurrection and I'd get to kick some magical ass.

TWENTY-TWO

Jacquie didn't materialize until the sun was well on its way past the horizon. At least a couple more hours were gone. She looked a little worse for wear, dark circles ringed her eyes. I sat up as much as the stitches in my belly allowed.

"I want to apologize again for lying to you about all the magic stuff and putting your job on the line," I said before she could speak. "If I could go back and do it again, I'd tell you everything up front."

She leaned on the foot of the bed. "Hindsight is twenty-twenty. I'm sorry too. By the way, the captain knows you were attacked. I had to make up some half-ass excuses why you weren't in a hospital."

"Damn, I'm sorry you had to lie for me."

"Something tells me it won't be the last time. I know you're still recovering, but we need to find out what you remember. Get the ball rolling."

"That's exactly why I needed to talk to you. I want to do a cognitive interview with you and see what we can piece together. Besides, J.T. said I have to stay here for another few hours at least."

She smiled at me in an almost motherly way. "You hate being cooped up, don't you?"

"Like you wouldn't believe. For a cop, I don't like being told what to do."

"So I've seen."

"That day I went running off from the scene, I was chasing Kevin's magical signature," I confessed.

"Oh. I guess that makes sense given everything we know about the case now."

"I have someone tracking him down," I said, trying to sound reassuring.

"At this moment, I'm more concerned with who attacked you. I'm not a fan of almost losing partners to serial killers."

"I'm not sure it was a serial killer."

"You just said—"

"Kevin's magic was all over the bodies. Every one that I examined. He's definitely the one doing the dirty work. His partner, whoever it is, has been handling the surveillance. It was that person's magic I've been dealing with."

"And what exactly does dealing with their magic mean?"

"The reason none of the video picked up what

happened is because our second suspect has been using magic to corrupt the files." I brushed my fingertips against my throat. "I took copies of the videos and was trying to undo the spell. It ... fought back. I may be the Savior, but I guess taking my training on myself at fifteen wasn't the best move. I'm strong, but not indestructible."

"So that's why you looked like shit."

"It's being handled by some people here. Hopefully they've had better luck than I did. Anyway, the point is it wasn't Kevin's magic that I sensed before I got turned into a human pincushion. It was the other guy's."

"Then let's see what you can remember."

Before I could respond, a knock on the doorframe drew both of our gazes. Desmond stood there, arms hanging awkwardly by his sides. "Sorry to interrupt, but I wanted to offer my help."

"I know you've got a degree, Doc, but I've been trained to do this," Jacquie said.

He smirked. "And I've been able to use my magical skills to facilitate a more complete memory recall in these types of interviews. One might say I've got a talent for it."

I appreciated the posturing from them both. I'd spent so much time putting distance between myself and anyone who gave a damn about me that having them fight over me now was a refreshing experience.

Note to self: letting people in doesn't always have to end in tragedy.

"Desmond can stay. As people keep reminding me, time isn't on our side." Not that I needed any reminder. "The sooner we get a clear picture of this bastard the sooner we nail his ass and find Kevin." I had the suspicion that Taggart should be the top of my suspect list.

"I'll get another chair," Desmond said without looking at me.

He returned and set the chair on the opposite side of the bed. I looked from my partner to the only living family that mattered and back again. "So, let's do this."

Desmond reached over and fluffed the pillows beneath my head, sliding one down so it propped me up about as much as my core muscles would allow. Next, he gripped my right hand with both of his.

"I know your instinct is to fight me, but I need you to let me in, okay?"

"I'll try."

"Close your eyes. Take a deep breath, count to ten and then let it out."

I did as I was told. Eyes shut, I took a big gulp of air and started to count to ten.

One...

Two...

Three...

My veins throbbed with Desmond's magic. It

raced through my body like a drug, sharpening every sense to the point that even thinking hurt. I lost track of the counting and blew out the breath anyway. My lungs ached with the effort.

"Too much," I ground out through clenched teeth.

A pulse jumped from my palm up through my arm and down my spine. The sharpness lessened enough to be tolerable.

"She's ready." Desmond's voice sounded a million miles away.

"Ezri, I'm going to ask you some questions now. Do the best you can to remember anything you can." Jacquie's voice in contrast was practically shouting in my ear.

"Okay."

"I want you to go back to the afternoon when you found the body. What led you there?"

Like old home movies, the day rewound on my eyelids. "I used the map and the other points to find the body." The scene materialized in my mind's eye. The woman lying prone on the sidewalk. People walking by oblivious. "I hoped I wouldn't be too late, but she was already dead."

"What was the scene like? What did you hear and smell?"

"Traffic. People walking and talking. Too much noise."

"Block that out, focus on what your other senses noticed," Desmond said from on high.

Like turning a radio down as far as it could go, the people and the cars disappeared. I was left in silence, but that gave my nose the chance to turn it up to eleven. Kevin's magic and that of my attacker were everywhere. How people couldn't smell it was mindboggling.

"I can smell their magic. It's stronger than I've ever felt before." I could feel my fingers pressing against something hard. "There's some kind of a barrier. I can feel it."

"Was it visible?"

"Yes. And no."

"What does that mean?" Jacquie's tone was laced with impatience.

"I can feel it, but anyone walking by wouldn't notice. Whoever put it up is good."

"What did you do next after you felt the barrier?"

My own magic wafted from my body. "I broke through. It shattered like glass. That's when I found her."

"Did you see or feel anything else?" Jacquie prompted.

"I started to call it in and then something hit me from behind." In one swirling motion, I was on my back again staring up at the blurry figure who'd nearly done me in. "He stood over me and then I woke up at headquarters."

"What did he look like?"

"I didn't see. My head was too fuzzy."

Another jolt danced up my arm, this time settling behind my eyes. Some of the outline cleared and I could make out a black suit and skinny tie. My would-be assassin held his blade over my body and I caught the whorl and scythe mark of the Order. "He's with the Order."

"Can you see anything else? Anything about the weapon he used?"

The pain in the memory washed over me and nausea tugged at my throat, but I refused to give in. I forced myself to block everything else out, even the man standing before me, until all that remained in the fuzzy black void was the knife. Its silver blade flashed before me, growing longer in an instant. But that felt wrong. It hadn't grown. Sweat peppered my hairline as I tried to rewind the memory and slow it down.

"Ezri? What are you doing?" Desmond's voice was still so distant.

"Trying to remember." Time rewound and the man's hand stopped mid-motion. All I saw was the handle of what looked to be an elaborate utility knife. The blade flicked from within the handle, sharp and straight. "Uh, it's like a utility knife. I don't see any logo on it. It's a straight blade maybe five inches long."

"Is anything else coming into focus? Can you make out anything about him now?"

"No." I pulled my hand free from Desmond and the room flooded back. "I need to stop for a minute."

"Of course. You did good."

"How long was I lying there before someone found me?"

"Not long. As soon as you sent me the address, I left the precinct. And ... I think I caught the attack on the dashcam."

"Please tell me you are running facial recognition."

"I wasn't close enough to get a clear image."

Time to share my theory about Agent Taggart. "You said Agent Taggart wasn't there when I called, right?"

"Right. Why?"

"During the news conference, I swear I spotted the Order's brand on his wrist. And my attacker was dressed like a Fed. In a dark suit and tie."

"If you're right, he's been pushing us in the wrong direction the entire time," Jacquie said, anger tightening the corners of her lips.

"I don't doubt the FBI has people on the payroll fighting against us. Even so, why would they bother trying to stab you or at least not stick around to make sure the job was done?" Desmond asked.

"What? Instead of shoot me? Less evidence to leave behind." I turned back to my partner. "How certain are you that you didn't get a good look at this son of a bitch?"

"I was out of the car as soon as you went down, but Taggart or whoever attacked you was fast. And cloaked themselves. Like you said, they've been putting up barriers around the crime scenes to mess with surveillance."

"I need to see that tape." I was already kicking aside blankets. I needed to confirm that the lead agent was manipulating this case and me along with it.

"Avery's working on it," Desmond said.

"Has she had any luck with the other videos?"

"I'll check in. But I think, right now, you should follow doctor's orders and get some more rest."

I shook my head. "I can rest when I'm dead. We still have too much to do."

I kicked the sheets off and swung my legs over the edge of the bed, narrowly missing Desmond's chair. Only the IV hooked into my arm stopped me from making my planned escape. I dug at the medical tape, wincing as it took a layer of skin and hair with it. The IV itself stung even more coming out of my arm, leaving a tiny pool of blood to dribble from my elbow.

Jacquie was on her feet and blocking the door the moment my feet hit the ground. "Jacquie, please don't stop me. I need to do this. I need to have some damn control over what's happening to me. I'm done being kept locked up while everyone else saves the day. Ever since I learned what destiny had in store for me, I knew I couldn't let anyone else save me. It's my job."

"You can check in with the tech guys, but you might want to get cleaned up first. And don't blame me if J.T. tries to usher you back to bed," she said.

"I'll take my chances."

"There's a bathroom down the hall," Desmond offered with a vague hand gesture toward the left.

Jacquie stepped aside. I tugged on a pair of sweatpants and trotted into the hallway and made a sharp left. The first doorway turned out to be a linen closet and the second was another bedroom. Lucky door number three held the bathroom and a shower.

Stepping from the bathroom fifteen minutes later, I felt like a new person. I pulled on a clean pair of pants and a T-shirt someone had laid out for me. When I returned to the bedroom, my gun and badge waited on my pillow.

"Thank you, partner."

The fabric of the T-shirt rubbed against the fresh bandage on my abdomen and I pulled it up, tugging on the edge of the medical tape to get a better look at my battle scar. The two wounds were red, the stitches dark threads against my skin, but the pain had lessened.

"Those should dissolve in a day or so," J.T. said from the doorway to the bedroom.

I reapplied the tape and settled the shirt back in place. I made a show of strapping on my gun and badge. "Thanks again."

"I'm just sorry you're going to have a scar."

"Hey, a scar is better than a slab in the morgue. I owe you my life." I closed the distance between us and pulled him into a hug. "Thank you."

He returned the embrace lightly, putting just enough pressure to tell me he accepted my appreciation. "I was really worried there for a minute. You had us all pretty damn scared, Ez."

"See, you all were better off without me around. Less potential for near-death calls."

"Don't joke. Anyway, I came up to say you can leave if you're feeling up to it. As your personal paramedic, I'd caution you against extreme physical activity for a while, but we both know that's not in the cards." He fished a scrap of folded paper from his back pocket and handed it to me. "In case you need me, here's my cell number."

Our fingers touched as I took the paper from him and that schoolgirl crush returned. "Thanks." I cleared my throat in an attempt to divert his attention from the blush creeping up my neck.

"You know, maybe once things are settled, we could grab dinner," he said.

I stared at him, not believing he was asking me out after all this time. I didn't respond right away.

"Or coffee," he added quickly.

Part of me wanted to accept wholeheartedly, but my future was still uncertain and I didn't want to promise him something I couldn't deliver. "Assuming I survive the next few days, I'd like that a lot."

"Great." He remained where he was, barring my exit.

"I was actually on my way to check in with Avery and her people in the tech department."

"Oh, good."

I gestured for him to move and he scrambled to give me space. I pocketed his number and wound my way through the upper floor until I found the double doors leading to the meeting hall. I stopped short of the doorway, unsure whether I'd be bursting in on a private meeting. I stood there equivocating for longer than I needed before deciding to throw caution—and decorum—to the wind and pushed the doors inward. The space was empty, cast in shadows from the heavy curtains lining the windows. I veered right and followed the path I'd taken to get to the tech hideaway the first time. The whir of technology drew me in and I found Morgan sitting there, headphones slung around his neck. I could barely make out what he was looking at around his beefy torso. I'd half-expected Jacquie to be with him, but she was nowhere to be seen.

"Hey," I said as loudly as I could.

He didn't respond.

I moved to stand closer and nudged his shoulder. Still nothing. I finally snapped my fingers in front of his face and he blinked slow, as if he were just waking up. Surprise registered on his sweaty face and he jumped, the entire rolling chair skidding backward with the effort.

"What are you doing here?" His voice was an octave higher than I remembered from a few days ago.

"I thought I'd check on your progress with my evidence."

He swallowed—his Adam's apple bobbing in his throat—and patted at the sheen on his forehead. "Right, sorry. I was just ..."

"You were just what?" I pressed.

"I was just cleaning up some footage and it was you. He just attacked you out of nowhere. I don't see stuff like this a lot."

"Show me."

He didn't move. Bypassing him, I turned to the computer and the black and white dashboard camera footage. Fear danced down my spine and I gripped the edge of the desk to keep from letting my legs turn to jelly. The video was zoomed in as much as possible, but it was still a good distance away. I hit "Play" and watched as the air—which appeared empty— rippled as I approached it. I could just make out the dead body on the sidewalk as I watched myself crouch down. The video flickered as a figure appeared and struck me on the back of the head. My wound throbbed in sympathy with my recorded self. My hindbrain warned of danger, but I couldn't look away. There my attacker was in broad daylight trying to end me.

"Can you make his face any clearer?" My voice rasped against my vocal cords. I needed hard proof of Taggart's involvement before I could do anything through official channels.

"Not without losing resolution."

"There's got to be something magical you can do to enhance it," I snapped.

"Sorry. There isn't."

"This isn't good enough. I can't see who he is."

For a large man, he seemed small when he cowered. "I'm sorry ... I did what I could."

"What about the other videos?"

"We've made some progress on those," Avery said from behind me.

"Please tell me it has something useful," I said.

She nudged Morgan aside and cued up the video of Mrs. Mendoza's scene. "We haven't finished, but this one's pretty clear."

She hit "Play" and I watched as I saw Kevin—all made of stone—knock our first victim to the ground, hands pressed to her chest until the life left her eyes. His accomplice stood just out of view of the camera angle. All I could make out was a black-suited shoulder and the back of his head. Still, I'd seen that pomade-coifed head of hair before. Taggart wasn't stupid enough to let his face be caught on camera even with magic concealing the scene.

"Trenton, we've got good news," Jacquie announced, moving into the already crowded space.

I wouldn't let my body relax until we were back down on the first floor with the front doors and open spaces in sight. She handed me a coat, which was definitely not mine, and waited.

"Where are we going?"

"Your friend Kayla found Kevin."

J.T. appeared at the top of the staircase to the second floor wearing a jacket and carrying a first aid kit in one hand. He descended to meet us and eyed Jacquie. "You ready?"

"What's going on?" I fought with the zipper on the coat, finally giving up after three futile attempts.

"Well, your suspect is a gargoyle. From what I know, you're going to have to expend some serious energy to get him talking. I'm just tagging along in case either of you needs medical attention."

My jaw hung open a little at his statement. In all of the craziness of nearly dying and being saved by the people I'd sworn to hate, I'd completely over-looked what needed to happen to actually solve the case. Did I even have the ability to make Kevin talk? And even if I did, I couldn't exactly arrest a gargoyle.

Sure, Jacquie would understand, but the FBI—minus Taggart—and the general public couldn't know about the undercurrent of magic in the city.

"I ... I have no idea how I'm going to do this."

"You'll figure it out. You're pretty resourceful," J.T. said and gave me a gentle shove toward the door.

Time to interrogate a gargoyle.

MARCH 17, 2017

TWENTY-THREE

It was after midnight by the time we got back into the city and found Kayla waiting for us at the entrance to the Arlington T station. Her hair looked almost black in the darkness. Maybe it was because she was barely visible. She said nothing to our trio as we approached. Instead, she turned and started walking into the gardens. The memory of running through, chasing Kevin's magic flickered across my mind's eye. I'd been so close and I hadn't fully realized it.

I didn't have time to recount all the little ways things could have gone different if I'd just paid a little more attention or if I'd had the added resources of the Authority. I didn't have to like working with them, but I couldn't deny that they had managed to find the killer when the police and FBI had fallen short. Without their aid, we likely wouldn't have found Kevin until the Order had tried their hand at whatever resurrection they had planned.

The grounds of the garden were quiet except for the distant, distinct screech of the T. The streets beyond the park were pretty busy for a Friday night with college-aged students drunkenly enjoying the start to their weekend. I spotted a few homeless people lingering beneath the sparse streetlamps and flaked out on benches. They didn't seem to notice us. The moon hung low in the sky, almost full.

"Is he much farther?" I asked, a stitch developing in my side with every step.

"We're close." Kayla's voice had an ethereal quality to it thanks to her still-translucent status.

I pressed my left hand into my side, trying to surreptitiously ease the pain, but I wasn't subtle enough. The telltale "snip" of a zipper opening and footsteps thudding a little faster on the pavement revealed J.T. at my side before my eyes registered his presence.

"What's wrong?"

I shook my head, trying to mask the discomfort. I had a job to do and I didn't need him babying me. "It's nothing."

"Bullshit." He grabbed my arm, yanking me to a halt. "We're going into something I'm pretty sure neither of us has dealt with before. If you can't handle it, I need to know."

"It's just a little cramp. It will pass."

He ushered me to stand under one of the street-lights. "Show me."

Jacquie and Kayla's specter stood a few paces ahead of us in silence. A chill wind blew over us and I shivered. I didn't want to unzip my coat in this weather, but he was standing there so intently I had no other option. I yanked the zipper down and rolled up the hem of the T-shirt and rubbed the sore spot under my ribs. "See, just a cramp."

He poked at them and I winced at the pressure. "It may be some bruised ribs."

"Really, I'll be fine," I protested, but he pressed his palm to the spot and the air suddenly hung heavy with his magic.

The stitch disappeared and an invigorating jolt of energy zipped through my core, sending my heart hammering in my chest. I felt like I could do a five-minute mile. I bounced on the balls of my feet and didn't bother zipping up my jacket. "That was amazing," I said.

J.T. reached down and pulled the coat's zipper back into place. "It's only temporary. It will wear off in a while."

"Yeah, got it." I bounced—yes literally *bounced*—over to Jacquie and Kayla. "So, let's go wake us up a gargoyle."

I took off at a power walk and left them all in my wake. It was only after about thirty seconds I realized I had no idea where we were going. I heard

Jacquie ask J.T., "What did you do to her?" and smirked.

"He fixed you up good," Kayla said, appearing at my side and looking more corporeal than I'd seen her since my apartment.

"I guess. And, uh, I never said thanks for helping patch me up before and for finding Kevin. I kind of took your head off before. I shouldn't have done that."

Her eyebrows almost disappeared into her pixie hairline. "I was not expecting that from Miss I-Can-Do-Everything-Alone. You're welcome."

"I'm working on asking for help. It's a new skill for me."

"I get that." She stopped walking and I outpaced her before she called after me. "He's right here."

I backtracked just as J.T. and Jacquie joined us. The light was dim in this part of the park, but I could make out the statue standing before us. Jacquie switched on a flashlight and illuminated the stone figure's face. I didn't need to compare it to the photo in the missing persons file. It was definitely Kevin. I tasted the dampness of his magic on my tongue, as if he were shaking at our arrival. Like he was scared.

"What exactly are you supposed to do?" Jacquie asked. "We can't arrest a statue."

"Well, whoever he's working with clearly made him mobile so we know it's possible. And most magic is about getting your intent and the will to perform the action expressed in the right way. So, I just need to figure out how to get him talking."

"I don't care how you do it. But the evidence shows he's still got stone dust on him. Hell, he may still have been made of stone when he was killing those people. Even if he moves and talks, there's no way this holds up in court."

"Calm down. Let me at least question him before we get that far," I said and stretched my arms over my head and across my chest. "Give me some space, but hold that light up for me."

The beam of light narrowed as Jacquie backed up, but it was still enough to see by. J.T. and Kayla flanked Jacquie, forming a semicircle around me and Kevin. I stood there staring into the slate-grey face trying to devise a plan when I felt a presence beside me. I glanced to my right to find Eleanor as she'd been in my dream.

"Be calm. They cannot see me. Not even the Whisperer," she said, inclining her head in Kayla's direction.

"So, I'm talking to myself right now? Awesome."

"You have never conducted such a spell as this. You're going to need some guidance."

Who was I to say no to a powerful ancestor's spirit offering help? "Guide away," I muttered out of one side of my mouth. I secretly hoped the three people behind me didn't think I'd gone insane.

"First, you must clear your senses. Then look

around this place. It has been heavily touched by magic. See what has been done," she instructed.

"Won't you disappear?" I whispered.

"I will be here as long as you need me."

I nodded and gripped the sandalwood charm and let it wash over me. The foul stench of my attacker vanished. I hadn't even realized how much he'd left behind. Desmond and J.T.'s soothing balms went next and I was left a blank slate.

Without the other layers of magic vying for my attention, my surroundings came into sharper focus. The grass around Kevin's statue was still mostly brown from the winter, but I could make out a circle of dead foliage wreathing the base of the statue. I bent down and brushed my fingertips along the arc nearest my left heel. "They cast some sort of binding circle. But why?"

"Influencing another being takes a lot of power and concentration. Binding the ritual within a circle allows the caster to control the space and ward off intruders."

"Right. That makes sense." I stood and Eleanor gave me a side-eye. "What?"

Before Eleanor answered, I heard Jacquie whisper, "Who is she talking to?"

"Shh. Let her work," Kayla hissed.

Eleanor smiled. "I like her. I do not understand why she presents herself in such a wild way, but I like her spirit."

"Yeah, she's unique. Why were you looking at me that way?"

"I told you what you must do to begin communing with this young man."

I eyed the dead ring in the grass. "I can't use dark magic."

Her face fell a fraction of an inch. "You should know by now, it is the intent that determines good or evil, not the act itself."

Embarrassment spread down my neck and I averted my gaze. Of course, she was right. I'd known that for most of my life, at least since I learned magic was real and I'd been born to wield it. Rubbing my hands together, I turned my attention to the circle in the grass. Tendrils of my magic slithered forth from my hands and wove among the blades of grass. First, I urged them to grow and revive the brown brush within its confines. The grass rippled beneath my feet, growing green and lush.

"Focus on the task at hand," Eleanor said.

Now that I knew that good magic could heal this place, I set about establishing a barrier. I glanced over my shoulder and my gaze met J.T.'s. "You guys are going to need to stay beyond the circle. Otherwise, your magic is going to interfere and I'm honestly not sure what happens if it does."

He said nothing but took several large steps backwards. Jacquie and Kayla mimicked his movement. I gave them a wide smile and went back to work. The magic I'd seeded into the ground called to me, waiting for instruction. I poured my will into the ground, needing it to form a barrier to the outside world and to keep this space safe and clean of dark magic. The magic burned bright through the circle like a lit fuse, twining into a knot behind me. With a "whoosh" the barrier came into place and rippled skyward. Testing the barrier, I pressed my palm to the air to my left and came up against solid matter.

"So, this is how they kept people from seeing what they were doing," I murmured. I hadn't noticed any circles burnt into the ground around our victims but, then again, they had been temporary spots that needed protecting. I had to assume Taggart had come here many times. Repeated magic always left its mark.

I crossed the short distance to stand within arms' reach of Kevin. "Now, how do I get him talking?"

Eleanor tipped her head upward to study the moon hanging low in the sky. "The light of a full moon naturally makes those of stone wake. So long as the light strikes them."

"Sure, let me just manipulate the moonlight."

"Your demeanor is most certainly a family trait, one you seem to share with Theodora."

I laughed. "I'll take that as a compliment. Okay, I can do this."

I wasn't sure how I knew what to do, but I let sight and sense of touch take over, letting the others fade to nothingness. It was just the big disc of the moon and me and my outstretched hands. I imagined the moon within my grasp and it grew larger and closer. I was vaguely aware of the sense that the earth was shifting underfoot, but I blocked it out. Silvery moonlight danced across my hands and stuck to it like syrup.

"Just a little more," I begged under my breath and the sphere obliged.

Soon, I had a viscous pool of shimmering light cupped in my hands. Eleanor's instruction to make sure the light struck Kevin played in the back of my head, but I had other ideas. Her way seemed to expend more energy than needed. I let the moon go back to being distant in the sky and the ground beneath me settled again. I did my best not to spill the gathered light as I separated my hands and placed them atop each of his. The light squirmed between my skin and the roughness of the stone, as if it wanted to act. I'd been counting on that. With just the tiniest of pushes from me, the light spread over Kevin's body, covering every visible inch in pale light.

"What have you done?" Eleanor's tone was more intrigue than annoyance.

"Let the light do the work for me. I hope."

We stood there, waiting with baited breath as the light dulled until it was hardly visible. I said a silent prayer that it had been enough to wake Kevin. No sooner had the thought left my mind than the light pulsed and the statue that was Kevin blinked. He stepped down from his plinth and turned a slow circle. He moved with remarkable fluidity given that he was entirely made of stone.

"Kevin?" I said, holding my hands palm up to show him I wasn't a threat.

He came to face us again, and if it was possible for a statue to blanch in terror, he did. "Please, don't make me do it again," he wailed, tears falling from unseen ducts.

"I'm not going to hurt you, I just want to talk."

"You have magic. I can feel it. You ... you did something to me."

"Yes, I do have magic. And I just used the moon-light to wake you up. I don't want to hurt you. But you have answers that I need. So, please, can we talk?"

"Okay." He shuffled back to the plinth on which he'd been perched and sat down.

There was enough room for me and I squeezed in beside him. "Do you know why I'm here, Kevin?"

"The people I killed."

"That's right. We found conclusive evidence that you were at the very least involved. And we know you weren't alone. Can you tell me why you chose those people?"

"I didn't choose them. God, I didn't want any of this. I thought, after what they did to me, that was it and they'd leave me alone, but then he came and told me if I didn't…" Fresh tears dribbled down his cheeks, giving off the smell of damp limestone.

That explained the scent of his magic. I let his rambling words sink in. There was a lot to parse there. "Okay, why don't we go back to the beginning to when you went missing? Tell me what happened then."

"Missing? I didn't go missing! I've been here in this park the whole time."

"Your parents didn't know that. They filed a report with the police."

"I never even told my mom about the magic, you know? I figured she would think I was crazy."

"She wouldn't have thought that for a second," I said and placed a hand atop his.

"You're just saying that because you're supposed to make me feel better."

"No, I'm not. And I know that she wouldn't because I talked to her. She had magic too. It doesn't just randomly appear, Kevin. It's always passed down through bloodlines. You could have gone to her."

"Well, it's too late now."

I wanted to tell him that it wasn't too late and he could still see his mother, but I also knew if we had any shot at closing these cases, he was going to need to spend time behind bars. Even with a plea deal, there was no way he would likely see the outside of a prison cell for a very long time.

"So, if you didn't go missing, what happened? You said they did something to you. Who are 'they' and what did they do?"

He wiped at his cheeks and stone grated on stone. "I was dating this girl, Gabrielle. About six months in, we discovered we both could do magic. It was amazing at first. And then she started hanging out with people I didn't trust. They convinced her that she was better off with them instead of me. I followed them one night and saw them performing some weird ritual. I'd never done anything like that. Just small things. I wasn't supposed to be there, and when they found me, they freaked out. Gabrielle started yelling at me that I was ruining her time with her friends and that I hadn't been invited for a reason."

"She's fallen in with the Order of Samael," I whispered.

"I didn't know that's what they were called then, but yeah. They seduced her with promises of power. I told her if she didn't leave with me, we were over. She didn't leave."

"I'm sorry."

"I never knew what happened to her after that because a group of them grabbed me and knocked me out. I woke up and I was standing here and I couldn't move."

"Why bring you here?"

"I don't know. Maybe Gabrielle told them we used to walk here a lot. I like the feel of this place. It's a little slice of nature in the heart of the city." He dabbed at his cheeks again. "Anyway, when I came to, there was a man I hadn't met before standing in front of me. I couldn't see his face because he had one of those big hoods on. He told me that this was my punishment. I'd ended up a statue."

"By the fact that there are signs of magical interference here, I'm guessing someone from the Order came to you and convinced you to start killing people now."

"They didn't convince me. They said they would kill Gabrielle and my mother if I didn't do as I was told. They promised that if I did what they wanted, they'd change me back."

"Are they planning any more murders? We've found five so far."

"No. That was it. I'm so sorry. All those people didn't deserve what I did to them. I tried to make it as quick and painless as I could. I really did."

"But they made sure you left DNA behind. If they did set you free, they ensured that you'd be found and arrested for the murders."

"Are you going to arrest me?"

"I have no choice, Kevin."

"But I told you I didn't want to do it."

"That's not for me to deal with. That's for the

District Attorney. If you come in with us and cooperate, I'll make sure that gets to the prosecutor and I'll do what I can to get them to give you a lighter sentence. But you have to know someone needs to pay for what happened here."

"What about him?"

"The man who forced you to commit the murders. What can you tell me about him? Did you get a name?"

"I don't know his name, but I know he's law enforcement."

"How do you know that?'

"I saw his badge once. He caught me looking and covered it up, but I'm sure it was law enforcement."

I unclipped my badge from my belt and held it up. "Did it look like this?"

He shook his head. "No, it was shinier. And a different shape."

The sense memory of my assailant's magic clogged up my nose and I shivered. I had to be sure. I fished my phone from my pocket and flipped through images on Google of different badges until I found one for the FBI. "Did it look like this one?"

Kevin shrunk back from the image. "Yes. That was it."

Another shiver danced down my spine as I looked at the image of an FBI badge on the screen. That meant one thing. The suspicions I'd had weren't just my imagination. I'd definitely seen the

Order's brand on Taggart's wrist and it had been his magic I'd tangled with. I pulled up the first photo of Taggart I could find and showed Kevin. "Is this the man?"

"Yes." He took the phone from my hand and I winced as he pressed his fingertip to the screen and scrolled down. "I never knew his name. He never told me."

"Did he have the Order's mark on him? A triple spiral and a scythe?"

"On his wrist. I don't think he cared that I saw it." He handed the phone back and, even though he was made of stone, when he hunched his shoulders, he looked significantly smaller. "What happens now?"

"First, I make good on their promise. I'm going to free you from his curse. And then we're going to go down to the precinct and you're going to give a statement about your involvement. You're going to leave magic out of it. And then I'm going to arrest Taggart and put an end to this."

"I want to help. I really do, but going up against an FBI agent ... they'll kill me."

"They won't. Because, FBI or not, he's just a man and he's going to pay for what he did to both of us."

"Both?"

I pressed one hand to my belly. "I found the last body and he was still there. He tried to kill me."

"Oh, no. Wait, you're her. The Savior. The one they're trying to stop."

I stood up and crossed my arms over my chest. "Damn right I am. And they need to know that the only way to stop me is to actually kill me, and if Taggart is their best guy, then they're seriously going to need to up their game. Now, let's see about getting you back to normal."

Before I could even contemplate how to reverse Kevin's condition, Eleanor stage coughed and nodded to the edge of the circle farthest from the gargoyle and my waiting compatriots. Kevin didn't seem to notice the ghostly presence as I stood up.

"Just give me a minute. I've never done this before." The truth in my words didn't appear to inspire any confidence.

I shuffled to the edge of the circle, careful not to break the barrier pressed into the grass. Eleanor eyed Kevin warily and said, "As much as you feel for this young man, you have more pressing matters to attend to."

"No, I don't," I argued.

"You were born for more than this. You have a destiny to fulfill."

"I know that. Believe me, it's been drilled into

my head for years. And I appreciate your help, but I'm a cop, too, and this man is a key suspect in a quintuple homicide and I need him to bring down a corrupt FBI agent who also happens to work for the Order. If I can take him out of play, don't you think that would throw a wrench in their plans?"

"Assume neither this boy nor the agent is a key component to what the Order has planned. Do you know when their ritual is to take place?'

"Obviously it's going to happen when the eclipse is at its height and the meteor shower is in view."

"And where?"

"I'm working on it but probably somewhere on the Common."

"You cannot hope to stop them if you are not there."

"I get it. I'll see what he knows. But I'm reversing what was done to him and I'm closing out this case."

"Be mindful of the price to be paid." With those parting words, she disappeared, leaving me alone with Kevin in the confines of the protective circle.

"Uh, are you okay?" Kevin's question made me jump.

"Shit, sorry. Dead relative ... sort of."

"Oh." He looked at his hands. "You aren't going to fix this, are you?"

"Of course, I am. I just need to know anything you do about where they're going to be conducting their ritual."

"I don't know anything. All they did was take me to the places where the dark practitioners died and force me to kill people. They didn't share their plan with me. I wasn't important enough. Or, I guess, they figured I was expendable."

Add narrowing down the location of a dark cult's ritual resurrection to my to-do list. Check. Sweat broke out on my palms and I wiped them on my thighs before motioning for Kevin to stand up.

"Fair warning, I've never done this before so it's going to be a trial and error kind of thing."

"Some Savior," he muttered.

My ego wanted to fault him for his remark, but he wasn't wrong. What had I done to prove myself to be this great champion of light magic? Been born into the right family at the right time with the right gender, that's all.

"Okay, let's try this. I'm going to take your hands. I want you to use whatever magic you have and put it out there into the universe, will yourself not to be stone anymore. I'm going to do the same on my end, and, if we're lucky, it will work."

If anyone could manage a skeptical eye roll while being made entirely of stone, it was Kevin. Deep down, I understood his apprehension. I'd just said I'd never done this before and I could think of a myriad of ways for this to go horribly pear-shaped for both of us. But if I was going to have any shot at getting out of this situation with at the very least my career intact, I had to give it the old college try.

I let Kevin's magic bubble up around me, taking in the sharpness of the smell. The question of whether his magic had always smelled like this fought for my attention, but I pushed it down. I would have time for questions later. His hands trembled in mine with the effort and, even though he was presently made of stone, I could see his legs growing weak from the exertion. He hadn't done anything like this before. In fact, he probably hadn't used his magic in five years. Time to put on my big girl pants and show him it could be done. The sugary smell of strawberries fresh off the plant bloomed to mingle with the earthier scent of Kevin's will. I could feel my magic tugging at the edges of his, trying to establish dominance. Kevin's power flared in response.

"I need you not to fight me," I said, squeezing his hands tight with mine.

"I'm trying," he ground out.

I shut my eyes and tried to focus with my other senses, feeling the magic flow around me as the energy it really was. Almost intangible but just solid enough to be manipulated. Like air through a car window on the highway. Instead of pushing the energy toward Kevin, I urged it out. I willed the stone to detach from every molecule in his body, to be replaced with skin and bone, and slowly stone began to crumble beneath my fingertips giving way to rough flesh.

My magic grew stronger, buoyed by some unseen hand keeping me afloat as the magic being expelled from Kevin swirled in the air around us, confined by the binding circle. It had nowhere to go. I squeezed hard on Kevin's hands again and heard more dust hitting the ground. I didn't want to risk opening my eyes for fear of ruining the moment and the fluidity of the spell. What I was doing was actually working and my heart fluttered an extra beat in my chest at the realization.

"I don't feel..." Kevin's voice grew weak and I couldn't keep the world shut out any longer.

The visual overload from opening my eyes so quickly made everything tilt and come rushing up to meet me. A bright pop of magic—my own but somehow not—burst around me, cushioning my fall and giving me enough time to right myself and reset my equilibrium. When the world was no longer off its axis and my eyes had readjusted to taking input, I finally saw Kevin's face. It was ghostly pale and dampened by sweat. His eyes—no longer made of stone—were glassy and unfocused. If I'd just passed him on the street I would have assumed he was just hungover or in need of a fix. The boundary of our protective circle was still unbroken, but my senses knew something was off. They just hadn't communicated it to my brain yet.

"What happened?" Kevin's voice still retained some of the gravel from his previous state.

Our hands were still clasped together and I felt the soft skin beneath my fingertips. By sight and touch he was definitely human. He was really Kevin Ellery again, as he'd been before his run-in with the Order. The markers of my magic were stronger than they'd been before and I relinquished the grip on his right hand to center myself with a hit from the sandalwood charm at my throat. My senses came into focus as the remnants of the spells I'd worked were wiped clean. The effects of the spells remained, but I could sniff out the signatures with more ease now.

"Oh shit." My brain caught up with my senses finally. The only hint of magic I could find was my own. It was as if Kevin's magic had been erased. But that wasn't possible. *Was it?* Fear beat a frantic path through my veins, turning them ice-cold. I looked to Kevin and said, "Try to use your magic."

"For what?" He sounded tired.

"Anything. It doesn't have to be big. Just *something*."

His face scrunched up with the effort, only serving to add a new layer of sweat to the sheen on his face. I waited with baited breath, searching the air and surrounding space for any sign of his magic. None came. Not even a hint to say it had once been there.

"What did you do?" His body shook and his legs went out from under him.

I wasn't quick enough to catch him as he crumpled to the grass. I'd need to get him up and moving at some point, but he needed a minute. And I needed help. Time to break the circle. With deliberate movements, I bent at the point where the spell had knotted itself together and I exerted my will, telling it to break. With a sizzle, the spell vanished.

The added sounds of nature and people and cars threw me for a loop. My ears ached from the sounds and my nose stuffed up at the gas fumes pluming in the midnight air. Even the moonlight above and the nearby streetlamps were too bright for my eyes. I could only imagine how sensitive Kevin was to everything. I waited to the count of ten before turning to face Kayla, Jacquie and J.T. They remained where I'd left them in their semicircle a safe distance away.

"You need to check him out," I said, jutting my chin in J.T.'s direction and pointing to Kevin behind me.

J.T. raised a brow at me but shouldered his medical bag and went to check on Kevin. Kayla trotted after him, concern etched on her face. I stepped out of the bounds of the circle and my body suddenly felt like it weighed fifty pounds more than it should. I tried to shake that feeling as I fell in line with Jacquie.

"He told me everything. He's going to give us a

formal, signed statement and he's pointed the finger at someone we thought we could trust as his accomplice."

"Uh, Ezri..." Jacquie trailed off, but I could see even by the weak moonlight above that she'd gone pale.

"What?"

"Your feet are turning to stone."

I blinked. I couldn't have heard her right. She'd said my feet were turning to ... stone. I didn't want to look down but knew there was no other option. So I did and I barely muffled the shriek building in my chest.

"J.T. Help!"

He looked up and his eyes widened to the size of half dollars. Kevin lay on the ground, but I could see the shallow rise and fall of his breathing. Kayla cradled his head in her lap, stroking strands of hair out of his eyes. He'd be okay. My own condition worried me far more. J.T. approached me, circling me once before asking, "What exactly did you do to him?"

"I don't know!"

"Well, when we got here, he was a statue and now he's not. So you did something."

I glared at him. "I tried to change him using magic. I mean it had to be possible. The Order turned him to stone in the first place. I told him to use his own magic to help the process along. Everything was going fine and then somehow ... it's like his magic is gone."

"I'll be honest, I've never seen anyone attempt what you did. Changing someone against their will is never a good idea. But it looks like whatever spell they cast to turn him to stone was tied to his own magic somehow. If you're right and if his magic is gone, it latched on to the nearest, strongest source it could find. You."

"As if I didn't have enough problems this week," I grumbled.

"I might be able to temporarily reverse it, but I can't say for sure that it wouldn't come back in some other way."

"The original caster could reverse it permanently, right?" I could feel a small ember of hope burning within me.

He nodded. "More than likely, yeah."

"Great."

"How is that great?" Jacquie chimed in.

"Because Kevin confirmed that Taggart was his accomplice," I answered as the feeling of being encased in stone crept up my ankles.

"You were right. But why would he do this? I mean he had to suspect after you survived that Kevin could blow his cover."

"For all we know, he thinks he succeeded in killing me."

"Did Kevin explain why he went along with this?"

"Taggart threatened his family and his ex-girlfriend."

"I never liked her," Kayla interjected from behind us.

"You knew her?" Jacquie asked.

"The three of us went to college together. At least for a while. Gabby got her hooks in Kevin before I could even tell him how I felt."

"I'm sorry." The words felt hollow leaving my mouth.

"You couldn't have known. But he's going to be okay, right?"

"Hopefully. And I think they left Gabrielle out of things. I overheard her on the phone when we were at the restaurant and she didn't know Kevin was around."

J.T. had managed to rouse Kevin while we'd been talking. Kayla clung to his side, helping him to stand and regain his equilibrium. He looked at her and a genuine smile broke out on his lips.

"Hey stranger," she said, resting her head on his shoulder.

"Hey." He took one look at me and went, "Oh. I didn't mean to do that."

"I know. It isn't your fault. If I'd paid better attention then maybe I'd have seen what they'd done to make you stone in the first place."

"I feel strange."

"You need some food and a shower. And maybe some rest. It's been a while since you've had any," J.T. said before I could drop the truth on the kid.

Kevin nodded, his eyes still glassy. Jacquie moved to support his other side and said, "We'll meet you in the car." She and Kayla led Kevin away through the park, generating a wide berth from any nosy onlookers or any of the homeless population. Jacquie exuded "cop" even if they couldn't see her badge and they didn't want to get snatched up in the dead of night.

That left J.T. and me alone in the middle of the park with my body slowly molding itself to take Kevin's place. J.T. bent down and pressed his hands to the affected spots on my legs. I felt his magic more than smelled it this time and I drank in the warmth and healing touch. With every fiber of my being I urged my own magic not to fight back, to accept the help for once. Mercifully, it complied. His working had the intended result. The stone disappeared, leaving me normal again. If I thought about it, I could still hear the whispering of the spell in the back of my head—in Taggart's voice no less—taunting me that it would have me bound with my own magic yet. I silently told him to fuck off.

"You okay?"

"Yeah. I can still feel it there in the background."

"Come on, we should really get back to headquarters."

I stayed put. "I'm not going back, J.T. I appreciate what they did for me ... what you did for me, but I got what I needed from them."

"You need rest and sleep almost as much as Kevin. And I know you, remember. When you get focused on something, everything else falls away. Besides the soup, what's the last thing you ate?"

"I ate when we questioned his ex-girlfriend." But that had been a couple days ago. I had let myself go in the pursuit of the killers and my own attacker. I was lucky I hadn't been killed due to low blood sugar and exhaustion. But I wanted to be in my own bed.

"I'll make you a deal. I'll go home and sleep and get something to eat and I'll meet you at headquarters in the morning so Jacquie and I can bring Kevin in, okay?"

He looked like he wanted to protest, but his shoulders sagged and his head dipped a little. "Fine. But if you aren't there by ten, I'm sending a search party."

"Deal."

"You're going to have to come back to headquarters tonight anyway though," he said as we started back toward the entrance to the park.

"You just said I could go home."

"Unless you feel like taking a lift."

"Shit, my car," I groaned. I hadn't even thought

about it stranded there in the middle of the city. It had probably gotten a ticket and was towed to a lot somewhere.

"We managed to get your car from the scene," he said, as if reading my mind.

"Oh, thank God."

By the time we reached the car, Kevin had been secured in the backseat. His hands were free, which meant Jacquie hadn't put him under arrest. Yet. She was leaning against the front passenger door, keeping an eye on the street and the traffic still managing to come through at this late hour. Time to get everyone situated and some much-needed rest. And after that, kicking the Order's collective asses.

TWENTY-FIVE

The clock read a little after two o'clock in the morning by the time I'd retrieved my car from Authority headquarters and made the trek back home. The residual bit of Taggart's magic was there in the back of my head all the while, though it hadn't reasserted itself. Maybe a little sleep would do me some good after all. I stripped down to my underwear and crawled into bed, snuggling down under the warmth of the layered blankets. The world fell away as I passed out.

Everything was cast in hues of grey, like a black and white movie. Sound was nonexistent or maybe there was nothing to hear. I stood in the middle of an abandoned street. The buildings felt familiar but I couldn't place them. For a fleeting moment, I feared I was alone and then I felt a presence come up behind me. I turned to greet my new companion, but my mouth hung open in horror at the sight of the man with a blade. His face was too angular to be human, everything so exaggerated that he belonged in a funhouse mirror's reflection. He sneered at me and waved the knife in my face, taunting me. I wanted to move, but I was stuck in place.

Between one breath and the next we were surrounded and this time the bodies moved to defend me. Women in all manner of dress formed a barrier to keep him and his knife at bay. My shoulders relaxed and my fingers inched out of the balled fists I hadn't been aware I'd made. He took a tentative step forward and, like fog, the women vanished. One by one he stepped through my defenses until he was again within reach. With one powerful hand on my shoulder, he forced me to my knees and then the blade found its new sheath—my belly.

A pained scream died on my lips. The women rematerialized around me and I watched in silent dismay as one by one they turned to stone. The man laughed, throwing his head back so the sound could only go up into the air. I pressed my hands to my stomach to staunch the blood but none came. Instead, I, too, was made of stone. Only my eyes remained unaffected so that I could watch the destruction he was causing. Statues around me crumbled to dust until I was the only thing remaining with the man. He danced around my immobile body, jeering at me until he finally stopped at my side. With one *powerful kick to the sternum, I, too, dissolved into dust.*

"No!" I sat upright covered in cold sweat. My hands flew to my stomach, but there was no knife protruding and the fact that I could move my arms meant I hadn't turned to stone.

I still struggled to free myself from the bedsheets and staggered to the bathroom, flicking on the light with a sweaty palm. The mirror showed a disheveled redhead with dark smudges under her eyes. But everything about her was decidedly flesh and blood and bone. I gripped the edge of the sink to steady myself as relief washed over me. It had been a nightmare no doubt brought on by the trauma that had been heaped on me in the last few days. The details were already beginning to fade, but what I could remember sent fresh chills through my body. Taggart had succeeded in killing me and somehow all of the witches in my bloodline who'd come before me—even though they were already long gone. He'd wiped us out with a simple, well-placed knife and a spell meant for someone else. My chest ached where his heel had struck me and my fingers made contact with the pentagram at my throat. The metal was cool to the touch, but knowing it was still there, still intact, eased my apprehension a smidge.

"It was just a dream," I murmured over and over to my reflection, hoping if I said it enough times it would quash the nugget of fear behind my ribcage. I pressed my right hand to my ribs and shock made me stand upright. It wasn't an imagined lump below the bones and cartilage. There was actually a solid mass situated beneath my ribs. I probed the spot with my fingertips. The spot even appeared ashen, the same color that Kevin had been.

"You aren't going to win, you bastard."

It didn't appear to be spreading like it had with my feet in the park. But that didn't mean it wouldn't become more aggressive if I let my guard down. Anxious about what new terrors would plague me if I went back to sleep, I padded into the kitchen and set about throwing together something to sate the hunger gnawing at me. I came away twenty minutes later with a sandwich, some leftover potato salad and a questionable microwaved burrito. I really needed to go shopping.

The DVR told me I'd only been asleep for an hour before making my trek to the kitchen. That had been neither long enough nor restful, but I was too freaked to go back to sleep yet. So, I settled on the couch with my makeshift snack and stuffed my face. My stomach balked halfway through the burrito, but I managed to keep it down. At some point, I must have turned on the TV because early morning news buzzed in the background. Whatever station I was on was replaying Taggart's press conference. I reached for the remote and paused, unsure whether to just turn it off or toss the remote at his smug, lying face.

A cooler head prevailed and I turned the TV off. The lack of sleep was catching up to me again, weighing down my eyelids and tugging at my ability to stay awake. I gave sleep a valiant fight, but it won out in the end and I slumped over on the couch, half-eaten burrito still in my lap.

A SHARP KNOCK on the door to my apartment jolted me from a restless but thankfully dreamless sleep. My hand went to my hip on instinct, but there was no gun. Panic rose momentarily until I surveyed myself and the early hours came back to me. I was in my underwear because I'd been too lazy to actually put on night clothes. The burrito still sat in my lap. Setting it aside, I got to my feet and went in search of clothes. I pulled on an old pair of sweatpants and a tank top from the laundry pile and went to the door. Holding my breath, I undid the bolt and eased it open.

Kayla stood on the other side of the threshold. She was solid and wore an impatient expression. "You aren't planning to go to work in *that*, are you?"

"You knocked."

She smiled. "I guess we're both capable of

change. Anyway, Des and J.T. wanted to make sure you arrived on time."

I scrubbed the drowsiness from my eyes. "Give me a few minutes." I stepped aside, leaving the door open as a gesture she was welcome to come in. She'd seen me bleeding and bruised in my home. Some dirty dishes and half-eaten food seemed like nothing.

"You know, J.T.'s not the only one who's never seen what you did to Kevin. How'd you know how to do it?"

"I didn't, not entirely, but it seemed logical enough," I answered as I grabbed a set of work clothes from the closet and headed into the bathroom again. This time the circles weren't quite as pronounced under my eyes and even the spot on my ribs looked like normal skin tone. Almost. I jumped in the shower, letting the water work its own kind of magic on my muscles.

When I emerged ten minutes later, the apartment had been tidied up and I even heard the "swish" of the dishwasher starting up. "Wow, thanks."

"You saved Kevin's life. You gave us a second chance. Figured I could be nice and clean up your mess in here as a thank you."

"I'm not sure I saved him. He's going to be spending quite a long time in prison for what he's done."

"But it wasn't his fault."

"And that's why the law considers mitigating circumstances and actions under duress. But that's what his lawyer is going to have to deal with. Magic or not, he committed a whole lot of crimes and he needs to be held accountable."

I grabbed a jacket from the back of the door and gestured at her. "Come on. Let's go before they release the bloodhounds."

Kayla remained solid all the way to the car, going translucent once she was buckled in the front passenger seat. I eyed her as I pulled into traffic, hoping the fact that most people were already at work—and if they weren't they were at least going in the other direction—meant it wouldn't take forever to get to our destination.

Eager to fill the dead space between us, I asked, "So, what's it like being a Whisperer?"

She snorted. "You know, I hate that name."

I shrugged one shoulder and flipped the blinker on, merging into the lane to my right. "I didn't come up with it. Blame the old dusty corpses from eons past."

"Yeah. It's ... fine. I don't really think about it much."

"Magic made you this way, right?"

"Mostly. Let's just say I grew up in a very paranoid family and my parents overdid it in teaching surveillance spells. One backfired on me and here I am."

"Sorry."

She waved a see-through hand dismissively. "I'm over it. It has its advantages. Shopping is super easy what with humans not seeing me." Color drained from her face—what little color there'd been anyway —and she shrunk against the seatback. "Crap, I just admitted that to a cop, didn't I?"

"Yep. Not my department though."

"I still have a bank account and stuff. I could live like a normal person if I wanted to. Most of the time I do, actually. Still, being invisible and walking through things can be fun."

"So, the whole punk rocker thing is what ... a fashion statement?"

"Hey, I don't judge you, ginger."

I couldn't help but let out a hiccup of laughter. "Okay. Fair enough. Can I ask you something else?"

"Sure."

"You and Desmond. He only lets people he's really close to him call him 'Des'. And I know he's dating Avery. What's the deal with you two?"

"He does some consulting work for the Authority. I needed someone to talk to after I ... changed and we became friends. I actually introduced him to Avery."

We passed the rest of the trip in companionable silence and I was grateful. My mind raced with everything I had left to do to finally find some peace. Top of the list was, of course, taking Taggart down. It was probably too much to hope that whatever ritual the Order was planning would be foiled simply by detaining their lead FBI agent. So I still needed to pinpoint the exact location of the spell. At least I still had a couple of days to sort that out. They weren't going to chance it before the eclipse and the meteor shower. What better way to mess with the Equinox than to blot out the sun completely?

In the light of day, headquarters was far more bustling. Half a dozen cars were pulled into the circular drive and the front door sat open and welcoming to a steady stream of people. I half-recognized some of them as members of the Council. Others were unknowns, dragging young children in tow, no doubt to get their magical education.

"You really don't like it here, do you?" Kayla said in a hushed tone as we left the car behind and followed the stream of people up the front steps.

"Too many bad memories," I murmured.

She said nothing as we stepped into the foyer and had to pay attention to children darting between us. Kayla had enough time to shout, "They're in the library," before getting shoved out of view. Or maybe she went invisible to avoid being run over.

I shouldered my way through the throng gathering outside the library and slipped inside. As promised, Jacquie and Kevin were sitting at one of the tables. Desmond stood by one of the windows studying a photo on one of the shelves. I caught a glimpse of a teenage boy with dark hair and olive skin near the left edge of the frame. J.T. was nowhere to be seen. Kevin must have recovered enough from losing his magic to no longer need a healer.

"So, now that we've had some rest, let's get this show on the road," I said, hoping my call to action would spur people to their feet.

Jacquie was the first to acknowledge my presence. "We need you to see something before we go. And the Council wanted to speak with you about what you did to Kevin."

"They can wait until Taggart is in custody," I snapped.

"You can't avoid them forever," Desmond offered, still facing away from the rest of us.

"I'm not. Work comes first. If they want to work with me, fine. But they have to know that I'm a cop first."

He turned on his heel to face me. "We still need to show you something. Come on."

"We aren't leaving Kevin alone," I blurted.

"He's coming with us," Jacquie said. On cue, Kevin stood and held his hands loosely at his sides, no doubt doing his best to show that he wasn't a threat anymore.

It was only as I followed Jacquie and Desmond up the spiral staircase that I noticed Kevin's change of clothes. It was a good move. It would be hard to explain how he'd been in the same set of clothes for five years when we brought him to the precinct for booking. Our quartet ended up cutting through the Council chamber—which was vacant yet again— through the door to the tech room. Avery spun in her chair at our entrance. She looked exhausted, but she wore a triumphant smile. "We finished cleaning up the tapes."

"All of them? Even the dashcam footage?"

"Yep."

"But Morgan said he couldn't get a clear image of my attacker."

"We just had to use a little magic to nudge the file along. You've got crystal clear footage. And ... I'm sorry for what happened to you."

"Thanks."

Her gaze slid over Kevin and he took a step behind me. "You know you're on these, right?"

"Y-yes."

"You should really consider joining the police force or at least freelancing. We'd have a much better shot at getting usable footage," I said.

"May just take you up on that offer, Detective. But maybe after we survive the coming shit show that Mother Nature is heaping on us." She held out a pile of writeable CDs to me to take with us.

I accepted her offering and turned to Jacquie. "You ready to put this one to bed?"

Her lips turned up in the tiniest of smiles. "Lead the way."

Stepping back into the Council chambers felt like I was stepping out into a brand-new day. Things were finally going our way. We had the evidence we needed to nail Taggart for his involvement in the murders and my attempted murder. We'd caught Kevin, even if it had meant stripping the magic out of him, and we still had time to stop the Order.

"I'm going to call Captain Beech and let her know we've got someone in custody. Just so we know for sure the FBI will be there," Jacquie said, phone in hand.

"Good. The sooner we can get him in cuffs the better."

"You said you can protect me and my family." Kevin's voice was small and strained.

I clamped a hand on his shoulder and gave it a firm squeeze. "We will. I promise. Besides, he's going to have to worry about being law enforcement in prison. They aren't exactly the most popular of people."

"But he's not alone." It came out as a whine.

"We are going to do everything we can to keep your mother safe," Jacquie added as we escorted him out to the waiting patrol car she must have arrived in.

As I rounded the front of the car to take the wheel, Kayla flickered into existence on the front steps and beckoned me with one hand. "Give me a minute."

Jacquie settled Kevin in the back seat and I

crossed the distance to Kayla. "Do you know where he's going to end up?" she asked.

"I'm not sure yet. But I can let you know."

She nodded. "Thanks."

"He's going to need someone to be there for him while he rebuilds his life."

"I can do that."

"I'll see you around, Kayla."

I headed back to the car and she called after me. "You aren't as big of a douche as I thought."

I didn't respond, but I cracked a smirk that she couldn't see. We'd gotten off to a rough start, but she was growing on me and I suspected she would become someone I could rely on. Buckling up behind the wheel, the realization dawned that it might be nice to have people I could trust around me. I didn't have to go it alone.

"Everything all right?" Jacquie snapped me out of my musings.

"Fine. Just thinking." I started the engine and eased the car through the obstacle course of other cars in the circular drive to get back to the street.

By the time we made it to the precinct, we were only a few hours shy of our regular shift starting. We pulled into the side lot and let the engine block cool. I eyed Kevin through the rearview mirror. I expected him to be a bundle of nerves, but he sat calm, hands already cuffed behind his back. I got the impression he was trying to remove the bonds, but not even a whisper of wet limestone filled the car. I'd really taken his magic from him. My heart hurt at the thought that, if I'd done it to him, someone more powerful than I could do the same to me. It sent icy fingers clawing down my back and I opened the door with more force than strictly necessary to get out of the confines of the car.

"We're about to walk into a room full of pissy cops and Feds. So maybe don't go shouting Taggart's guilt to the rooftops just yet," Jacquie reminded me as I led Kevin from the back of the car and around to the side entrance.

I mimed zipping my lips and throwing away the key with my free hand while she opened the door. The moment we stepped into the bullpen the electricity of the place struck me. Every cop and Fed in the room turned as one to look at us. They'd all seen Kevin's face plastered on the news. They knew who he was. As we moved toward one of the interrogation rooms someone started a slow clap. It picked up steam for a few seconds but died out as Captain Beech appeared in the doorway of her office. She gave us a satisfied nod but said nothing.

I glanced around, but there was no sign of Taggart. We still had the element of surprise. Maybe we could catch him off guard. We settled Kevin in the interrogation room, transferring his cuffs from behind his back to the bar on the table in front of him.

"Do we have to make a show of you questioning me?" Kevin asked in a low whisper.

It seemed silly given that he'd already told me everything, but if we wanted this to stick, we needed to do things by the book. So Jacquie and I sat down across from him.

"Mr. Ellery, we're going to give you another opportunity to hear your rights," Jacquie began.

"I don't want a lawyer," Kevin said, his voice stronger this time.

"Are you sure?" I prompted.

"Yes. I know what I've done. I don't want to waste your time, Detective. I want to make a full confession."

"You sure you don't want to think about this for a little while?"

He shook his head. "No. I just want this to be done."

I nodded at Jacquie and she retrieved a pad and pen and set it in front of him. He picked it up and pressed the tip to the first line but paused. "I didn't do this alone."

"Okay. If you identify your accomplice, we can tell the prosecutor that you've cooperated," I said.

Kevin licked his lips and his gaze darted to the two-way mirror on the wall to his right as if he expected someone to come through it as he spoke. "I didn't want to kill those people. He made me. He threatened to hurt my family."

"Who?"

"Agent Jamison Taggart."

No sooner had the words passed Kevin's lips than the door burst open and Taggart loomed there, filling every available space. His eyes went wide at the sight of me, but he covered his shock by turning to look at Jacquie. "How dare you conduct this interrogation without my people?" he bellowed.

Captain Beech appeared behind him, giving him no choice but to join us in the room. Not built for comfort in the first place, the space was beginning to feel claustrophobic—or maybe it was my proximity to the man who'd nearly succeeded in murdering me.

"I don't think you have the right to go accusing my people of anything. Or did you not just hear who this young man fingered as his accomplice?" Captain Beech snapped, placing herself in his path.

"He saw me on television. He's clearly lying to mislead you all."

"Oh, I don't think so." I was on my feet before my brain realized the impulse had been sent. "He's confessed to his part in the murders." The wound in my belly ached at the nearness of him. "And we have evidence you were involved, *Agent*."

The nauseating scent of his magic seeped from his pores. "What evidence?"

"Yes, I'd like to know what you've got too," the captain said. Her tone was far more inquisitive than his.

I reached into my jacket and pulled out the CDs with the cleaned-up footage. "Our techs were having trouble with the surveillance footage so we took it to a freelancer. She's very good. Cleaned it right up. Why don't we watch it together?"

Taggart started to argue, but Captain Beech held up a hand to silence him. Her eyes were focused on Kevin who sat there, his body quivering at the sight of the man who'd forced him to do terrible things. "You say this man forced you to kill people?"

"Yes, ma'am. He said he'd hurt my mother if I didn't."

She seemed satisfied with his response and turned her attention to me. "Get someone to sit with him while he finishes his statement. Then meet us in my office. We're going to do this in private."

"Yes, Captain."

Jacquie was around the edge of the table and flanking Taggart before the words finished leaving my mouth. They ushered him out of the room and out of view, leaving Kevin and me alone.

"You're doing the right thing," I told him before finding someone to watch him.

I settled on a uniformed officer who I was almost certain had no magical bone in her body to babysit Kevin. Walking into Captain Beech's office minutes later, I felt the tension wrap around me, trying to weigh me down. Taggart sat on one side of the desk while Jacquie and Captain Beech bent behind the computer, getting the first disc ready to play.

"You have no idea what you're getting yourself into," Taggart growled at me.

I didn't respond. I took up residence on the captain's other side. She hit "Play" and swiveled the monitor so that Taggart had a good view. It was the camera right near the Orpheum Theater. It played along depicting pedestrians making their way along Tremont Street. Sure, I hadn't been at this scene, but it didn't matter. I didn't need to see Kevin end another innocent person's life. I intently watched Taggart's face transform from smug to a hint of fear as the recording inched closer to the time of death and didn't cut to black. Kevin appeared in view. Taggart paled and he fiddled with the hem of his left shirtsleeve, no doubt tugging it down to cover the Order's mark on his wrist. I glared at him and he made a break for the doorway. There was no chance in hell I was going to let him get away. Sure, there was an entire bullpen full of cops who would react if I needed them to, but he'd made this too personal.

I darted around the corner of the captain's desk and dug my hands into the meat of his upper arm, dragging him to the floor. He bucked, but I managed to get a knee into the small of his back, pinning him down. I felt something damp dribble down my front. I'd probably popped another stitch. I yanked his left arm behind his back and he grunted in pain. I hadn't grabbed him that hard, but then I remembered our sparring sessions as I'd tried to undo his magic on the videos. He'd beaten me pretty good, but I'd winged him too.

Bending low so the other people in the room couldn't hear, I hissed in his ear. "Hurts, doesn't it? That's what you get for trying to kill me."

"This changes nothing," he snarled, spittle dripping from his lips.

"You bet your ass it does." I looked over my shoulder. "Captain, you're going to want to take a look at the last recording." I let up the pressure on my prey just enough to get my handcuffs free and latched around his wrists. In the process, I pushed up his left sleeve far enough to reveal the triple spiral and scythe mark.

The image on the computer screen changed. This time, it was me finding the last body. I wanted to look away and avoid the sense memory of the knife rending flesh and muscle, but I forced myself to watch. I had him in custody and he wasn't going to hurt me again. In horrible black and white he knocked me down and stabbed me, leaving me there to die with the last victim.

"Get him up."

I dragged the man to his feet, not caring if I put extra pressure on the wound on his shoulder. Let the bastard feel my pain. I swung him around to face Captain Beech and if I hadn't known the fury in her gaze was meant for him, I'd have shrunk back in fear.

"Jamison Taggart, you are under arrest for conspiracy to commit murder and attempted murder. I think you know how the rest of this goes."

He struggled against my grip and I had to eke out a little of my will to keep him in check. With Jacquie by my side, we marched out into the bullpen leading our captive to the other interrogation room. The rest of the FBI contingent stared, mouths agape, as their boss was led away in cuffs. His second in command glared daggers at me and I just stared at her, trying to keep my expression neutral. Giving him a shove between the shoulder blades into the room gave me a sense of satisfaction I hadn't thought possible.

"It's all fake!" he yelled, but I slammed the door on him.

"You better get all of those tapes authenticated by department techs. This needs to be ironclad," Captain Beech said.

"Already on it, Captain," Jacquie said.

"You need to get checked out. You're bleeding, Trenton."

I looked down to find yet another blouse ruined by blood. "Yes, ma'am."

The adrenaline of the takedown was beginning to wear off and the pain of having ripped out a stitch seeped in. I bit my lip and tried to pour a little will into it, easing the desire to cramp up. I'd never been so grateful to have an ex's phone number in my phone than right now.

The line rang only once before J.T.'s voice said, "Are you okay?"

"Uh, not really. I popped a stitch. Not sure it's the best idea for me to drive right now and I don't have my car anyway."

"Where are you?"

"The precinct."

"Stay put and put some pressure on it. I'll be there as soon as I can."

"Okay." A pause and then, "We got him, J.T. The bastard who orchestrated all of this, we got him."

"You can tell me all about it when I get there."

I ended the call. I should have rested until my ride arrived, but there was one more thing I needed from Taggart. It was a risky move given that the cameras were still on and I didn't want to shut them off because it could jeopardize our case. Still, the weight under my ribs throbbed and I needed to try. I slipped into the interrogation room to find Taggart standing in the corner, hands still cuffed behind him. I wanted to trust that they remained locked, but there was every possibility he'd unlocked them. The charming façade had dropped away, but an image flashed in my mind and I realized why he'd looked so familiar.

"You can't question me without my attorney present," he snapped before I could speak.

I stayed at the other end of the room and answered, "Lucky for you I'm not here to ask about the case." I had no choice but to get up close and personal with him, so I crossed the distance and pressed one hand to the spot under my ribcage. "I know you turned Kevin to stone."

His eyes lit up and he smiled. "Yes, I did note he was far more mobile in there."

"I undid what you did to him and now it's trying to change me. You cast the spell. You can make it stop."

"No."

"Excuse me?" I wanted to throttle him, but I kept my hand pressed to my side.

"I said no. It won't kill you. You've proven stronger than I anticipated and the spell wasn't meant to bind you. But even if I wanted to, I can't. Let it serve as a reminder, Savior, that even your heroics carry a burden. You're fighting a losing battle. It's going to cost you dearly one day."

"It's certainly cost you your freedom."

He shrugged. "Perhaps."

"I remember you now, you know," I said and took a few steps back to lean against the table behind me. "It didn't click at first, but then I saw the photo of you at headquarters. You were one of us. Why would you throw in with those lunatics?"

He bristled and his lower lip curled. "Those lunatics, as you call them, have the right idea. Using our gifts how we want. You can't tell me you never thought about it."

I wanted to deny it, but, of course, I had wanted the freedom. But not the anarchy the Order represented. "So, you just turned your back on everyone?"

"Isn't that what you did?"

"No ... we're nothing alike."

"I embraced my gifts and the people are willing to accept me. What did you do, Savior? You ran and hid away from the world."

His words hurt and I backpedaled out of the room. Barely holding back angry, hot tears, I slammed my fist into the wall outside the interrogation room. Taggart was wrong. I hadn't run and hid. We were not the same. With that line repeating in my head, I went and sat at my desk for lack of anything else to do. The mountain of paperwork could wait until I wasn't bleeding from an open wound and had saved the world from going to hell.

"I thought the captain told you to get that looked at?" Jacquie said.

"I'm waiting for J.T. to get here."

"You took him down faster than I think I've seen anyone move before."

"I was highly motivated. I'm just glad this case is over."

"It won't be over for a long while, Ezri."

"For now, it's done. I can worry about a trial when it comes to it." I wasn't convinced Taggart would want all that publicity. The Order may want to fuck with people, but even they weren't stupid enough to let one of their top people get dragged through a very public trial.

I let the buzz of the precinct lull me into a sense of calm as I waited for my personal medic to arrive and patch me up. Before long, the desk sergeant stuck her head in and asked, "Did somebody call for an ambulance?"

Jacquie was nice enough to help me to my feet and walk me out. I didn't think a torn stitch required an ambulance ride, but I didn't argue as J.T. helped me into the back of the rig. Jacquie shut the door once I was perched on the edge of the gurney and we pulled away.

"I don't think this is necessary," I protested as he pushed me onto my back and wrapped a blood pressure cuff around my left bicep.

"I was just coming off shift and this seemed faster. Now, let me take a look."

I tried to relax as he peeled the fabric of my shirt away from my stomach. It wasn't nearly as bad as it felt. Either I was going into shock or his magic was numbing the surrounding skin and muscle because I barely felt him poking at the wound, pinching it back together and securing it with a fresh set of sutures.

"I hope you have a good dry cleaner."

I laughed and winced. "You know, I may have to

find one who isn't squeamish about blood because it seems I'm covered in it more than usual."

He smiled at me and it was a genuine expression of adoration. Maybe I hadn't totally broken his heart all those years ago after all. Or maybe he'd been more empathetic than I'd given him credit for. "Thanks for saving me again."

"Any time."

I lost track of time as the ambulance trundled through the city streets. I hadn't even paid attention to the direction we'd taken out away from the precinct. When we finally came to a full stop, I looked around. J.T. popped open the back doors and offered me his hand.

I shouldn't have been surprised to find myself back at headquarters. I was really starting to get sick of the place. I let him guide me up the front steps and into the foyer. He nudged me toward the spiral staircase and, with reluctant steps, I trudged up them to the waiting Council. They weren't going to let me leave until I answered their questions about Kevin. That was fine. They were going to answer some of mine.

I pushed the double doors inward and marched into the spacious room to find them all sitting in their stupid semicircle. One chair—mine—vacant on the end. There was nowhere else to sit that wouldn't have given the impression I was coming back to them entirely. So I remained standing.

"You should have a seat, dear," Belladonna said from her seat near the middle.

"I'll stand," I answered, my body tensing in anticipation of her magical push. None came.

"We wanted to congratulate you on solving your case," said a man I didn't recognize.

"Just doing my job."

"Saving that gargoyle wasn't. Tell us, how did you manage it?"

The mass beneath my ribs pulsed as I swallowed. "They'd used his own magic to turn him to stone. I pulled it out of him. All of it."

"That's dangerous. Did he consent?" This time Wallace's voice came from my left.

"I don't think he realized what was happening. And why does it matter if he consented?"

Wallace's eyes bulged. Had I really said something so shocking? I'd made Kevin a promise to try to free him and I'd done so. Sure, it had taken more from him than intended, but I didn't think that was entirely a bad thing.

Belladonna's face softened and she said, "Yes, it matters a great deal. Magic is a part of us. It's in our blood and our DNA. Taking it without consent can have disastrous consequences."

"Such as?' A lump formed in my throat.

"The spell designed to lock him into the form in which you found him could latch on to you or another practitioner. Spells don't like to be just dismissed without the right intent."

"Did something like that happen?" Desmond's voice came out as a strained tenor instead of his usual baritone.

My fingers massaged my ribs before I could stop them. "I tried to get the original caster to reverse it, but he refused. It's been contained."

"For now," Desmond murmured.

Great, a ticking time bomb was now nestled in my ribcage, ready to go off with a moment's notice. Maybe Taggart was right and this was my punishment for meddling with magic I didn't fully understand. I'd grown up knowing I was supposed to save the world. I thought I knew better. I'd honed my skills in the last decade but clearly not enough.

"Look, I'm sorry that what I did was against the rules or unethical or whatever, but I needed Kevin in a state where he could be brought into a police station without raising mortal eyebrows. And even if he was an unwilling participant, it got a murderer off the street. You have got to see that as a win."

"We aren't questioning your motivation," Desmond began to the scoffs of some of the other Council members. "But we are relying on you at the moment to fulfill the prophecy. A task which would be far more difficult if you were, say, encased in stone."

The argumentative part of me wanted to spring

into action. To be contrary to these people just because they'd ruined my life. But Desmond had a point. Damn him. So, I held my tongue. "I'll get us through the Equinox." *Or die trying.* I surveyed the twelve people assembled before me, meeting each of their gazes in turn. "If that's everything, if you can't reverse the stone magic put on me, then I need to get going and make final preparations for the Equinox."

"You're free to go," Belladonna said with a small, dismissive flick of her wrist.

I was already halfway down the stairs to the first floor when Desmond called my name. I didn't stop. Instead, I let him come to me. His footsteps thudded heavily on the stairs as he caught up and grabbed my left arm, halting my escape.

"I need to talk to you. It's important."

"They said I could leave."

"And you can. This is better if we don't do it here anyway. Come on, I'll drive."

TWENTY-SIX

He gave me no choice, dragging me out into the late afternoon sunshine and away from my car parked in the driveway. He thrust me at the passenger side of his car and I climbed in.

"Where are we going?" I asked as we eased to a stop in a line of traffic.

He didn't answer. By the hard lines of his shoulder muscles and his white-knuckled grip on the steering wheel, I knew I wasn't going to get any answers while we were still on the road. So, I settled back against the seat and watched the traffic pass us by. Turning my attention to the sky, I took in the late afternoon sunlight. Only three more days until the world experienced a rare phenomenon and a dangerous cult was going to use it to ... do what exactly? I wracked my brain trying to decipher what they needed five souls for, but nothing obvious came to me.

"Do you know where the best spot is going to be to watch the eclipse?" I asked, hedging my bets that he might want to talk about our impending doom.

"The Common probably."

"Yeah, but where exactly? I mean if I'm a dark magical cult and I'm relying on this eclipse and the meteor shower hitting right at the Vernal Equinox, I'd want the best view to do my dark ritual."

"We can look at a map." He glanced at me before turning his attention back to the road. "It's a shame you won't be able to really enjoy it. From what I've heard it's supposed to be pretty spectacular."

"Oh, I'm sure I'll see some of it before they try to kill me." I couldn't help sounding glib about my potential death. I'd survived this much already that I had to find humor in it somehow. It didn't mean I wasn't silently screaming in terror. I'd accepted my role in all of this, but I really wasn't sure what I'd be up against and that chipped away at my confidence a little more with every day that passed, bringing me closer to the final battle. But they all needed to believe in me. I couldn't show weakness now.

"Don't do it alone."

"I think I kind of have to. That's the deal with being the Savior, right?"

"I meant don't go by yourself. Bring backup. If

you manage to stop them, you're going to need help rounding them up."

"Oh, right. That makes sense."

Our brief conversation was enough of a distraction that I hadn't noticed when we crossed the Charles River into Cambridge. Desmond pulled to a stop in a short driveway leading to a split-level, brick fronted house. Without a word, he climbed from the car, leaving me to follow after him. He produced a silver house key from a pocket and slid it into the lock on the front door as I'm sure he'd done a thousand times before.

"Nice place," I said, eyeing the décor in the front hall.

"Thanks."

"You rent?" I realized with a pang of sadness I knew very little about his private life. That had been my own fault as much as his.

"I bought it a few years ago." His hands darted from under his arms to in his pockets and then hung limply at his sides.

As much as I wanted to ask for the grand tour— we were getting reacquainted with each other and that was the sort of thing you'd do with a guest—he didn't seem in the right headspace.

"So, what was so important we had to drive all the way to your house?"

Color drained from his cheeks and he jutted his chin toward a hallway to the right. Giving him some serious side-eye, I headed down the hall and stopped at the closed door at the end of the short hall.

"In there." His voice once again had gone tenor. He stayed put.

"Are you coming?"

"Trust me; you're going to want to do this alone. I'll be out here when you're ... ready."

The quiver in his voice as he finished speaking made me doubt I wanted to see what was behind door number one. Fear flashed in my cousin's eyes as he took a step back and out of view. Was he afraid of what was waiting for me or was it *me*?

I wasn't going to get answers staying rooted to the spot in the hallway. Swallowing down my anxiety, my hand trembled as I opened the door. It swung inward on silent hinges to reveal a small study with a desktop computer set up on a small table set beneath a window looking out on the street. A TV with a DVD player sat against the far wall away from the glare of the front-facing window. The TV was on but covered in static, waiting for a connection to be made.

"What am I looking for, Desmond?" I muttered.

The answer came almost immediately as a bright orange Post-It note caught my attention. The note, reading "Play Me," was affixed to a slim case housing a burnable DVD. Opening the case, I powered up the player and inserted the disc. I pulled the chair over from the desk and sat down, waiting for the TV screen to resolve into whatever content the disc held.

It took forever for the disc to load and the anticipation started to grate on my nerves. The walls began to press in on me and I became all too aware of the seconds ticking by, bringing me ever closer to the fate that had been foretold for me since before I was born.

The picture finally loaded and I let out a small gasp. It was the living room of my family's apartment. The tiny time and date stamp read March 11, 2007 at 8:21 p.m.—only hours before my birthday and the worst day of my life. I was with Desmond and J.T. at that very moment, blissfully ignorant of what was coming. I could hear footsteps on the recording and my mother came into view, settling down on the couch, so close to where I'd find her the next morning. Tears welled uncontrollably in my eyes at the sight of my mother alive and smiling. So full of life.

She smoothed the creases on her pants and looked at the camera. She wore the pendant that now hung around my neck. Her hand reached up to squeeze it and I mirrored the gesture, transfixed by my mother's image. After a breath, she spoke. "Hi, Ezri." She stopped and pressed her free hand to her lips. I could see the moisture tracks of tears that had almost dried on her cheeks as she leaned into the light from the ceiling above her. "Oh, this is going to be harder than I thought." Another pause as she collected herself. She cleared her throat and started again. "You've known for a while now that Eleanor Pruitt's prophecy is about you. And you've taken it in stride, my beautiful girl. I've taught you what I could and there are people you're going to need to rely on as you get older. I know you didn't ask for any of this, but tomorrow is going to change a lot of things."

I scrambled for the remote and slammed my thumb down on the "Pause" button. The recording halted mid-sentence. I didn't want to hear what she had to say. I had a million ideas about what came next and none of them made what was coming any easier or what had happened any less painful. People didn't record videos like this unless they knew what was coming. But she'd made this for me and Desmond obviously thought it held useful information. I couldn't let my childhood fears dictate my adult actions any longer. I dried my tears and resumed the video.

"You are going to be fifteen tomorrow. I know kids these days are more worried about sixteen and learning to drive, but for you this is the important year." She looked away from the camera and down at her hands, which were now clasped in her lap. "We didn't want to scare you, but the Council has been tracking the Order and there is a possibility that they've found us and they've figured out who you are. I know that sounds frightening and I'm sorry, but sometimes the truth is scary. The coming days are going to be very difficult for you, sweet girl, and for that I cannot apologize enough. But you have to understand that I'm doing what I'm doing to protect you and keep you safe just a little longer." She stood up and took the camera with her—off whatever tripod she'd had it on—and maneuvered it to the table on the other side of our living room. There was the knife I'd found plunged into her chest the next day and the candles I'd found strewn about her body. She picked up the blade and said, "Tomorrow, I'm going to die. I need you to know, Ezri, that I am doing this willingly. A life and magic freely sacrificed can protect the object of the caster for a time. I'm doing this to hide you from the Order so you have time to grow into your power. So that you'll be ready when the fight comes."

I hit "Pause" again and this time the tears had fallen freely down my cheeks, leaving matching tracks to those on my mother's face. I'd been so wrong about everything. She hadn't been murdered. She'd given up her life to keep me safe, to give up her magic to ensure I lived long enough to use mine to save everyone else. I'd pushed everyone who could have helped me away. I thought I'd known what tore my family apart. It turned out it was *me*.

The lack of police and interference by the Authority made sense now. They'd been in on it from the beginning. Their own paramedics would have been called to see about her body. I tried to dredge the memory of the aftermath from the depths of my subconscious, seeking out any hint that the men who'd come and carried away her body in a body bag had any hint of magic on them. I couldn't recall.

"Oh, Mom," I sobbed, clutching the DVD player remote to my chest.

She still stood frozen on the screen, blade in hand. I couldn't stand to look at her like that. I needed to finish watching. I hit "Play" again and she continued her explanation.

"There are going to be five people here with me. They're going to channel my magic into this pendant and they are each going to give up a year to protect you. Until you are twenty years old, the Order won't be able to find you. Even so, I beg you to be careful, Ez. Please." She set the knife down and turned the camera back on her face. "You're going to be hurting for a while, baby girl, and that's perfectly natural. But don't push people away."

Too late for that one.

She smiled into the camera and then zoomed in on the pendant at her throat. "And remember, no matter what, your family is always with you. You can always rely on that strength. Let it build you up. You are stronger than any of us, but your heritage goes back further than you realize. Be safe, my beautiful girl, and happy birthday." She refocused on her face and blew a kiss.

The recording ended and I sat in stunned silence, letting her words sink in. She'd given up her life to protect me from the bad guys before I was ready. And at least five other people had given up some of their lives to keep me safe too. And I'd shut them all out. Now I understood Desmond's glint of fear and the reason he'd kept his distance. He'd had possession of this recording for at least some length of time. He knew what I hadn't and he'd assumed it would send me into a fury.

I wasn't angry. Maybe I should have been and maybe the anger would come. Right now, all I felt was numb. At some point the numbness faded enough for me to regain use of my legs and I forced myself to stand and leave the room. To his word, Desmond was sitting in the living room directly off from the main hallway. It was a spacious room with two full couches and an armchair. A functioning fireplace lined the wall opposite me. He was fidgeting with his hands, looking far more like the young man I remembered than the psychologist I'd so recently become acquainted with.

"How long did you have that?" My voice cracked on the last word.

He gave me a plaintive look. "Ezri—"

"How long?"

"Since she recorded it. She gave it to me. I was supposed to show it to you but ... things went wrong. God, you weren't supposed to find her. That was never supposed to be what happened. You were supposed to hear from your dad that she'd died and then I was supposed to show you the recording so you'd understand, but you insisted we go back to your place that day. J.T. and I couldn't stop you without making you suspicious. I'm so sorry you've had to carry this with you for so long."

The anger that had thus far eluded me was beginning to seep into my consciousness. I wanted to hurt him for keeping this from me. Everything would have been different. Everything *should* have been different.

"Why didn't you tell me? You had the information. So, I found her, you should have still shown me what she'd recorded. It would have helped. Do you have any idea how isolated I felt after she died? When my dad did nothing and just moved on like it hadn't happened? Like it was just normal that she'd had a knife plunged into her ribs in a ritual circle?"

He didn't seem fazed by my outburst. If anything, there was relief in his expression. He'd been bracing for this reaction. "You were a kid. You needed time to grieve."

"Bullshit. Maybe you didn't think I could handle it, but my dad should have known better. He should have made you show me. I thought the Authority covered up her death. I blamed them as much as the Order for her death and I wanted nothing to do with them. Everything that's happened on this case could have been avoided if they'd been there."

He wouldn't look at me.

"Did you watch the video?" I pressed.

"No. She said it was for you to see and you only. I knew what they were doing in general terms, but she only wanted me to be the messenger. I really am sorry I didn't show it to you sooner."

"If you'd tried to show it to me when we first reconnected, I'd have probably walked out and I'd be out of a job right now. But why show it to me here?"

"There were some on the Council who weren't involved in the ritual back then who didn't think it was necessary. You had the motivation of the prophecy hanging over your head. They assumed that was enough to make you act in their interest. For what it's worth, Belladonna and the others involved disagreed. The Council rarely does anything without a unanimous vote."

The proverbial genie was out of the bottle now. I wanted to know who besides Belladonna had been involved in the ritual. Who else had been with my mother in her final moments? Had she been scared? I tried desperately to remember the last time I saw her alive, heading over to Desmond's the night before my birthday. I wanted to believe she'd held me a little tighter and longer than normal. If the Council had been so divided about sharing the truth with me, there was only one place I was going to get the information I sought. But I was so tired. Sleep was what I needed, even though it was still only evening.

"I have to go," I said and struggled to my feet.

"Where?" He sounded tired too. As if the weight had lifted but he'd carried the burden so long it had worn him out. But the question also bore a note of hope. Like maybe he could come with me.

"Home. I need to sleep and think." I could just drive, but then I remembered my car had been left behind at headquarters. My anger at Desmond was starting to ebb, but there was no doubt in my mind that if I went back to the mansion, even without speaking to anyone, the feeling would intensify and I didn't think I could handle that much negative emotion right now.

"Let me take you."

I shook my head. "No. I'll catch the T. I need to think." After a moment I said, "You knew Taggart was one of us, didn't you? I saw you looking at the photo in the library."

"He was one of our best guys once upon a time."

"What drove him to the Order?"

He shook his head. "I wish I knew. He just left one day and never turned back."

I started for the door and he trailed after me, hands shoved into his pockets. He kept a respectable distance and I could tell by the hunch of his shoulders and the cords of tension in his neck that he was trying to keep himself in check.

"Thank you for showing me this."

"I just hope it wasn't too late."

MARCH 18, 2017

TWENTY-SEVEN

The events of the past week had finally caught up with me on the T ride back to Allston and I'd passed out as soon as I'd made it home. Fragments of my mother's final goodbye video swirled with the recurring dream of Taggart turning me to stone and killing me plagued me until the early hours of the morning. I'd finally given in and taken one of the pills Belladonna had prescribed days ago. It knocked me out into a land of dreamless rest well into the early afternoon hours. I woke to a too bright sunbeam hitting me in the face. I moaned and threw an arm over my face in protest.

The light persisted and I rolled over, catching sight of the clock on the night stand. My heart jumped into my throat. I groped for my phone, snagging the charging cord on the edge of the night table.

"Damn it," I muttered and yanked the phone free.

To my surprise I only had one missed call from Jacquie. No voicemail. It must not have been urgent. Hitting my partner's number from my "Favorites" list, I rolled back the other way and propped my head up with my free arm.

"Finally, you're answering your phone," Jacquie said as the call connected.

"Things got complicated yesterday and I came home and crashed."

"The lab techs have verified the video files and logged them back into evidence. I've started on the reports. Taggart put up a fight. That's going to be nasty."

"Somehow, I'm not all that surprised. I mean, sure, a rational person would see the evidence we've got plus a sworn statement from his co-conspirator and cooperate. But when you're a high-level member of a murderous dark magic cult, rational isn't really in the vocabulary."

"No, it's not. Did J.T. get you all stitched up again?"

"Yeah. As long as I don't go tackling any more errant FBI agents I should be okay." And maybe another day would give me time enough to heal up to face the Order's ritual without risking my internal organs deciding they want to try existing outside of my body.

The line went quiet for a minute. I could hear Jacquie breathing on the other end. I knew that sound. She was trying to find a way to break bad news to me.

"What's wrong?" I prompted.

"Captain Beech is catching some heat from the top brass for having you back without medical clearance. You'll be getting the official word at start of shift, but you're off active duty until you are medically cleared by a doctor of the department's choosing."

I'd been so wrapped up in taking down the bad guy I hadn't even considered the mundane things like getting a doctor's note to return to active duty without restriction. My cheeks flushed with embarrassment that I was grateful she couldn't see. "Oh. Yeah, that makes sense."

"If I were you, I'd see this as a blessing. It gives you time to formulate a plan of attack," she said.

"Yeah," I agreed, not really listening.

"Ezri."

"Huh?"

"What happened yesterday after J.T. came and picked you up?"

I wasn't sure I was ready to share this with anyone who wasn't family, but Jacquie had had my back even when I didn't think she did. That made her more family than a lot of people. "My mother left me a recording. She wasn't murdered. She sacrificed herself and her magic to protect me." It also made sense why Tricia hadn't found any other fingerprints besides my mother's on the knife.

"Damn."

The anger welled up in me again and I fought back the hot tears that pricked the back of my eyes. "Thanks for letting me know about the medical leave. There's something I need to do."

"Let me know if you need anything else."

I hung up and lay there staring at the ceiling. I wasn't sure I was going to get the answers I was looking for today, but I had to try. And there was only one place I could think to go. After dressing in jeans and a loose shirt to allow the stitches to breathe, I headed out. A quick stop at Dunkin for a bagel and coffee and I was off.

The cemetery was practically vacant when I pulled in. That was fine. I needed privacy for what I was planning. I made the familiar trek to my mother's gravesite. It was unchanged from earlier in the week. Even so, I knelt down and brushed some stray foliage from the headstone. I took one last look around me to make sure I wasn't going to be disturbed.

"Hey, Mom. I'm not really sure how this works when I'm conscious, but if you're there, I really need to talk to you."

Nothing happened.

When Eleanor had appeared, she'd just sort of

been there without thinking about it. Or had she? I centered myself, putting my intent out into the world. Needing my mother to be there to answer questions. Wanting that last chance to touch her and feel her embrace. Even if it was an afterimage and all just a product of magic.

The air around me pushed back, pressing against my skin like a film. It covered my nose and mouth, cutting off my supply of oxygen. I struggled against the force keeping me from getting what I wanted. The scent of burning ozone warred with fresh fruit as my magic battled whatever unseen force was fighting me. Finally, my ears popped like I'd just reached altitude on a plane and the air calmed down. I looked to my left to find my mother standing there as I'd seen in my dream. To my right, Eleanor settled on the ground, legs crossed beneath her.

"I saw the video," I said, turning my full attention on my mother.

She remained silent, her eyes sad and the corners of her lips turned down in a frown. Wind whipped at the ends of my hair, but she remained insubstantial to the elements. "You understand what I did." No hint of questioning in her tone.

"I get you wanted to protect me. And I understand if you'd told me what you were doing ... when you were doing it, I wouldn't have let you."

"Sometimes being a parent means sacrificing for

your child to ensure they have a happy and fulfilling life."

"And in our family line, heartbreaking as it may be, that often means death," Eleanor offered from her spot on the ground.

"I miss you, Mom," I said and a breath caught in my throat.

"I've never been far from you, sweetheart. I've been right here." She pressed her fingers to my chest, her palm resting against the pendant, and despite the fact she was a spirit made of magic, I felt the brush of her fingertips against my body. They were warm and comforting.

The pendant.

"I've been having this dream. The man who tried to kill me was turning me to stone and then he crushes me and everyone I love. He steps on my chest. I didn't realize he was actually destroying the pendant. I remember you wore it all the time."

My mother turned her hand over and cupped the necklace. "It's been in our family a very long time." Her eyes darted down to Eleanor's face.

"In the video, you said that our family's blood has strength. I'm guessing it's tied to this pendant."

"You always were a smart girl."

"This is how I'm able to see you, isn't it?"

The corners of her mouth turned into a smile. "Nothing carries magic quite like objects with a lot of meaning and shared history."

I looked down at Eleanor. "So why isn't Theodora here? She's our direct ancestor, not you."

Eleanor stood gracefully, not even ruffling her skirt. As she stood there in the early afternoon sun, she looked younger than she'd been in death. We hadn't been that far apart in age when they'd hung her for witchcraft. "The necklace belonged to me before my death. I knew my sister's children would need its protection and power, and so, on the eve of my death, I gifted it to my sister with the promise that she would give it to her firstborn child. I imbued it with enough of my magic to keep my connection to it alive through her descendants."

"This necklace has been passed from mother to daughter since the 17th century. It carries the magic and the strength of every witch going back to Eleanor," my mother said, still holding tight to the pendant.

"Prophecies are tricky things. They are maddeningly vague and often do not say what they truly mean," Eleanor said, looking rather annoyed at her own words. She'd been the one to spit out the prophecy back in the day.

"So, what are you saying? I'm not the Savior?"

"Oh, no. The prophecy was specific enough about the sex of the Savior, but you will not stand alone to face the rising of the Druids. You have the power to harness our family's collective magic and wield it as your own," Eleanor explained.

"That's ... wow."

I took a few steps away from the ghosts of my mother and ancestor and leaned against a nearby fencepost. The metal was cool against my hands and I rested my head against the blunted tip. This was more to take in than I'd been expecting. Sure, I was getting the information I needed to fight the battle ahead of me. I'd just never expected to have access to an entire bloodline's worth of magic to do it. And it raised more questions in my head than I wanted to contemplate. Not least of which was: can just anyone do this or is my Savior status the key to it? Does the Order know what I'm capable of?

"Am I the only one?" I might as well put the question out into the world.

"The only one what?" Mom tilted her head the same way she'd done when she was alive whenever I asked a vague question.

"Am I the only one who can harness this blood magic?"

"The world would not be in need of a Savior if anyone could do it," Eleanor said dryly.

"But the world exists on a balance. That's why when the seasons change, the world shifts, never giving one side more of an advantage over the other. Having a practitioner powerful enough to use the built-up magic of an entire bloodline going back centuries, using it for good or bad, seems like the kind of thing that the world wouldn't be happy about if it wasn't balanced out."

Eleanor shrugged one shoulder and crossed the distance to stand beside the fence. "Sometimes the world cannot balance out and there are the rare occasions when the need for good is so great that it outweighs the need to have an equivalent evil to balance it." She pulled me into a tight embrace and kissed my cheek before vanishing, leaving me to stare at my mother's ghost.

"I know you're scared of what's coming," she said.

"How?"

She gave me a sad smile. "I'm a part of you, deep down where your hopes and fears reside."

"Oh. I know I have no choice in all of this but ... what if I don't know what to do? What if I screw it up?"

"You may feel like you aren't ready, but I believe in you, and that belief, like our magic, lives within you," my mother whispered, the wind carrying her words to me.

I couldn't meet her gaze so I studied the headstone that marked her grave. "I wish you didn't have to die. There had to have been another way."

"Ezri, we looked and this was all we could find. Shielding you from the Order was the best we could do until you were old enough to take this burden on."

I let out a hiccup of hysterical laughter. "I spent so much time being angry at everyone around me that I didn't even realize stripping someone's magic from them without their consent would probably end up killing me. That's something I should have known."

In a rush of air, my mother appeared at my side and pulled me into a tight, comforting embrace. "You reacted how any teenage girl who lost her mother would. I'm sorry you didn't get the explanation until now. That isn't on you."

I blinked away fresh tears. "Am I going to be able to see you like this after what's coming is over?"

"Honestly, I don't know. But even if we can't, we will always be with you in your heart. I need you to know how proud I am of the woman you've become. You are exactly who you are supposed to be. Now, you should rest. It's going to take a lot out of you."

"I have one more thing I have to do first," I said. I didn't want to move from her embrace.

"Good luck, my beautiful girl." Her lips brushed my cheek and then she vanished. But, unlike Eleanor, it felt as if she flowed into my body, her essence and magic covering me like armor.

I stood there, letting her power sink in and strengthen me. The added power made the mass of stone beneath my ribs feel less painful. I still needed to figure out where the Order was planning to hold their ritual. They'd clearly had a plan of where they'd made their offerings to call forth the spirits of the dark practitioners. I needed the map sitting at home in my living room. I closed my eyes, imagining myself back home sitting on the couch. I poured out as much will as I'd ever exerted and when I opened my eyes again, I was standing outside of my apartment building, my hair windswept around my face.

"I can't believe that worked," I said with a broad grin. The satisfaction of having effectively teleported across the city dampened as the world caught up to me and knocked me sideways into the building. "Need to work on that," I muttered and let the vertigo pass before heading inside.

I took the stairs two at a time and shouldered the door to my apartment open in my hurry to get the information I needed. The printout of the five locations sat waiting for me on the table, as if someone had known I was coming and what I needed. For a moment, I wondered whether my will had managed that feat as well. I was working with another person's magical strength added to my own after all.

Tucking my feet beneath me, I settled on the couch to study the map. The points definitely created a focal point on the Common. Tracing the lines connecting the five points led to a tightening pentagon around the Soldiers and Sailors Monument and the bandstand. It was only a hunch at this point, but it wasn't like I could just march up to Agent Taggart to confirm my suspicion. There was no way I was risking a solid case in court just to ensure my curiosity. Besides, my gut told me I had the right place. Now I just had to wait.

MARCH 20, 2017

TWENTY-EIGHT

It turned out downing Nyquil and one of Belladonna's pills was not the greatest of combinations when you wanted to do anything but sleep. March 19th was a complete blacked out space in my memory. I barely even woke up long enough to shovel some soup down my gullet before passing out again. But it meant I woke up the morning of the Equinox bright-eyed and ready to kick some evil ass.

As I pulled on loose fitting pants and a long-sleeved shirt a little after eleven o'clock, a knock at the door signaled I had visitors. I took in a breath and caught the honey scent of J.T.'s magic and the floral scent of Kayla. At least the Whisperer was starting to respect my boundaries and things like a locked door. I tossed my hair into a messy knot at the nape of my neck and went to answer the door.

"You look better," J.T. said with a smile.

"Sleeping for a day straight will do that for a girl," I answered and beckoned them in.

Desmond and Jacquie brought up the rear. Five people made my one-bedroom feel slightly cramped, but going into battle, it felt good to feel the closeness of the people who were going to have my back.

"How are you?" Desmond looked nervous.

"I'm okay. I worked some things out over the last few days and I'm ready for this. Assuming we all make it through, I think it might be a good idea to keep talking. I may understand what happened, but I suspect I'm going to need more time to sort out how I feel."

"Whatever you need."

"Do you know where they're going to try pulling off this ritual?" Jacquie's turn to pepper me with questions. Kayla remained silent.

"My best guess is somewhere near the Soldiers and Sailors Monument on the Common. The points linking the scenes crossed around there so it's as good a spot as any. And I'm pretty sure it's going to be hard to miss a power-intensive magical working. I have to believe most of the Order is going to be there."

My partner nodded, her hand resting on the holster at her hip. "We'll be waiting to take them down."

"Not to put the kibosh on your plan to arrest

anyone involved, but what exactly would you be arresting them for?" Desmond questioned.

"If we can link them to Taggart, then conspiracy to commit murder. Even if he's high up on the chain of command, I don't believe for a minute he did this all on his own," she answered.

"We'll take down whoever we can, but stopping the ritual is the goal," I interrupted.

"You're sure you're ready for this?" Jacquie's face bore a maternal look.

"Yeah. I was literally born for this, as cliché and cheesy as that sounds. I've got all of you backing me up and I've got my family." My hand clutched the pendant and it flared warm with energy. A cacophony of magical signatures filled the air around me. Like when my mother's spirit had disappeared, they settled over me, hardening into more layers of protection.

"We should go," Kayla said.

Taking a steadying breath in, I led our small group down to the street where we split off into two cars and wove our way through traffic on Commonwealth Avenue, racing the inbound B line train until it disappeared underground at Kenmore Station. We peeled away and ended up on Charles Street. The sky above us was starting to darken as the moon slowly moved into position, ready to block the sun. I peered out the passenger side window of Jacquie's car and tried to spot the meteor shower, but it was either not in view or was waiting for the sun to disappear to make its appearance.

"Maybe this is a good thing," Jacquie blurted as she found parking near the church outside of Arlington Station.

"What do you mean?"

"Think about it. Everyone is going to be so preoccupied with the eclipse and the meteor shower that no one is going to notice a magical battle going on."

I could almost see the benefit in her argument. Almost. "That's what the Order's counting on. That everyone would be so distracted they could just bring forth their ancient Druid buddies without interference. Besides, what better time for them to work such a huge spell than on the day the world is supposed to be balanced and it's thrust into darkness?"

She shook her head at my pessimistic view. "We'll do what we can to keep the civilians out of your way. And try not to die, okay? I don't need that on my conscience."

I snorted. "I'll try my best. It would really suck for you to have to break in another new partner."

Her face lost its jovial look. "Yes, it would."

An awkward silence fell between us and I broke it by climbing from the car and heading up Boylston Street toward the Common. The rest of my entourage fell into step around me as we marched to meet our opponents on a literal field of battle. They weren't going to pull any punches and neither was I. Whatever had to happen to quash their plans I was ready and willing to do. Too many lives were at stake to be cautious.

I felt the binding circle before I saw the wavy edges of the barrier. That same feeling of the air pushing in around me hit me just as the monument should have come into view. The rest of the group stopped a few paces behind me.

"This is definitely the place," I said and reached out a hand to test the barrier.

It wasn't solid like the ones Taggart had erected around the crime scenes, but it wasn't pliable either. It was going to take some effort to take down. And this one may not shatter entirely like Taggart's.

I turned to Kayla, J.T. and Desmond and said, "I'm going to need your help getting through their circle."

Jacquie kept an eye on the street as the other three moved to stand beside me. I waited for them to give me a nod that they could sense the barrier before we poured our collective energy into the task of breaking through it. I had the impression that my family's magic could have tackled it without much issue, but I wasn't sure how long that connection would last and it was counterproductive to waste it on getting to the fight.

Overhead the sky continued to fade to black and, if I squinted, I could make out the fiery chunks of space rock hurtling towards the planet. To my right, Kayla flipped between her solid and insubstantial states as she poured her flowery magic into weakening the barrier. Sweat broke out above her lip.

"The eclipse is messing with our powers," Desmond said as he balled his hands into fists and his cheeks turned pink with exertion.

J.T.'s face was similarly flushed. *Okay, family magic, let's see what you're made of.* I turned my attention inward, feeling the different strands of magic from every woman who'd worn this necklace and contributed a piece of themselves to bolster mine. My mother's magic was strongest, but I could sense dozens more. In my mind's eye, I braided the strands around the core of my own magic until it pulsed bright. I sent it out into the world like a wrecking ball against the barrier.

Instead of shattering, the barrier rippled beneath my palms, spreading out in a spider web of weak spots until all I had to do was push and it created a hole for me to slip through. I slid one arm through to ensure it didn't collapse before I was through. With one last glance back at my friends, I stepped through and into a horror show.

Within the boundary of the Order's binding circle, the sky had already blackened to midnight. The moon was halfway across the sun and I had to blink spots from my vision from looking directly at it. Faceless figures in hooded robes stood in a loose circle. Seriously, why do bad guys have to always go with the robe trope? A shorter figure stood in the center of the gathering and I could see the five spirits of the dark practitioners they'd already raised. The hood hung low over the person's face, but the robe was open to reveal the curve of breasts and a bare midriff. As I followed the line of her body down, I saw she was only clad in a bra and underwear beneath her robe. The sleeves were pushed up over her elbows and she held a blade in her left hand.

No one noticed me; all of their attention was focused on the woman in the middle of the grass. Collectively, their heads turned up toward the sun. Maybe it was a trick of the light but as I glanced skyward—careful not to look directly at the sun this time—I noticed that the light was almost entirely gone. The meteors were in clearer view too. Their ritual was about to happen. Time to fulfill my destiny.

"Hey, psychos," I called and strode forward with purpose.

I couldn't tell if the group was surprised to see me, what with their faces obscured, but a few of them turned at the sound of my voice. I gave them a little smile and wave and waited for them to go on the defensive. They tightened their ranks around the woman with the blade, making it crystal clear that she was my objective.

A group of four moved forward into a line, fire

swirling forth from their palms. It coalesced into a giant ball before shooting straight for my head. The limited training I'd received as a child kicked in. I held up my right hand, willing the molecules in the oncoming fire to turn to ice. Even though the odds were against me, my will won out and the fire turned into a giant ice ball. Unfortunately, it was still coming speeding toward me like a rocket.

Raising my left arm up, I turned my intent into a solid shield. The ice slammed into it, sending me staggering a step or two back. The barrier held, the ice shattering into tiny crystals on the grass. My opponents were already preparing for another attack. If I could bring down their barrier for good then Jacquie and the others could handle them.

I reached out with my senses for the knot keeping the binding together. It was at the far end of the circle and naturally that meant through the throng of bad guys. Taking a big breath in, I sprinted at a diagonal around the cluster of Order members, throwing up a shield at my back to deflect any passing shots. I felt the heat disperse over my body as a fireball collided with my protection.

Tapping into the surplus of family magic, I extended my reach as I moved, letting it snake along the grass in front of me until it reached the anchor point. With an outpouring of will and a mixture of my own magic and that of my ancestors, I ripped it free.

The barrier fought to stay alive, no doubt pulling from the confluence of phenomena around us, but it did die and with it the protection from my allies. The pack of Order members looked amongst each other and splintered off, some producing weapons like knives and guns while others simply harnessed their magic into a solid mass around themselves like shields.

I left them to do battle with my friends and set my sights on the woman they'd been guarding. Only three people remained to separate us and, with the boost of the barrier coming down, that seemed like nothing to me. One of the robed figures, who was tall and lanky by the way they moved, came at me with a fist drawn back to hit me. I easily side stepped and slammed my heel into the small of their back, sending them sprawling to the ground. With a wave, handcuffs bound their wrists behind them, effectively immobilizing them. I urged the grass to rise up and ensnare their legs for good measure. The other two were a little more calculated.

"Come on, let's do this!" I shouted at them.

They came at me in tandem. I ducked their blows and, when one came from behind, lashing out with magic that smelled like gingko berries, the blow bounced off me as if they'd actually struck armor. I still stumbled from the contact, but the force doubled back on my attacker and it sent them flying through the air. They slammed into the base of the monument just beneath the placard. They didn't move, but their hood fell back enough to reveal a man with greying temples. I thought I spotted flecks of blood on his lips.

The woman's other protector lunged and hooked their forearm around my throat, catching me off guard and hauling me to the ground. They used their other hand to land a few shots to my kidneys. Even with the protection of my magic, I still felt the pain. The urge to breathe—and therefore choke—was strong, but I held my breath and wormed my hands up to dig into the meaty exposed flesh of the person's arms. My nails drew blood, leaving violent red marks as I dragged them upward. It was enough to loosen their grip and I rolled free, coming up in a crouch. In my peripheral vision, I saw the woman drag the blade across her right forearm. I expected the blood from the wound to drip to the ground, but it slithered along her pale skin and out to one of the five waiting spirits. The blood tethered the spirit, forming a visible connection. Behind the spirit I caught a flicker of something else ... someone else moving through a haze. It appeared to occupy the same space as the dead woman and drawn, gaunt features over-laid across the woman's face.

My throat went dry as I realized what she was doing. These spirits would become the vessels for the Druids to return to the land of the living. The woman drew her knife across her right thigh next and another connection snapped into place with the second spirit. Like the first, a shadowy figure came to occupy the same space. The woman's final protector pushed their hood back to reveal a young woman with jet-black hair hanging in loose curls around her face.

"You're dead, bitch," she howled, sprinting towards me. As she moved, magic weaved from her hands into thick ropes. She snapped them and they snaked around my legs, dragging me down. They cut into my legs, inching their way towards my middle as I struggled.

"I don't have time for this," I muttered and grabbed the closest rope. I willed it out of existence and, after a tense few moments, it gave in to my intent. I scrambled to my feet and put up a barrier between us. She charged, bounced off the barrier and crumpled to the ground. It was my turn to sprint and I took off, ready to tackle the knife-wielding woman. I came to a skittering halt a foot from her. She paused in her self-harm long enough to shake the hood from her face. Taggart's second-in-command sneered at me.

"Jamison may be out of the picture, but you're too late to stop this, Savior."

I held out my hand and willed the blade from her hand. Nothing happened and she let out a peel of high-pitched laughter, slicing into the meat of her left leg. My heart began to thud against my ribs in an ever-increasing beat as I tried to figure out what needed to happen.

"How am I supposed to stop her?"

I didn't expect an answer or the feeling of hands grasping my shoulders. I turned to see Eleanor and my mother at my sides.

"Sacrifice comes in many forms," Eleanor said, sadness etched into the lines of her face. "You are strong, my child. But this is only the beginning of the fight. You must protect them from the darkness ahead."

"No. You don't have to do this. I'll figure something out," I protested as they both stepped forward. I didn't have time to process her other words. My mind was too focused on stopping the shit going down here and now.

My mother gave my hand a squeeze before moving to grab the tether between the FBI agent and the first spirit. The scent of my mother's magic overwhelmed everything. The connection between living soul and spirit burned bright and then began to crumble to ash. The shadowy Druid vanished. My mother's specter flickered for a moment—long enough for her to look at me and smile—before she, too, disappeared. Instinctively I knew she was gone for good. I couldn't feel her magic within me anymore.

In my periphery I saw one of the Order members send a knife flying right at Kayla's head. She vanished and the knife went with her. On the other side of the monument, Jacquie was in hand-to-hand combat with a man who'd forgone the robe altogether. She currently appeared to have the upper hand as she slammed him to the ground. Desmond and J.T. were double teaming a group of three Order members. J.T. had an oozing cut above his left eyebrow and I could see Desmond's lower lip was swollen, but they were holding their own.

Turning back to my own situation, I watched as Eleanor moved to take on the next spirit. "No, you don't have to do this. Stop!" I begged her, but she didn't listen.

Rosemary flared in the air and another connection turned to ashes, leaving only one connection left. A woman who turned out to be my grandmother strode past me, and with a wink, she severed the final connection, her magic disappearing along with her. I clutched at the pendant as if I could keep their magic contained a little while longer. I didn't want to lose any more of them.

Taggart's second-in-command and I stared at each other. She made a move to keep cutting herself, but my reflexes kicked in. With the connections to the spirits—and by extension the Druids—broken, I could approach her. I charged to her left, catching her off guard. Once I was behind her, I grabbed her right forearm and twisted it behind her. She struggled in my grasp, slamming her head into my nose. I tasted the blood running down my lip but let it fuel me. Looping my leg around hers, I dragged us both to the ground. She scrambled to get free, wielding the blade in front of her. Blood still ran down her arm and legs in little rivers of red.

This close up I could see the detail on the knife and my chest tightened with a moment of panic. It was the same knife Taggart had used on me. With a wicked grin, the agent raised her arm and threw the knife straight at my chest. Before I could throw up a barrier, the pendant at my throat burned with cold blue energy. The knife's tip connected with the metal and went careening back at its owner, slamming into my attacker's chest. She dropped instantly, eyes wide in shock. I scrambled to her side, pressing my fingers into the side of her neck. Her heartbeat had slowed faster than I'd have guessed possible. A shadow passed over her face and then she was gone.

With her lifeless body now lying on the ground, I stood to face the spirits. Their accusatory looks even with hollow eye sockets were all they gave me. Perhaps they were robbed of their voices in death and they'd have gotten another chance at life if the ritual had been completed. Overhead, the rim of the sun flared around the moon. I reached up to that light and let it fill me up. The pendant at my neck turned white hot as if from the forge. The sunlight channeled through the diamond at the center, calling to the magic within me and I let it out with a single thought: *Go.*

Before my eyes, beams of sunlight struck the spirits straight in the chest. Their mouths contorted in silent screams as the light burned them up, dissolving them until they were banished back to whatever hell they'd come from. Not even the brimstone scent accompanied them out of this world. With the last one gone, I released my hold on the sunlight and my ability to stay upright went with it. The world went monochrome before I collapsed.

TWENTY-NINE

The world came back slowly. First the murmur of low voices tugged at my consciousness, urging me to join the conversation. Then my nose filled with the sweet honey scent of J.T.'s magic, bringing me closer to the surface. Finally, my eyes caught up to the party and opened. At first, everything was a technicolor blur. I blinked a few times and my surroundings resolved into the same bedroom I'd come to in days ago after Taggart nearly killed me. The disorientation passed faster this time. I sat up and looked around the very crowded room. Desmond, J.T. and Jacquie were present along with Belladonna.

"We did it," I said, the words feeling thick in my mouth.

"*You* did it, Ezri," Desmond corrected. His smile

reached from ear to ear. The pride in his voice rang clear. I'd done good.

"I saw you all fighting there with me. If you hadn't been there to back me up, I couldn't have stopped them."

I rubbed at my head as a dull throb began to pulse right above the bridge of my nose and nape of my neck. "How long was I out?" I glanced to the windows to see the sky was dark, which told me absolutely nothing.

"It's a little after eight at night," J.T. answered.

It could have been worse. The thought that we'd all made it through died as soon as it formed. We hadn't all made it. I could sense the absence of the magic of the three women who had sacrificed themselves to stop the Order. And Eleanor's warning still echoed in my head. *This is only the beginning of the fight. You have to protect them from the darkness ahead.*"

"What is it?" Jacquie settled on the edge of the bed.

"Taggart's second-in-command. She was sacrificing herself, or at least a part of her, to raise the Druids. It's hard to explain, but she was establishing a living connection between herself and the spirits they raised from the murders. My mother's spirit was there along with my grandmother and Eleanor Pruitt. They gave up their residual magic to break the connections." It was as if I'd lost my mother all over again.

J.T.'s hand wrapped around mine as I fought to keep my composure. The pressure from his touch was enough to let me take a few shaky breaths and look to Belladonna. "I need to thank you. For giving up some of your magic to protect me."

She smiled at me. "It was worth it. You should get some more rest. The Council will want to be debriefed when you're up to it. And when you're ready, your seat at the table is waiting for you to fill it."

Slowly, people began to trickle from the room. Belladonna gave me a smile and stepped from the room in one fluid motion. Jacquie moved to stand next to me and patted the top of my right hand. "Take some time, you deserve it, and I'll see you back at work when you're ready, partner."

"How many did you arrest?" I asked before she reached the door.

"Not enough. They took some casualties, but we got a few in cuffs."

For the first time, I noticed a bruise on her cheek and a bandage on her left forearm that hadn't been there before. "Did any civilians get hurt?"

"No. We got lucky."

I pointed to her injuries. "You sure about that?"

"I'll bounce back. And I knew what I was getting into when I partnered with you. Now, get some rest."

And then there were two. J.T. raked a hand through his hair and looked at me with a quizzical expression. He'd obviously had time to heal the cut on his head.

"Did you know about what my mother was planning all those years ago?" I asked before he could speak.

His mouth opened and closed a few times and he glanced to Desmond as if asking for help. When none came, he looked anywhere but at me and said, "Not the details. I knew you were going to be hurting for a while. But I was a kid too. I didn't know what to do about it. I'm sure Desmond told you that you weren't supposed to find her."

"I know."

"Anyway, when you pushed away, I didn't fight it. I figured that's what you needed and you'd come back when you were ready. I didn't think that would be a decade." The last sentence came out at barely a whisper.

"I'm going to be saying this for a while, but I'm sorry I pushed you away. It wasn't your fault and I'm really glad you were there with me today. I wouldn't have made it through this without you."

"Apology accepted." He bent down and kissed me on the forehead. "And since we both survived this thing, you owe me coffee."

I grinned. "It's a date."

He gave me a mock bow and slipped out of the

doorway, pulling the door partially closed behind him. Desmond moved to stand by the window, his attention turned outward. Neither of us spoke for a while until the tension hung so heavy in the air between us that I kicked the sheets and blankets aside and stood beside him.

"Can you believe we made it? We spent so much of our lives waiting for the damn prophecy to come to pass and now that it has things feel..." I said.

"Empty," he finished without looking at me.

It wasn't the word I would have chosen, but I understood the sentiment. It definitely felt as if part of me was missing. Maybe it was the hole left by my mother and other ancestors who'd given up so much to help me beat back the rising darkness. Or maybe it was that I'd fulfilled the purpose I'd been told I had since I was eight years old.

"Something like that," I finally said.

"You're free now. You can just be Ezri Trenton, detective," he said.

"I'm not sure I ever was just a cop. I used my powers to help me get to where I am. I think it's time I step back into the community. There's a lot of healing still to be done. I don't entirely trust the Council, but that's not going to change if I keep them at arms' length."

Desmond turned and looked at me. "I'm surprised to hear you say that. Glad but surprised."

"You were right about a lot of things, Desmond. I

need the Council. We wouldn't have been able to get the evidence we needed to solve the case without them. There are benefits to having a governing body to back you up. And this week has shown me that there is a lot I still don't know about our world. I'm going to use this to become a better cop and a better witch. I may not be the Savior anymore, but that doesn't mean I can't still save people."

"Does that healing include your father?"

For the first time in a decade, thinking about my father didn't make me want to punch things. "He's top of the list."

"I'll be there if you want."

"I'd like that."

He pulled me into a tight embrace and I returned the gesture. I'd been lying to myself for so long that I was better off alone. Now I knew I was stronger with my family at my side. Together we would face whatever came next. And I had no doubt there would be new trials to face. There was still darkness out there to be defeated.

QUICK AUTHOR'S NOTE

THIS BOOK HAS BEEN a long time coming. First drafted in 2012, it has gone through many drafts and rewrites to get to where it is today. Believe it or not, it was first conceived during a Criminal Procedure class in law school. If memory serves, we were discussing search and seizure. And somehow, my weird writer brain decided "hey, what if a cop had magic and was forced on leave because of their actions on a case". And thus, the very early version of Ezri was born.

Her story looked a lot different in those early days. She had a brother, and a familiar! But, I have to say, thanks to an amazing developmental editor, I found the core of Ezri's story and it became what you just read. I find it amusing that the character who stayed mostly intact the most over the six drafts was Desmond. Although, in early drafts he was Aussie. I think I just liked the foreign appeal. But, thank goodness that went by the wayside, too!

I would be remiss if I didn't mention the Kickstarter backers who helped fund the publication of this book, too. And my awesome beta readers who have stuck by me with this series from the jump.

While Spring's Calling might feel like a complete story (if I did my job right), there is still so much more of Ezri's tale to tell. I dropped a few hints along the way of what's to come, but turn the page to get a glimpse of what battle she faces next...

Averting the apocalypse was only the beginning.

Three months after saving the world, Ezri is still finding the balance between being the Savior and a cop. When young girls in the magical community go missing, she doesn't hesitate to take the case. Not when one of the victims is her partner's niece.

The investigation leads her back into the orbit of her greatest enemy. With leads drying up, Ezri needs all the allies she can get. But can she trust the new FBI agent assigned to the case? Will the rapidly shrinking window to bring the girls home alive close before Ezri can summon enough power to counteract the dark magic at play?

Read on for a sneak peek of *Summer*...

Debts and Debtors

Have and Hold

Saints and Sinners

Hunted

Hunted

Allied

Fated

Muse Song

Muse Song

Reverend Margot Quade Cozy Mysteries

Into the Lion's Den

The Sacrificial Lamb

Cast the First Stone

My Brother's Keeper

Love Thy Neighbor

Brothers In Arms

Seasons of Magic

Spring's Calling

Summer's Stolen

Autumn's Legacy

Winter's Reckoning

Standalone

Unplanned

ABOUT THE AUTHOR

Sarah Biglow is a *USA Today* bestselling author. She lives in Massachusetts with her husband and son. She is a licensed attorney and spends her days combatting employment discrimination as an Investigator with the Massachusetts Commission Against Discrimination.

You can find an up-to-date list of all my books here